MURDER ─ IN ─ MELLIFONT

A De Cenza Murder Mystery

ARTHUR COLA

ARPress
45 Dan Road Suite 5
Canton MA 02021

Hotline: 1(800) 220-7660
Fax: 1(855) 752-6001

Ordering Information:
Quantity sales. Special discounts are available on quantity purchases by corporations, associations, and others. For details, contact the publisher at the address above.

Printed in the United States of America.

ISBN-13:   Paperback   979-8-89389-894-1
           eBook   979-8-89389-895-8

Library of Congress Control Number: 2024923888

Cover Concept and Design by Connor Christopher Smith

DEDICATION

To my wife and family who are the constant
source of support for my work.

Mellifont Abbey Ruins, Ireland

TABLE OF CONTENTS

St. Peter's Square, Vatican City

CHAPTER ONE

ARRIVEDERCI ROMA

The stones of the Gothic revival Slane Castle glowed in the morning sunrise as it stood perched on a knoll commanding a view of the countryside of County Louth in the midlands of Ireland. At the rear of the castle that knoll descended into a natural slopping amphitheater as may have been see in ancient Roman times throughout the empire. Its majestic gardens took on an almost magical appearance as its merry month of May blooms received the sunlight as they turned ever so slightly to catch the rays. Walking amongst them was the Earl of Mount Charles, the 7th Marquess Fredrick Conyngham, his fourteen year old son Henry and a woman dressed in a long flowing morning gown covered with a silk coat also floor length. She was wearing a wide rim hat covered with a translucent veil which covered her face. The entire ensemble from hat and veil to leather walking boots was totally black in color as if she were in mourning.

Despite the rather somber looking attire, the young Lord Henry was ecstatic as he was acting as the tour guide. He effused his dream about the amphitheater which one day would be the site of great concerts. His father was delighted with his vision to preserve the history of the castle and its estate. The woman listened with interest but it wasn't until the teen got to the part about the Hill of Slane and how St. Patrick stood upon it to light the Paschal (Easter) fire in defiance to the Pagan High King of

Tara, a short distance away from where they stood, that she took particular interest.

That same warm sunshine bathed the waters of the Irish Sea and extended across Wales and England over the Channel and onto the coast of Normandy down to the French Riviera and onto the Mediterranean Sea. Finally, its bright rays brilliance filtered through a small window behind the great Basilica of St. Peter's in Rome. There in the heart of the Vatican the small convent turned into an Inn to house assistants to the Bishops and Cardinals of the Church attending the Vatican Council slept exhausted seminarians. In a grand ceremony reflecting the centuries of history of the ancient Church the session had ended for the summer recess. The Prelates, Abbots, Mother Superiors and Heads of Religious Orders were on their way to their home dioceses around the world.

As the light of the new day made its way through the shutters of that window it illuminated a booklet set upon a small wooden table just under the window. On the cover was the title Travel Guide in small letters above large green letters spelling out Ireland. These were superimposed over various historic images of the Emerald Isle. Among those were the High Cross of Muiredach at Monasterboice, the tall Round Tower of stone of Clonmacnoise with its pointed stone peak and the "Lavabo" of the 12th Century Mellifont Abbey ruins. Placed between the various images were the names of the Midland Counties which the book highlighted, Meath, Louth, Westmeath, Cavan, Monaghan, Longford, Offaly and Laois.

The image of the Round Tower set against the backdrop of the Shannon River and clear blue sky seemed ready to take off like a rocket as the golden sunlight shone on it as it reached the bedside of Ron De Cenza one of those seminarians who acted as clerical assistants to the Prelates of the Council. On that wooden framed cot-like bed and twisting and turning in its sheets was that trim young man with his bushy almost black hair popping out of the sheets and digging into the white pillow under his head. The sunlight was just about to touch his head and announce the arrival of a new day and what was to be a new adventure away from the summer heat of Italy.

A knock on the door disturbed Ron. He rolled over to check his Mickey Mouse wrist watch lying next to the tour book of Ireland. "Who the hell is coming at 7:00 a.m.?" Throwing off the linen sheet, he jumped out of bed realizing that he was only wearing his Jockey shorts. The knock came again. He grabbed hold of his cassock and began to button it up. It was a task he never quite managed without cursing, for each button, and there was at least fifty of them, was a challenge to him. "I'm coming, hold your horses…" he pulled up the latch and opened the door.

There standing in a white chiffon negligee with a satin lining flowing down to her ankles was Susan Liguri. The daughter of the manager of the Latin School Abbey Gift Shop back in Wisconsin, which was his college home, she was originally from Georgia. She was quite good at effusing that southern belle charm and well did he know it. Despite this alluring nature which was a distraction to Ron she had been involved with him on several crime solving incidents. She proved herself to be indispensable to him. At the same time she was a constant threat to his vocation though she only teased and never did anything like what he was seeing in that doorway. She was attending Loyola University in Rome with his sister, Jan De Cenza, which now made her presence all the more frequent.

"Susan, what the…."

She pushed passed him as he still fumbled with the remaining buttons on his cassock. "It's time to decide once and for all if this is what you want, Ron De Cenza," she pointed to the stark almost barren room walls. Then noticing his issue with the buttons went to him; so close that he could smell the Channel Number Five scent of her perfume. "Here let me help, you never could get this thing buttoned up properly." She flipped back her long over the shoulder crimson hair and grinned so slightly but just enough to make her green eyes sparkle like emeralds.

Instead of buttoning the final ones at the bottom of the clerical garb, she began to unbutton them. He froze and then shuddered as she got to those at his knees. A couple of more and she'd see his Jockeys but more than that what was happening within them as his manhood rose to the pinnacle of rigidness like that of the Round Tower on the guide book. "Oh my word, honey child; do I see a little problem arising here?" She gently fingered her way up from the knee to his thigh.

It was over; he had made his decision in a fit of passion. Grabbing her in his arms he caressed her and kissed her with a fervor that was about to explode in his loins. Inch by inch he pulled up her nightgown and pressed against her pale smooth body as the remaining buttons were undone and the cassock fell to the floor off his shoulders. "I don't want to be a priest anymore Susan, I want you, I love you." He was breathless now and without fear or embarrassment.

A loud pounding on the thick oak door made his Round Tower manhood shoot off its pointed top. He jumped out of the bed but it was too late to stop the explosion of life force. He began to jump around not knowing what to do as he pulled off his Jockeys and went for the hand towel on the sink across the room. In the process he tripped over the desk chair and crashed onto the marble floor with a yell, "Oh shit!"

From the other side of the door his pal, Bob Wentz, shouted. "What the hell is going on in there Ron? Are you all right, I'm coming in." After all they had been through in chasing down Socialist Communists and saving Renaissance Treasures (found by the young man standing next to him with his mentor, Professor Andrew Pettigrew of Oxford University), he was taking no chances. Bob used his rather large body to push open the door. It was with some difficulty that he did so as his friend's feet were counter pushing against the door. Squeezing through he found his buddy on the floor his legs tangled in the toppled chair and the hand towel stuck between his legs. He knew immediately what had happened and slammed the door behind him almost catching the Professor's assistant one Dominic Fontana in the doorframe. Ron was now mortified to see the Professor's assistant starring down at him not knowing if he should laugh or show pity or simply remain stoic. He chose the latter and did and said nothing.

"What the hell Ron, can't you ever just have a wet dream like every other guy in the world?" Bob grabbed the cassock now on the floor as it had been on the chair. He draped it around Ron's shoulders. "Come on take my hand, we'll leave now if you're not hurt." He hoisted Ron to his feet.

All the while, Dominic stood without a word but his eyes could not avoid what was right before him. He smiled within himself as he thought of those days when such would happen to him when he thought of a certain Swiss Guard named Andreas Berne who was now the love of his life.

"You think this is just too funny don't you," he looked into those dark eyes the twins of his own actually speaking to Dominic. "Well it's not. I'm supposed to be holy and everything like that."

The Research assistant finally felt compelled to speak. "Ron, you're a guy with an issue like other guys. It's just that you made a mess of things so to speak." He smiled as he pointed to the discarded underpants.

"Come on Dominic, let's get out of here and leave him be. He doesn't handle manly things well." He placed his hand on the door latch.

"Fuck you and sure just up and leave me like this." Ron pulled the cassock around him like a bathrobe.

"Ron De Cenza man up and get on with getting cleaned up. Yelling at me won't stop the issue. You love her and that's all's to it." Bob signaled to Dominic to leave the room and turned back to his friend closing the door behind him. "Okay he's gone, the gay guy is gone and has seen your thing, so what is really bothering you?"

Ron slumped down on the edge of his bed. "Asshole, he didn't see my thing anyway. I was holding the towel over my junk."

Bob just stood at the door and watched the pitiful sight before him. "Fuck you, I'm here to help and you call me an asshole because I speak the truth and you can't take it. Just meet us at the Bernini/Fontana Fountain in the Piazza San Pietro. The girls are waiting there for us."

"Please don't go. I'm sorry for calling you an asshole. You are my Watson, my Tonto so I know that you're here to help me." He shot out a sickly smile but it was sincere.

"Apology accepted; so now go get showered and dressed. I hope that you have another cassock in the closet. This one around you is… well it's not clean." Bob opened the wardrobe closet and pulled out a black cassock. "Good, you have a spare."

"Why do we need our cassocks? We're going on a holiday to Ireland not doing Church stuff. In any case, don't you get it? You say that I don't want to hear the truth and maybe you're right. But the truth is that Susan drives me crazy and sometimes I like it when she does, if you get my meaning." Ron walked into the bathroom and turned on the shower. "So can't you understand that even if we should, I can't wear the cassock thinking that," he stepped into the shower. "Oh shit, I forgot my underwear. Would it be too demeaning for Watson to get Sherlock his Jockeys?" Shouting over the splashing stream of almost hot water, "and another thing, if we are going along with this duo may I point out that Sherlock wouldn't have minded Dominic seeing his thing as he would think that to be a compliment, if you get my meaning. So I think we'll stick with Tonto and the Lone Ranger."

"You are such an idiot. Okay than Tonto will fetch your underpants but I am doing it out of pity because the Lone Ranger is hurting right now."

"In more ways than one; I think I may have broken my dick in the fall."

"Don't be so full of yourself, it doesn't have a bone so it can't break like that; maybe you bruised it." Bob's hand popped through the doorway and hung the Jockeys on the doorknob on the other side of the door, "Anything else Kemosabe?"

There was silence as the water had been turned off; after a short time Ron's now softly spoken voice answered, "Well there is one thing pal which hasn't been addressed." Ron appeared in the bathroom doorway in his Jockeys and drying his hair with a large towel.

"Now what? Everyone is waiting for us."

Ron set the chair upright and placed the towel over it, walked to the wardrobe and pulled out a pair of black polyester pants. "That's my point, how can I even face her after…"

"After what, you didn't do anything."

"That's not the point here. I wanted to and did it with her. Dream or no dream there's a problem with all of this. How can I hope to become a priest after what you said?" He zipped up his pants and began to pull a light blue polo shirt over his head.

"Really that's how you're going to Ireland, like a little boy going to Catholic School." Bob spotting the suitcase on top of the desk opened it. "Holy God in heaven; Ron this is like a priest's suitcase. Everything is black and white." He dumped everything out and went to the wardrobe. "I know you have regular clothes. Can't you be like the rest of us and wear jeans and a tee shirt?" He began to pull out some jeans and a few souvenir tee shirts and a St. Benedict Abbey sweatshirt. "This will have to do. It can be cool at night in Ireland even in May."

"Are you through being my mother?"

"Po'g mo tho'in as they say in Ireland," throwing the clothes on the suitcase Bob made for the door.

Ron cut him off. "I'm sorry, but don't you get it?"

"I'm only trying to help, that's all."

"I know, so go if you want," Ron opened the door.

Bob pushed it shut. "Okay, so what's going on?" He parked himself on the desk chair and began to straighten out the clothes so that they fit properly in the suitcase.

"Will you stop putzing and listen?" Ron closed the lid as Bob quickly jerked his hands out of the way. "You said it yourself. I think that I love her despite her driving me crazy, but I love the Church too even though I swear a lot amongst other things."

A light bulb illuminated in Bob's mind. "So that's what the cassock and all these black and white clothes are all about. I get it. You're trying to keep in the clerical mood as a way to stifle possible feelings for Susan."

Ron smiled and sat back on the edge of the bed.

"It won't work."

"Bullshit, it's worked up to this morning."

"No pal, it's not and you're the one kidding yourself that it is or have you forgotten about all those erections you've had whenever she touched you with fondness and what about ejaculating all over yourself the first time you ever met, just like this morning but it wasn't a dream but real."

"I'm fucked up is that what you're saying? I can't separate a sex drive from being in love."

Bob pushed Ron a bit over so that he could sit next to him on the foot of the bed. "That's not what I'm saying. I'm saying that you may possibly have two loves and one of those does have a sexual attraction to it. You pal have to decide if it's more than just sexual attraction and you can't do that by hiding behind a cassock or black pants with a white shirt."

"Shit Bob, when did you get so philosophical and smart?"

"Listen to me," Bob pulled Ron by the shoulders and got into his face. "I've always been smart and as for the other, I hang around with a guy who thinks like Sherlock Holmes and is motivated to goodness like the Lone Ranger, so it kind of grows on you."

"Oh Christ, I don't know if we're having a bro-mance moment, a gay moment or an enlightenment but whatever it is, you're one hell of a friend to put up with this shit all these years." He gave Bob a hug and jumped from the bed, unzipped his pants and dropped them.

"Shit Ron, not a gay moment please."

"Asshole, I'm changing into my jeans. I'll never know how I truly feel unless I go out to that fountain and go to Ireland with her."

Whilst this test of true love was being planned on the Hill of Slane the Lady in Black stood with the Marquess and his teen son. "My Lord, this has been a special time for me. Your hospitality has been most gracious. I ask only one more favor."

"Certainly, my Lady, whatever I can do."

"You are too kind. The favor has two parts but they are related. I am told that within your library there is a collection of ancient maps one of which pertains to Mellifont Abbey. I would like to photograph it."

"Well that's easy enough; would tomorrow be acceptable? The map display case is just being refurbished and won't be back until tomorrow in time for the tourist admissions; and now as for the second part?"

"I need an introduction with Gabriel Konig."

"Konig...I am not familiar with that name."

"Father, sure you are, she's the race car driver. Her real name is Gabriel De Freitas of Beaulieu House."

"Oh that Gabriel, of course I know her. I shall give Gabriel a call when we return to the castle. Perhaps we might dine together with her. Leave it to my son to know of a lady race driver; he is thrilled with motor racing."

Thirty plus miles away from where they stood the phone rang in the archaeological offices of the Dublin National Museum. The exhibits were yet to be open for visitation. One of those in particular was of interest to the caller as the phone was answered by the assistant Curator, Bridget Tulley. Like Dominic Fontana back in Rome, she too was a graduate student who was working on research. Her work under the Museum Curator Hugh O'Neill, was focusing on the Medieval Period in the Midland Region of Ireland, in particular the area around the Mellifont Abbey ruins. It was the artefacts found in those ruins which were of importance to the caller.

Her milky pale slender hand reached across her desk to lift the receiver of the heavy black cradle phone so common across Ireland but being abandoned in homes across the United States with the lighter weight ones called the Princess phone. "Good morning, you have reached the Archaeological office of the National Museum of Ireland, how may I help you?"

"Here's how you can help," replied the all business and no time to chit chat voice. "I am Professor Andrew Pettigrew of Oxford University but I am calling from Rome at the moment. Your curator, Hugh O'Neill knows of me. In any case, I will be arriving tomorrow morning with a research group from the Vatican Museum Archives and must see the exhibit of the Midland area artefacts found near Mellifont Abbey. I need to speak with your curator."

"I am terribly sorry but he isn't available…"

"Young lady, this is of utmost importance. I need to speak with him."

"I understand Professor Pettigrew; however he's on the road to Slane Castle."

"I see; then can you contact him there and have him call me at Trinity College this evening. My flight is due in Dublin around 4:00 p.m. that would be three o'clock your time. Therefore I should be at the University around five in the evening."

The giant bells of St. Peter's were announcing the 8:00 a.m. hour as Dominic arrived and greeted the others. Susan, Jan and Andreas were nervously standing around the recently renamed Bernini/Fontana Fountain and checking their watches as he approached them.

"So where are Ron and Bob?" Susan got right to the reason for their anxiety.

"And Buon Giorno to you as well Signorina."

"Oh okay, Buon Giorno, now where are those two."

Jan decided to enter the fray. "Dominic, we're all a bit anxious about getting to Da Vinci airport in time for the flight."

"I think you worry too much or am I wrong to say that the bells are telling us that it is eight o'clock?" Dominic walked over to Andreas who was in civilian clothes of jeans and a gold polo shirt with the Vatican Coat of Arms embroidered on the upper left quarter of the shirt. "So I see that even on holiday you cannot help but to announce who you are." He brushed his hand across the finely threaded emblem and smiled.

"You embarrass me Dominic," whispered Andreas into his lover's ear. "It's all I have."

Dominic suddenly got serious as what he just experienced with Ron and Bob flashed before him once more. He didn't want to place Andreas in a situation which he saw Ron being in over how to express one's love. "Mi dispiacere amico, I should know better. After all you're just on holiday leave from the Swiss Guards." Turning his attention to the initial question, he shot a smile at the girls. "Ron and Bob should be here momentarily. There was a wardrobe change needed, so I am told."

Jan began to laugh. "I'll bet anything that Ronnie was in black pants and a white shirt just like a priest off duty."

"And you would be half right, only the shirt was blue."

"Oh I see, so instead of a priest he looked like a student going to a Catholic High School, right?"

"Signorina Jan, with such a look I am not familiar but I must say that he looks young enough to still be in the secondary school instead of the Apostolic College."

The bantering helped to ease their worries about catching the flight especially when Dominic asked the whereabouts of the young Count of Pianore whom they all knew as Alessandro, a graduate student at the University of Bologna whom they met in the Palazzo Spada Galleria just a few months ago. For Jan, it was the opposite of Ron. There was no struggle, no questioning, she fell for his Adonis looks sure but also for his wit and smarts and all of that happened before anyone knew that he was from a noble family in Umbria, a northern province of Italy. He was informed that Alessandro was fetching the Professor at the Vatican Museum.

The young Count of Pianore flashed his Museum credentials in front of the Swiss Guard blocking the rear entrance alleyway leading to the archives offices. He too had heard the peeling of the bells and began to rush to the iron doors from which tourists would exit the museum on their way to St. Peter's without having to go all the way around the museum and to the other side of the Piazza. It was a short cut coming right after viewing Michelangelo's amazing ceiling of the Sistine Chapel which ended a long tour. That easy access route was appreciated by the visitors. Rather than rushing up the marble steps into the Papal Hallway leading to the chapel, Alessandro ran down the ordinary stone steps to the lower level into the archives area. In a small office piled high with research documents and randomly placed artefacts which the Professor was cataloging he found the Professor just hanging up the phone. He rubbed his short cropped beard and then his brow as if it was an effort. He seemed exhausted from just such a mindless effort as he plopped down onto a swivel desk chair.

"Professor, is all well with you?" Alessandro ran up to him and knelt before the rather young researcher and archaeologist nearing forty years of age. He looked about for a water fountain.

"Don't fuss Alessandro I just have to catch my breath. I'm not quite myself yet after being stabbed by that thief who wanted to steal all of this and more from the Vatican Museum. That was several months ago and still I'm not able to move as I wish to without an effort."

"Nonsense Professor, no one could have survived what you did and tell the tale of it. I shall tell the others to meet us here so that you don't have to walk across the Piazza."

Professor Pettigrew grabbed hold of the young man's arm. "No, please don't; if I am to take you on this research mission, I must carry my own weight. I am fully aware that without Ron, you and all your friends that I wouldn't even be here taking on yet another potential discovery of historic and artistic importance." He picked up a file folder and placed it into his briefcase. "We shall discuss the details again at the airport, now let's be on our way." He looked at his brown leather suitcase next to the cluttered desk.

"Don't even think about it, I shall carry it for you."

Halfway across the Piazza San Pietro Ron and Bob came running up to the others, now sitting on their suitcases by the fountain. It was not easily done as they both were holding their suitcases and Bob had his satchel hanging over his back while Ron had a backpack strapped around him.

"Hi everyone, sorry we're late but..."

Jan interrupted her brother. "That's okay Ronnie, we heard about the need for a wardrobe change."

"And may I say that those jeans just fit you so fine honey child," Susan laughed as she once again tried her exaggerated southern Georgia charm on him.

Only this time she didn't get what she usually got. "Yeah, cool aren't they. Look at my butt, it makes it look nice and firm and manly right?" He lifted his Roma tee-shirt and wiggled his back side.

Now it was Susan blushing and speechless. The others were just thrilled that just maybe this Holiday would actually be a fun time.

"So where are the Professor and Alessandro?" asked Bob trying to get the attention off Ron's butt.

"Right behind you," yelled out Alessandro.

The Professor looked at his saviors both of his life and precious artefacts. He even afforded them the distinction of possibly saving the nation of Italy as well but Ron pointed out that it was His Majesty Umberto II, the former King who actually did that saving.

"So let's get a move on Ireland awaits," the Professor pointed to the Bernini Colonnade behind them and slowly led them to the waiting cars which were to transport them to their BOAC flight.

CHAPTER TWO

BLOOD ON THE CHANCEL STONE

Hugh O'Neill, the curator of the National Museum of Ireland's archaeological unit was indeed on the road to Slane Castle. He arrived there with information for the guest of the Marquess Fredrick Conyngham at the same time that Professor Pettigrew and his entourage arrived at Trinity College in Dublin. That time was 4:00 p.m.

Greeted by the Chief Butler the curator was brought to his room immediately as the Marquess and his guest hadn't arrived back from the Hill of Slane. Ascending the wooden staircase he marveled at the collection of art pieces which adorned the hall resplendent with fresh flowers from its formal gardens. The butler placed his bag on a luggage rack next to the four poster bed and informed the curator that tea would be served in thirty minutes on the veranda as the last of the tourists would soon be gone.

"You are most gracious, I look forward to it."

Once the door closed, O'Neill placed his briefcase on a rather ornate Victorian Era desk set under the window which looked out over the gardens and veranda where tea was to be served. His hand was drawn to the phone situated on the desk so that he might contact his assistant Bridget Tulley. It was his intent to reach his assistant to inquire as to whether or not the Oxford Professor had tried to contact him. Glancing at his brief case once again, he thought better of it and opened the brief case. A knock on the door disturbed his thoughts. He quickly closed the lid.

"Yes, I'll be right there." Looking around the room as if to insure that no one could see what he was doing, he then slipped the briefcase under the bed. Opening the door, there stood the Butler still dressed in his formal attire with coat with tails and white bow tie. It was all done to impress the tour groups; normally he would be wearing an ordinary sport coat. "I was just getting ready to come down."

"I do apologize for the interruption. However, I thought you should know that His Lordship called to say that he would like to meet you at the ruins of Mellifont Abbey if that would be convenient."

"Indeed, I didn't hear the phone ring. But in any case I shall just freshen up and if you would be so kind as to write down directions to the ruins, I will be on my way."

"I will indeed have it ready for you sir." With that the butler turned and walked toward the staircase never addressing the fact that the phone in O'Neill's room hadn't rung.

Closing the door behind him, he immediately went for his briefcase placing it back on the desk while looking at the phone. This time he picked up the receiver. There was no dial tone. "Now isn't this strange?" he asked himself and then dismissing the thought. After all, the castle only had electricity for just twenty years, right after World War II. The phone lines are probably not up to par or perhaps the Marquess had a private line. Given his position, that seemed the most obvious answer. He visited the bathroom to freshen up, relieved that he was making too much out of nothing.

Splashing some water onto his face, he looked into the mirror above the porcelain sink. "My Mr. O'Neill, ye are beginning to show your age of fifty-five." He combed his long dark hair back with a brush revealing strands of grey. Next he focused on his beard which he was pleased to note had no signs of that aging color but rather had reddish highlights. "There now Mr. O'Neill ye are ready to be seen in public."

Feeling good about himself, he grabbed the brief case from under the bed and made his way out of the room. At the bottom of the staircase the butler waited with written directions in hand.

"It's quite easy sir, just stay on the N2 until you see the Mellifont turn off," he handed the directions to the curator.

Coming up that same N2 road was a van with Andreas at the wheel. Professor Pettigrew was correct in saying that they would be at Trinity College by five o'clock. It was actually four o'clock when they checked into the Dorm rooms which the Dean of Antiquities had arranged for Pettigrew's party. They just about had time to drop off their bags, use the bathroom and they were off to explore. The professor didn't see any need to review the documents he brought with him from the Vatican archives. They were to have a free evening. Amongst the seven of them, only Alessandro, the young Count had any knowledge of Ireland. He and his father had visited Trinity College several years ago when he first considered attending an English speaking University. Catholics were just being allowed to enroll back then and he wanted to be one of the first to apply.

"Not since Queen Elizabeth I established the college was that allowed and then that all changed in 1961. In the end, I didn't get to come," Alessandro noted. "My father felt that… 'the unrest in Ireland between the Catholics and Protestants was not conducive to a productive educational experience,' as he said. So I ended up at Bologna in my own province and a stone's throw away from Pianore. But never fear I'll get us to one of those quaint real Irish villages and out of this city."

They piled into the Trinity College van as the young Count took the wheel which was a stick drive. "Mama mia, I had no idea that this would be so complicated. This is a diesel vehicle." The grinding and crunching of gears drowned out his words but he got the van in gear and off they went toward the Liffey River and the highway called N2.

Ron instead of taking his usual navigator position up front had purposely sat next to Susan which forced Jan, much to her delight to be seated next to Alessandro up front. Bob, Dominic and Andreas squeezed in the third seat. Jan held the map of Dublin on her lap. Once out of the city, she could flip it and have the entire of Ireland's roadway system shown.

"Okay big boy, let's get going. Turn left out of the Trinity gates and head for the River. Once we cross it bear to the right." She felt quite accomplished taking over her brother's usual role. "The next question is do we want to stop at a village right on the N2 so that we don't get lost, like this Slane town or maybe go to one on the Irish Sea like this village called Drogheda." She lifted up the map so that Ron and the others could get a visual of what she was looking at. The wind from the slightly open window just about caused it to be lifted from her hands.

The weather report had been accurate. Thus the windows save for hers were closed.

Before anyone could decide, Alessandro pointed out that the Slane town was actually a castle and that his father knew the 7th Marquess of Mount Charles.

That pretty much made the decision as Bob got all excited. "Holy shit Alessandro, does your father know all these nobility families and royals?"

The poor guy who was just trying to be one of them and not the Count they now saw him as didn't know how to answer that without sounding snobbish, so he didn't. He just left it as his father having met him when they were in Ireland exploring Trinity College back in his undergraduate days.

"Well I say, let's stop in Slane and maybe we can knock on the castle door and say hey, we know the Count of Pianore and just dropped by to say Hi." Bob was quite pleased with himself as he grabbed hold of Ron's arm up on the back of the seat so that it came above Susan's shoulders.

His posturing was all part of his experiment to test his vocation and to discern as to whether it was love or sex drive that made him react to Susan as he usually did. If that meant he'd get an erection then so be it. Luckily Bob's taking hold of his arm precluded his finding out, at least for the time being. At that very moment Ron's arm fell onto Susan's shoulder and his hand came down over her chest. In one swooping motion Susan turned and slapped Ron's face.

"Ron De Cenza, are you trying to cop a feel? How dare you; and you being the holy one so everyone thinks." She pushed him to the door.

The red faced Ron could hardly blurt out his innocence let alone explain that it was Bob grabbing for his arm that made it look like that but it wasn't so. He held onto his face while the rest of his friends sat in shock and silence not knowing how to react without offending either Ron or Susan. Jan however had no problem sticking up for her brother.

"Don't be asses about this; my brother would never take advantage of a girl let alone Susan who is his friend. Susan, you should know better."

The guys tried to avoid eye contact with each other as Susan responded.

"Well yes that's true Jan, but his hand came mighty close to my breast and…well that's just not him. I don't know what's gotten into him, his being so fresh and us out for a good time and all." She fell into her Southern Belle accent without even realizing that she had. "It's just too much what with him shaking his butt at us right there in front of St. Peter's. Bob you come up here right this second. I'll go sit with Dominic and Andreas."

She waited for no answer but climbed over the seat and plopped onto the laps of the gay guys. In the process Ron, Jan and Alessandro looking into the rear view mirror got a bird's eye view of her posterior all tightly fitted in her green Capri pants which she had wished she hadn't worn as it was much chillier in Dublin than in Rome, in fact it was at least a thirty degree difference.

The guys couldn't hold it in any longer and began to howl at Ron's expense. Sliding into Susan's place on the seat he got up on his knees and helped Bob get over. "I knew this wouldn't work. I should have just stayed the Lone Ranger and away from women."

No one except for Bob knew what Ron meant by the analogy as three of them never heard of the TV character, they were Italian and Swiss. The girls, particularly Jan knew about the show as she had to put up with his watching its reruns from the time they were young kids and again all the way through high school when the series was rediscovered.

Alessandro put an end to the nonsense at Ron's expense when he announced that they were crossing O'Connell Bridge. "Look there, that's the statue of Daniel O'Connell, Ireland's freedom fighter."

It worked; all eyes were looking out the windows as Alessandro turned right along Eden Quay and followed the Liffey River.

Ron had to say it. "Let's not look too hard guys, we don't want to see some kind of attack on the banks of the Liffey like Bob and I did along the Tiber in Rome."

All of them were painfully aware of what had happened back in September when they first met the Professor and Dominic who was his assistant. That seemed ages ago to them and they didn't desire a repeat of it as back then the Professor almost died because of that attack on the Tiber River.

By the time Alessandro had the Trinity van clipping along the N2, after constantly being reminded to drive on the left side of the road Hugh O'Neill was entering his car at Slane Castle. As for the 7th Marquess and his son, they were saying good-bye to the Lady Devorgilla. It was her desire to be left at Mellifont Abbey to meditate, she told them. The Marquess would be sending a car back for her with plenty of time to prepare for dinner with them. He was anxious to return and greet the curator of the National Museum. Fourteen year old Lord Henry would have many questions to bombard his father with concerning the lady in black who was so mysterious about why she was dressed as she was and her need to be alone in the ruins.

Back in Dublin, Professor Pettigrew looked about the huge library of Trinity College, famous for its exhibit of the Book of Kells, an ancient Book of the Gospels found in a bog dating back eight hundred years. Surrounded by row after row of shelving both on the floor level and in a balcony area circling the research tables he felt at home. He spread out the documents from the Vatican Archives which were the reason for this excursion after a most deadly and traumatic school year for him and his assistants on this new mysterious quest. He was pleased that he allowed them an evening to be away from the work which lay ahead including the excavating of historic sites which may have clues to what he sought based on the ancient writings he now carefully placed on the table. What lay ahead of them was to be a delightful pursuit of a lost relic which would afford them a chance to enjoy Ireland with its mythology and faith foundation dating back millennia. There was no evil purveyor of black market antiquities, no murderous plots to reveal, no national histories to salvage, and certainly no hint of anyone seeking to undermine his work. He waited, for Drumond Shannon the Dean of Antiquities, with a light heart and excited vision for the work which lay ahead.

Whether it was the Formians of ancient Irish mythology at work with their destructive powers over nature or the Nuatha bringing sacred treasures to protect the people and their land was anybody's guess. One thing was certain as the sun began its descent, these lives along the N2, in the ruins of Mellifont, in a college library, leaving and arriving at Slane

Castle were about to collide. No force of nature would be able to prevent that from happening.

The Lady in Black walked from the parking area into the 12th Century Cistercian Abbey ruins. She paused at the foundations of the Abbey church and walked down what would have been its nave to the chancel and stood upon a flat stone facing the area where the sanctuary would have been located. Henry VIII saw that the Abbey was dissolved and Oliver Cromwell after winning the English Civil War saw that whatever was left of it was destroyed and turned into a private home fortress. It was almost a 190 foot walk for her when she arrived on that chancel stone. Surrounded by the Medieval stone foundations she could look in all directions to view the orange sun casting its final warmth on the day and illuminating the "Lavabo" where the Monks would wash before they went to dinner. Turning, she could view the Cloister pillars which led to the Presbytery and Chapter House of the 14th century. The ruins seemed to take on the sun's light and glow with a spiritual force which filled her with a quiet expectation that what she was about to do would actually help her fulfill her quest. She removed a parchment from her purse and held it up into the sunlight coming from what would have been the west transept of the Church. One would have thought it to be a prayer, perhaps the one used by St. Patrick himself on the Hill of Slane on which she stood not more than an hour or two earlier. It was not.

Rather that parchment held the words of the poem from the Lebor Gabala Erenn describing the arrival of the Nuatha with their treasures for protection. In a soft almost melodic voice she began to chant its verses.

"It is God who suffered them, though He restrained them
they landed with horror, with lofty deed,
in their cloud of mighty combat of spectres,
upon a mountain of Conmaicne of Connacht.

Without distinction to discerning Ireland,
Without ships, a ruthless course
the truth was not known beneath the sky of stars,
whether they were of heaven or of earth."

Though a song of pagan era Ireland it spoke of "God" and his gift to earth. She interpreted that poem to be a foreshadowing of what was to come when St. Patrick and his disciples preached the new religion of Christianity. Oddly God's gifts of the Nuatha came to that part of Ireland where Oliver Cromwell would send the Irish who would not give up their Catholic faith centuries later. He would say about the Irish, "Let them go to hell or Connacht," so barren and foreboding was its rock filled land in the west of Ireland.

When she had finished she knelt on the stone with the poem held in her right hand and silently prayed. Then taking a single red rose from her purse she then prostrated herself flat upon the stone of the chancel seeking enlightenment as to how to fulfill her quest. So withdrawn from all which surrounded her, she never noticed that her world was about to be torn asunder.

Behind the still standing wall on one side of the "Lavabo" a figure emerged. It made its way toward the foundations of the church. At the same time into the parking area of the ruins the Trinity College van had pulled in and the seven were jumping out of it. Alessandro had missed the turn off for Slane Castle and took the next exit which was Mellifont Abbey. The seven were excited when they saw the sign as it was the very place where the Professor was to take them for their working holiday. Each of them stood on the first line of stones from the foundation of the abbey ruins. They let the still brilliant sunlight hinder their view until some dark ominous clouds began to shade the waning sun and become like clouds bursting on fire and quickly turning into glowing charcoal briquettes floating above them. Awestruck they stood silently and with a bit of apprehension.

Susan still peeved with Ron nevertheless took hold of his arm. "Ron, isn't that a fantastic sight?"

Acting as if their spat hadn't happened he patted her hand. "It's quite cool for sure. Just look out there, see those Roman-like pillars taking on the red and oranges of the sun, it's like stained glass windows coming alive."

"My God Ron, that's poetic. I didn't think you had that in you."

He looked down at her, "There's a lot that you don't know about me because all you think is that I want to grab your boob."

Now he had done it, or so he thought. How will she react to that? But her response was not to let his arm go or to slap his face. Rather she looked up to his face glowing in the subdued sunlight, those big cocoa brown eyes filled with spirit and hope on fire in a way she couldn't explain but which drew her to him since the first day they met back in Wisconsin.

"That's unfair Ron, I don't think that, but I made a promise to your sister…"

Not more than four feet from them the other five had gathered purposely to give Ron and Susan some space. Jan was holding onto the arm of Alessandro as Susan was on Ron's arm.

"Oh my God, this is so beautiful. I hope those two can appreciate it and not kill each other."

"It is bella, so beautiful Jan, like you" Alessandro turned and lifted her up into his arms and kissed her gently on the lips.

She melted into his arms as the guys watched with broad smiles. "Now if only Susan and my pal can get their act together, this night would be perfect," observed Bob as it turned out to himself as Dominic and Andreas had been caught up in the moment and slipped away and were doing their own kissing. Once again he was the odd man out but it was okay this time. That is if his best pal finally found which love was to consume his life. Still he couldn't control himself and mumbled under his breath. "Well it's still too spooky for me all alone here with shadows moving everywhere."

"My sister, what the hell has my sister got to do with what you think of me?"

Susan didn't want to answer and reveal that conversation in the dorm of Loyola University in Rome in early fall when their world was being shaken by theft, murder and treachery. Ron broke his hold of her arm and stepped off the stones turning away from her and walking toward Bob who was still mumbling about it being too Halloweenish for his taste. "Look at those moving shadows like ghosts or maybe vampires," then turning to see Ron at his side.

"For crap sake Bob, cool it. It's just the fiery clouds creating the shadows over the stones in the walls." Suddenly he paused. He caught a glimpse of a shadowy figure moving across the ruins moving too quickly to be made from reflection through the glowing clouds. He grabbed hold of Bob and pointed to yet another something. A lump of black shadow like a shrouded rock lay in the other figure's path.

"Bob do you see that, over there," Ron pointed to the figure slowly moving toward the lump on the ground. "Oh shit guys look there quick, I think that thing moving out there is holding up something."

The kissing couples unlocked their lips as Susan ran up to Jan, pulling her away from Alessandro's embrace. "Your brother wants to know what we talked about, I didn't say a word."

"Well I don't think this is the time to bring that up…look out there," Jan pointed to the guys now running toward the figure with the uplifted arms with a roundish object catching the crimson rays making it to look as if a volcanic rock of molten lava was being held in those gloved hands for no flesh could be seen.

"Hey you," shouted Ron already coming upon the figure and seeing it to be a person dressed in black with a black stocking cap pulled down so that no hair was visible.

The Lady in Black heard him and her trance like state was broken. She turned and saw the figure coming down on her with a large rock, one of the actual stones of the ruins. She screamed. It was too late, with a crushing blow to her head the rock knocked her down. Blood flowed from the side of her head as she collapsed with a scream of pain.

Ron made a flying tackle at the ankles of the fleeing figure catching him briefly and causing him to stumble. They both fell but the person in black was able to regain his footing and run as the other guys pursued him across the ruins. Ron tumbled onto the fallen body of the Lady in Black. She moaned as he did so. Crawling around to her side as the girls arrived on the scene, he cradled her in his arms lifting her veil saturated with her blood. Her emerald green eyes were fading as she looked into his. "The library get to the library to save the Holy…" her voice failed as she shoved the paper with the poem into his hand and then she was gone.

"Oh my God, Lord, you cannot let this happen to me again," Ron shouted up to the darkening sky.

The girls were screaming, "Ronnie, Ronnie; are you okay?"

As they did so, gun shots could be heard echoing across the ruins. The guys came running back shouting for the girls to get down on the ground.

As they grabbed hold of each other they fell to their knees and then flat on the rocky ground.

"Shit, that guy is shooting at us." Bob was panic stricken as he fell next to Ron still holding the dead woman and wrapped his arms around him as if to create a protective shield.

In an instant all became quiet. Only the sound of a car engine could be heard and the scattering of gravel as it sped out of the parking area. Ron was now rocking the Lady in Black and praying.

"Hail Mary full of grace the Lord is with thee…"

Bob dropped his arms from his pal and joined in prayer with him. As the others realized that Ron held a dead person, they too prayed as they joined hands forming a circle around Ron and the Woman in Black. Through the Lord's Prayer and the Glory Be they knelt and followed Ron's lead until they reached the traditional ending of prayer for the dead, "May her soul and the souls of the faithfully departed through the mercy of God rest in peace, In the name of the Father and of the Son and of the Holy Spirit, Amen."

Six of the seven didn't know what to do. They all watched a scene all too familiar to them after that incident on the Colosso Statue of St. Charles Borromeo in Arona Italy in the Southern Alps. There too was a similar scene one which they hoped this holiday adventure would set aside from Ron's dreams and their own. Bob leaned into Ron.

"What shall we do now in the middle of nowhere?"

Ron lifted his head to scan the faces of his friends. That question could be read in all their eyes. Without a word, he gently lowered the body of the woman onto the chancel stone placing her hat behind her head to act like a pillow and pulling down the black net veil to cover the now serene face of the middle age woman with what appeared to be auburn hair. As he did so the burning clouds floated away and the bright sunshine of evening hours returned. The eerie shadows were gone save for their own and the realization that a murder had just been committed began to sink in. He held up the blood stained paper on which the poem she read was printed.

"She gave me this with her last breath." Ron examined it and folded it carefully then placed it in Bob's satchel still hanging off his pal's back. "Now we need to get a grip on this situation. The police will want to know exactly what happened here and despite it all being like a flash in darkness we need to remember every detail."

"Right, we need to contact the police, but how are we going to do that out here surrounded by nothing?"

Susan's heart was breaking for Ron as she saw him once again taking control of a horrific situation and about to plan the next step. But that wasn't what really touched her heart to the breaking point. It was the prayer he led all of them in that did it. She could never tell him what she told his sister and never prevent him from doing what he was called to do, serve the Lord.

"That's a good question Dominic. We are in unfamiliar territory but so were we in Arona on Lake Maggiore. So let's take stock in what we remember coming here."

Everyone looked at each other for that first memory which would get them going. Bob stated the obvious. "Well we're only here because we missed the exit for Slane Castle."

"That's it Watson, you're a genius. That castle is only what, ten minutes from here?" Ron turned toward Alessandro. "Well Count of Pianore, I think you have a job to do. You said that your father knows the Earl who owns the place. So it's just logical that you go knock on his door and introduce yourself and ask to use their phone."

It was done, the first step was taken. Alessandro would go with Andreas in the van after they made sure it was not hit by any of the bullets fired at them. They would call the police from Slane Castle. Everyone else would wait for them and watch over the Lady in Black.

It was in that vigil over her that they noticed a red rose partially concealed by the body. Ron pulled it from under her shoulder and placed it in her hands which he folded across her body. In that act of reverence he already knew that he had tampered with the evidence and his finger prints were on everything including the blood stained rock which he pushed aside as he placed her head down on the Chancel Stone.

Slane Castle

CHAPTER THREE

CHARCOAL BRIQUETTES IN THE SKY

That same eerie sky lighted by those charcoal briquettes floating in the sky lay over Slane Castle when the Marquess and his son arrived home. Oddly Shamus Sweeney was nowhere to be seen when they entered eventually letting themselves into the castle as no one had come to the door to admit them. Looking about the main floor from the reception hall into which they walked, then into the sitting room, followed by the dining room, they had just entered the library yet another empty room as far as people was concerned. However they did find something in that room which was unexpected.

Briefly abandoning their search for the Chief Butler who was actually the only one on permanent staff, they let their attention be drawn to what appeared to be a piece of furniture in the middle of the oak paneled library. They were unable to discern as to whether it was a chair or table as it was wrapped with a heavy quilted packing blanket and tied securely with a rope. Not expecting a delivery of anything until the next day, the 7th Marquess approached the item and began to loosen the ropes about it.

Outside on the gravel driveway a small dark car sped around the Trinity College van with Andreas driving and Alessandro in the passenger seat.

"Watch it Andreas; that guy is going to hit us for sure, he's driving like a madman." Alessandro hung out the window to try and catch a glimpse as to who was in the speeding car. "It's some older guy but I didn't get a good look at him."

Andreas had swung to the edge of the driveway and onto the grass border still damp from an earlier brief isolated shower. He now brought the van back onto the driveway; the sounds of small stones clinking against the undercarriage resulted. Slowing down to a halt as they approached the entrance doors centered between large windows on either side of them and up a few steps. There was no portico over the doorway just the steps leading up to them. The flat gray stone façade took on the shadows and an occasional orange-like brilliance from the waning sun. Reflecting in the glass panes of the windows were those floating burning coals now breaking up.

"Jesu, they could have at least left the light on for us," Andreas smirked knowing full well that they were not expected visitors. He turned to his passenger. "It's all up to you now, Count of Pianore. Go do your thing and get us into the castle."

Alessandro knew what he had to do but still he pointed out that it was his father who knew the Marquess not he, in fact he hadn't seen him since he was much younger. With that being said he opened the van door and jumped down. "Va bene, here goes nothing. What if he tells me to go jump in the lake or worse?"

"Really, do you actually think that someone coming to his door distraught over the death of some poor woman would be told that; just get on with it."

Alessandro took a deep breath and walked up the stairs. "I just hope that he is hospitable, and not cranky."

Inside the library the last of the ropes fell onto the oak panels which made up the floor as the bell was heard. The Marquess looked up toward the door leading into the hall. No butler came running out to answer the door.

"Father, he's not here. I'll go answer the door."

"You shall do no such thing, not with the troubles rearing its ugly head lately. You stay right here, I'll go."

Henry did as he was told and plopped himself down onto a wooden chair at the reading table in front of which was the item they were unwrapping. He glanced at the crossed swords on the wall opposite of him with the thought that his fencing lessons might come in handy should those at the door be unwelcomed.

The Marquess had closed the solid wood double doors behind him as he left. But as soon as his footsteps faded, Henry ran to the wall and then to the doors opening them slightly, in his hand was one of those swords from the wall. He hadn't time to think as to what side he would fight for in that famous Battle of the Boyne which took place not far from their castle. Would he be a Williamite, a soldier who followed William of Orange who was fighting for the throne of England or a Jacobite, a follower of the deposed Catholic King of England, King James. He wanted to be on the winning side that night for obvious reasons and took himself to be a Williamite as he watched his father cross the limestone floor of the foyer headed for the door.

Henry breathed a sigh of relief as from behind the wide staircase came running Shamus, trying to put on his black suit coat while rushing to head off the Marquess.

"I do beg your pardon, your Lordship, but things aren't running quite smoothly tonight. If you permit me, I shall get the door." He stood between the Marquess and the door.

"Good heavens Shamus, you look a fright, what's happened?"

"Yes sir, I do indeed, but shouldn't I get the door first as that pounding has not let up for a while?"

"Of course, let us find out what the fuss is all about. We shall talk later."

After a slight bow of the head, the butler turned and walked to the door, opening it slightly he knew what he would probably find as he had cut a van off as he entered the grounds in such a hurry. He was right. There stood a tall dark young man illuminated by the setting sun so as to glow like a god, make that two gods from Olympus as right behind him stood a pale skinned, blond young man in his twenties. Despite appearing to be shorter because of where he stood on the gravel being that the dark haired one stood on the top step, he was equally as tall if not taller from what he could tell. Seeing two handsome young men who were obviously distressed about something as they were nervously shifting in their stance and wringing their hands, he opened the door a bit wider. This allowed the casting of light from the crystal chandelier overhead onto the faces of the two standing outside.

"Good evening gentlemen, how may I be of assistance?"

"Buona Serra…I mean good evening to you. I am looking for the Marquess, Earl of Mount Charles."

"And why pray tell at this hour of the evening would you wish to speak with His Lordship?"

"Please tell him that Alessandro, the son of the Count of Pianore is calling upon him with a rather urgent need."

Before the butler had a chance to reply, the Marquess pulled open the door and stepped in front of Shamus. "Alessandro, my, the photos do not do you justice. How tall you are and a full grown man; do come in and tell me, how is your father and charming mother?" He pulled on the arm of Alessandro and pulled him through the doorway and into an embrace. He instantly felt the tension in the young man while noticing yet another lad behind him. "If you are a friend of the young Count do come in."

Andreas meekly followed them into the reception hall, stopping to look over the disheveled butler who definitely was an older guy.

"Now tell me Alessandro, what brings you to Ireland and why didn't your father tell me that you were coming with a friend? Henry look here, it's the young Count of Pianore," he turned to Alessandro. "Your mother and father were so kind to us, when we visited last winter at the villa but you were in Rome with a University class, I believe."

They were walking into the library where Henry was busily replacing the sword on the wall. Andreas followed them virtually feeling the breath of the butler who walked behind him on his neck. He rubbed the back of his neck as if he could wipe the feeling away.

Back at the Mellifont Abbey ruins Ron was still kneeling at the side of the dead woman in black. He leaned back on his legs and looked to each side of him where Bob and Dominic flanked him. The prayers were concluded and they didn't know what they should do if anything. Bob was pointing out that Ron's fingerprints were all over the rock which was the murder weapon as if Ron hadn't realized that already.

"Like I don't know that but what was I supposed to do? Just let the poor woman suffer her last breath without a hint of compassion to try to make her more comfortable."

Bob's face became saddened like that of a puppy being scolded. "I'm sorry, I just thought of what happened back at the Abbey last year and then again on that statue in Italy last fall."

Ron patted his buddy on the back. "I'm sorry too; this is a mess for all of us. We were supposed to get away from this kind of violence after everything that happened in Rome. I think I'm cursed or something."

Susan and Jan watched the guys at the body from a stone foundation on which they sat. Susan wrapped her arms around Ron's sister who was upset that her brother was feeling the way he did.

"Poor Ronnie, he was trying to help and she died in his arms just like that nightmare we lived through last fall," she paused for something had caught her eye. The purse of the Lady in Black lay not three feet from where they sat. "Susan, what's that?"

In the dimming light which ended the floating shimmering coal-like clouds as they faded in color, the smooth black leather caught the final rays as the long strap meant to hang over one's shoulder stretched out as if calling to her. Jan shot up and went for the purse before Susan could react. As she bent down to grab hold of the strap, a hand took hold of her wrist.

"No sis, don't touch it. It's bad enough that my fingerprints are on it, we don't need yours as well," Ron placed his arm around his sister and took her back to Susan. He turned and told the guys, "I think it's time to see if we can figure out who this poor woman was."

"Oh my God Ron, no don't touch it again," Bob pleaded.

It was too late. Ron had taken hold of the strap and lifted the purse up. He walked toward the *lavabo* ruin and placed it onto an arched window ledge which was still intact. His companions gathered on the other side of that opening and watched as he unzipped the purse and looked inside. The first thing he pulled out was a Passport of the United Kingdom. "So it appears that whoever she is, that she was English, Welsh, Scotch or Northern Irish."

Andreas and Alessandro were seated at the reading table of the library in Slane Castle. Opposite them were the Marquess and the young Earl, his son. Standing at the doorway was Shamus who was intently listening to their conversation.

"My dear boy, I am so sorry to hear of this. But who you've described can be no other than my guest. I left her at the ruins not long ago, it was still light. She insisted to be alone. I thought she wanted to pray or explore," he rose from his high back wooden chair with leather upholstery and walked to the still covered piece of furniture. "I remember that she was interested in some ancient maps I had in the castle collection but I couldn't let her review them as they were out being fixed onto a new display case, which if I'm not mistaken is under this blanket."

He pulled off the blanket revealing a mahogany case on four legs with the display area being rectangular in shape around three feet wide and two feet long. The display area was recessed about four inches down onto a velvet panel on which the maps were attached and glass protected. "And there you have it; as I expected the new display case and here inside are the maps. The issue is how did they get into my library when I wasn't home and obviously," he turned to look at the butler standing in the doorway. "Nor was Shamus if I am correct."

The butler seemed embarrassed as he slowly stepped forward. "If I may Your Lordship…you are correct. I was out briefly this evening looking for the Curator of the Irish Museum, Mr. O'Neill. I had given him directions to Mellifont but realized that he had turned the wrong way to get there. I tried to catch up with him but couldn't. I'm presuming he is still out there somewhere trying to find the Mellifont ruins."

"Thank you Shamus, but that doesn't explain how this display case got into the library." The doorbell followed by knocking on the front door of the castle interrupted the thought of the Marquess. "You had best get that." He turned to the silent young men at the table. "I am presuming that would be the Garda, our police."

"Yes sir, I hope so. All our friends at Mellifont must be worried as to where we are. They are stranded there with…" he wouldn't go on as he tried not to bring up the dead woman who was the guest of the Marquess.

"Quite right Alessandro, I understand that both of you wish to get back as quickly as possible. As soon as this matter is taken care of, I shall come with you."

The young Count of Pianore glanced at Andreas, who wasn't feeling much like a member of the Swiss Guard at that moment. The last thing they wanted was to drag the Marquess into a murder investigation and certainly not his teen son. The exchange without words ended when Shamus returned.

"Your Lordship, Sargent Carrick of the Garda wishes to speak with you."

Stepping out from behind the butler appeared a man in uniform about ten years older than the young men seated at the table. The two now stood as the officer entered the library. He removed his cap and placed it under his right arm revealing a thick bushy head of black hair. His dark eyes gave him the look of Alessandro from Italy rather than from the northern county of the Republic of Ireland.

"Good Evening Lord Conyngham and all present," he nodded to young Henry and the Marquess and then zeroed in on Andreas and Alessandro as he walked up to the obvious strangers to the community. "I am Sargent Lawrence Carrick of the Drogheda Garda sent by Chief Inspector Rory O'Connor to take your statements of the incident at Mellifont. He has decided to go directly to the Mellifont Ruins to inspect the scene."

As those words were being spoken by the Sargent, two black cars and an ambulance pulled into the parking area of the Mellifont Abbey ruins. The driver of the first car dressed in a police uniform jumped out of the driver's seat to open the rear door of the vehicle which did not have its lights flashing. Out stepped a rather robust looking man which even in the almost totally dark evening could be seen to have flaming red hair which would challenge that of Susan in brilliance. He was not in a uniform but a dark suit with black tie and white shirt. Despite his suit, the middle age man seemed a bit disheveled in that his tie was not affixed close to the neck and his hair hadn't seen a comb for the better part of a day to be sure.

"Thank you Carrick, tell the other men to follow us into the ruins with no guns drawn if you please. I believe that we're dealing with a group of tourists who found a dead body." He turned to the Coroner's men. "You two stay here with the stretcher made ready for my call."

At the body of the Woman in Black, Ron was reading her name from the UK Passport. "This belongs to the lady for sure," he held up the passport showing the photo. "Her name is Devorgilla MacMurrough…"

It was a strange sounding name to everyone standing around Ron. Only Susan was able to note that the name was of ancient origin. This she surmised because of its Gaelic spelling she was able to identify because of her perusing an Irish language text on the plane coming to Dublin.

A deep voice came from the shadows beyond their little group huddled around the *lavabo* ruin. Several flashlights behind him gave the man a ghostly appearance. "And thank you for that information young man, and how did you come to know it?"

Ron turned to face the direction of the voice as his friends became frozen in place with the beams of the flashlights now shining in their eyes. There was no way to tell if they were police at that point but Ron felt confident that it was a voice of authority speaking, he had heard such speech before back in Wisconsin, New York City and most recently from a certain Captain in the Carbinieri of Italy, all of them were police detectives. He thought that he was being respectful when he stated, "Well it says so right here on her passport which I know belongs to her as the photo on it matches that of the face of the victim."

The Chief Inspector took control of one of the flashlights and shined it on the passport which Ron held up. "And how did you come upon this Passport? But first let us get to know one another," O'Connor ordered Walsh to take down their names and contact information. He remained silent with the flashlight beams still shining on the Passport. When Walsh finished with Dominic, Susan, Jan and Bob he came around the broken wall toward Ron. "Thank you Walsh, please keep notes until the Sargent arrives with the others. And now young man exactly who are you and what brings you and the others to these ruins at night?"

After identifying himself as Ron De Cenza of the Apostolic College in Rome, he informed the Chief Inspector that they were all assistants to Professor Andrew Pettigrew of Oxford University on a research project.

"And is it normal practice to conduct such research in the dead of night? Where is this Professor Pettigrew?" O'Connor continued to shine the light on the Passport but made no mention of it as yet or of the blood on the Coliseum on Ron's souvenir shirt which it also illuminated.

It didn't take a Sherlock Holmes to figure out that he did so to cause a bit of anxiousness amongst he and his friends for they had tampered with evidence. Nevertheless Ron decided to simply answer the questions. He was interrupted by Dominic.

"Sir, I am Dominic Fontana also of Oxford University who works with the Professor. He has remained in Dublin meeting with the Dean of Antiquities at Trinity College… a Mr. Drumond Shannon, I believe is his name."

The Chief Inspector thanked him for the information and instructed Officer Carrick to radio headquarters. His intent was to have this Dean at Trinity tracked down as well as the Professor. Now he was ready to focus on the passport, the bloody shirt and the body still lying on the chancel stone in the chapel ruins. Being another officer short, he found himself with five suspects, two distant educators and the unknown of what was happening at Slane Castle where he had sent his Sargent. Nevertheless he directed Ron to take him to the victim.

Re-entering the car park area, Walsh immediately saw the two ambulance attendants standing next to the stretcher. "The Chief Inspector is viewing the body now. You should be summoned shortly to remove the victim." Receiving their acknowledgement he moved on to his car and took hold of the microphone to contact Trinity College at Dublin having little hope of reaching anyone given the time. His second call would then be to the Garda Headquarters in Dublin.

While making his call, the Trinity College van and Sargent's car pulled up next to the ambulance. From within the van Sargent Carrick came out of the passenger side. Another officer was driving the Garda car. He opened the side door of the van to assist the Marquess out. His son, Henry, was told to stay with Shamus at the castle as Carrick didn't feel it necessary to expose the young Earl of Mount Charles to what was sure to be a grizzly sight. His driver joined them with flashlight in hand as Andreas and Alessandro approached the Marquess standing next to Sargent Carrick. He having everyone in place then called to the ambulance drivers to follow them with the stretcher. Before they left, Andreas pointed out the direction from which the shots came at them when they chased the fleeing murderer.

From behind one of the last remaining clouds shone the bright Moon which made its presence noticed as it appeared against the back drop of the star studded night sky. Under this canopy of twinkling lights and moonbeams two processions made their way to the Lady in Black holding her red rose.

With Ron at his side, the Chief Inspector was led to the chancel stone on which the victim now known as the Lady Devorgilla lay in death. Bob, Susan, Jan and Dominic followed as in a religious procession, only this one had two uniformed officers holding flashlights and not candles behind them. The moonlight emphasized the red rose on the body as they approached. O'Connor instructed that everyone take the position they were in when the incident took place. This meant that except for Ron, everyone stood on the foundation stones of the outer wall of the Abbey ruins while Ron was near the body where he thought he had tackled the shadowy figure after the mortal blow was struck. Bob placed himself between Ron and where the others stood at the foundation stones, explaining that he was slightly behind his pal when the murderer was tackled; adding that wasn't unusual as Ron always could outrun him even in college gym class. The Chief Inspector nodded as he looked over the ample physique of Bob Wentz which certainly would require more of an effort to move at great speed.

Turning his attention to Ron and not the body just ahead of them, he asked a question. "So then am I to understand that it was only you who actually saw the blow being struck and only you who laid hands on the assailant?"

Instantly flashing in Ron's brain was a picture of the Abbey School volleyball court back in Wisconsin. There on that summer afternoon now more than a year past a wounded man came down that grassy knoll and fell upon him to die in his arms. He knew what that Chief Inspector was thinking and he had to dispel that theory and quickly too. For he knew the next questions would involve why he opened the purse and why he touched the bloody rock which served as the murder weapon.

"Chief Inspector, sir, I can't say what the others actually saw as it happened so fast and I was trying to shout at the guy dressed all in black hoping to stop him hitting the Lady with that rock." Ron pointed to the rock a few feet away from the body. "It was too late, he struck her and she fell where she is now while I tackled him at the ankles."

"And in this tackle you noticed nothing about the person; and you weren't able to keep this person on the ground, he was so much larger than you then?"

"I am sorry to say that I didn't have a good hold on him and he was able to kick his way out of my grasp by hitting me in this shoulder which isn't what it used to be. The kick made me flinch and release him before I knew what happened."

"So the assailant kicked himself away by kicking your right shoulder; does it still hurt?"

"Well kind of since he got me right where I was shot…"

"He shot you?" the Chief Inspector was taken by surprise.

"No he didn't Brother Michael shot me…"

"And who is this Brother Michael, one of those on the foundation stones or those who you said were out calling me to this scene?"

"Oh my God, of course not they are my friends; I think I was not very clear. Let me show you." Ron pulled the blood stained Roma tee shirt up and over his head. He called to one of the officers to shine the light on him.

The light flashed on his belly button at first.

"Not down there, up here on the shoulder," he pointed to his right shoulder area. "Now then, see this scar, that's where I was shot last year by this guy who pretended to be a Monk so that he could rip off the Abbey. To this day it's still sensitive especially to something like a kick which was right on target."

Susan gasped as the light flashed on Ron's belly button and up to his shoulder. "Oh he is so handsome even though he's rather thin, I can see his rib cage."

"Really now you have to evaluate my brother's looks while he's being interrogated; get a grip girl. We have to save him from himself, always trying to be the hero."

"Right, I got it. No more chest looking," Susan sighed then took a deep breath. "Let's go rescue him."

Off the stones the girls jumped, grabbed hold of Dominic and then Bob on their way to the Chief Inspector.

"I told you to stay where you were located when the attack took place."

Ron instead of holding his shirt across his bare chest continued his experiment in lust over love. He gave a tug on his jeans and brought them down a pinch to reveal just the slightest ribbon of pubic hair coming up and touching the bottom of his belly button.

Susan watched the move and couldn't help herself. She sighed, "Oh doesn't he have just the cutest little ole inner side belly button you ever saw?"

Jan poked her in the side. "Stop it." She turned her attention to the Chief Inspector. "Sorry sir, but we couldn't help hearing what Ron is telling you and need to clarify a few points for you."

"All in good time, young lady," then turning his attention back to Ron, "you may put that shirt back on young man."

The Inspector was interrupted by the arrival of Sargent Carrick and the others. "Sir, I've brought the stretcher bearers, the Marquess and the students."

O'Connor walked up to them. "Your Lordship, I am sorry that my Sargent brought you here, you are not a witness to the events here and needn't have come."

"Thank you Chief Inspector, but this poor woman was a guest in my house and I felt it to be my duty to be here."

"Then I thank you," O'Connor turned his attention to the others. "You two with the stretcher go stand on those rocks; be ready to come forward when I ask you to do so. And now for you two, I am to believe that you are Andreas Berne," he pointed to the blond Swiss Guard, "and you are the young Count Alessandro of Pianore in Italy, am I correct?"

"Yes sir," they jointly replied.

He directed them to join their friends lined up at the head of the dead woman in the sanctuary area. Ron still stood at the side of the body next to the rock he had moved. The Marquess remained at the side of the Chief Inspector and moved with him to stand next to Ron. He gave an audible gasp as he came upon the Lady in Black with the rose in her hands.

An ever more darkening night came over them as another wave of clouds came across the ruins. They were blocking the moonlight and constellations with a veil-like cover similar to that which covered the face of the dead woman. This allowed shimmering light to filter through the clouds and just the slightest features of the mature woman to be seen behind the black netting of the veil of her hat. In this dim light O'Connor had to procure the slightest details which might lead him to the assailant. While he placed everyone where he wanted them, he realized that the coroner himself was not present. He was told by the stretcher bearers that he was in Dublin for a meeting of Medical Examiners and would be returning later that night. He decided that the body should not be left out in the elements. She would be moved to the hospital in the village of Drogheda. Before that would take place however, he was to have the exact events from the time of their arrival in the Trinity College van to the attack to the chase to what took place after he got away acted out.

The enactment concluded with the five guys and two girls holding hands and kneeling around the body of the Lady as they prayed and Ron acted out the placing of the Rose in her hands.

The Chief Inspector was satisfied that he had gotten a clearer picture of what happened amongst the ruins of Mellifont Abbey. His next step was to have the students placed in a hotel or closest Convent or Rectory as they were all material witnesses and would be needed for further questioning. He would also be sending for Professor Pettigrew and the Dean of Antiquities to verify where they were when this incident took place. As this was being planned the Marquess offered to house the seven in Slane Castle. He felt that to be a logical place as the item the dead woman wanted to see was in his library and his other guest the Curator of Dublin Museum, Hugh O'Neill might be back from his excursion which had gotten him lost as he hadn't arrived at Mellifont which was his destination.

"Is that so, yet another person involved; we will get to him in due course," noted the Chief Inspector.

Before leaving Ron knelt at the side of the Lady Devorgilla, offered a prayer as all stood with heads bowed behind him. The coroner's men then sent them away as they gently placed her body onto the stretcher as the

Chief Inspector led everyone toward the cark park area. While the Lady in Black was taken to the ambulance Ron pulled Bob back behind the *lavabo*.

"What the…"

"Quiet Bob and listen to me. That paper I put in your satchel," Ron gave the leather bag a thump with his hand. "Say nothing to anyone, even the guys, my sister or Susan, at least for now. I don't want them to get into trouble if what I'm about to do goes awry."

Bob grabbed hold of his shoulders; Ron winced as the kick to it still hurt. "Oh sorry, he hurt you didn't he? Well the hell with him for now. You can't do this alone and you know it. You need Watson or am I Tonto today…whatever, you need me or I blab about the paper in my bag."

Ron took hold of him and squeezed him tight but briefly. "You big nutcase, I am just trying to protect you and everyone else. Of course I need you, always will but this isn't like what happened back home or even in Italy."

His voice quivered a bit but Bob disagreed. "Who's the nut case now? This is exactly how it was in Italy when you copied those notes in the Professor's brief case only this time you have the real thing and if the Chief Inspector finds out, you're in deep shit."

"Well then pal, that's your job, keep me out of the shit because we don't even know what's on that paper the Lady gave me with her last breath. She just said something about the library and pushed it into my hand."

Bob shuddered. "Oh Lord, then it's like her dying wish or something."

"Well it's something all right but what that is remains to be seen. Come on before the Chief Inspector gets suspicious."

"I think he's not as nice as Detective Sargent Malone back in New York or for sure Captain Verdi in Italy. He seems to be all business not much empathy."

"Judge not lest you be judged young man, as Father Gregory back at the Abbey would say. Come on." Ron grabbed Bob's arm and pulled him out from behind the ruin right toward the chancel stone where the body had been.

The moonlight suddenly became quite bright as the lingering clouds floated away without dispensing their usual soft shower. Unfortunately right in front of them was Sargent Carrick and another officer who were setting up poles and tape reading "crime scene" around the chancel stone. They immediately noticed Ron and Bob running from the *lavabo*.

"Hey, you two stop where you are," shouted the Sargent. "Okay, now come over here."

The frozen in place guys slowly thawed and moved toward the Sargent with Ron offering an excuse for their being away from the others before the Sargent asked the question. "We just couldn't hold it any longer; you know we had to take a leak."

"Is that so, well zip it up and help us out," the Sargent laughed. "So do you guys always pee together or what?"

"Well, we do everything together Sargent." Bob offered a thin smile realizing what he just said could mean something quite different as he checked his zipper thinking that's what the Sargent meant when he said what he said.

The Sargent glanced at the officer across from him and gave him a wink. "Okay, glad you managed to get it all out. So take this and jam it into the ground opposite me," he handed Bob a three foot long stick and then gave Ron another one. "You can put this at the top of this long stone where the victim was lying. Here, take this flashlight too. Make sure you stay away from the stone itself. The coroner and Chief Inspector will be back here tomorrow to check out the scene."

The guys went about their duties as instructed. After Ron stuck his stick into the ground, he used the flashlight to light up the chancel stone and get a quick peek at what the stone was all about. There had to be a reason why the Lady in Black chose to do whatever she was doing on that stone. The Sargent was worried that any rain from those clouds which kept appearing since their arrival might wash away finger prints and evidence. He pointed to the pool of blood still spread across the flat stone as he placed the crime scene tape around the stick and moved on to the next one. It afforded Ron the time to take a closer look at that blood spill.

What became clear to him was that the blood gathered in certain grooves within the rock but that they were more than natural crevices and formations within the stone's surface. There were letters faintly visible and the blood had filled those carved letters which made them more distinguishable. He called to Bob to help him with his stick feigning that the soil was hard to penetrate. It wasn't and Bob knew that but played along.

"So what have you found?"

"Look there where the light is shining but don't be obvious about it. What do you see?"

"Holy shit, are those letters carved into the stone? But this place is like nine hundred years old at least, so whatever those spell out is pretty old I'd say."

"Exactly, now turn your back to me so I can get a pen and paper from your satchel." Ron slipped his hand into the bag and found the paper which the Lady had given him, but pushed it to the side ever so gently so as not to get blood on his hand. In the inside pocket was a pen and pad of paper. "Ok, got it…now just keep me blocked while I copy down those letters."

The deed was done quickly. The letters he could make D…E…R… B…A…I…l…, it was obvious that some of the letters were so worn as not to be distinguishable even with blood filling in the indentation in the stone. "Done," Ron replaced the pad and pen just as the Sargent arrived with his roll of yellow tape with black lettering stating "crime scene- do not enter."

"Well now, praise God this sordid job is done. Thanks lads for the help. 'Tis time to return to Chief Inspector O'Connor."

On the way back, Ron poked Bob in the arm. "Christ almighty didn't I forget it back at those rocks."

"Huh, what are you talking about?"

"You know, my camera, I put it down to pee and now I left it there on that rock so I didn't pee on it by mistake in the dark." He winked at Bob as he pulled the instamatic camera out of Bob's satchel and slipped it into his pocket.

"Ah, that rock, sure I saw it there." He ran up to the Sargent. "Sargent Carrick, my friend forgot his camera back at that thing called the *lavabo*, he needs to go get it."

"Indeed, it might rain so okay but make it quick; I see the Inspector pacing by the cars."

Running back to Ron he sent him off blocking him so that the camera now in his hand could not be seen. Back at the chancel stone Ron crawled under the crime scene tape and knelt exactly where he was when he held the dying Lady in Black who obviously had been lying over the letters. Bending over with the camera stretched out over the blood filled lettering he snapped some shots. Then just before leaving he took a photo of the entire chancel stone. It was rather dark despite the moon having come out from behind the clouds. He prayed that the letters would be visible once he had them developed. The next thought as he turned to run back was where he would find a camera shop out in the middle of nowhere.

His thought was cut short as he ran right into Sargent Carrick. "Oh shit, I'm so sorry, sir."

The Sargent toppling over was grabbed by Ron and righted himself on his feet. "For a skinny lad you certainly pack a forceful body slam. Now go on with you, I have to take some photos of the crime scene just in case it rains and everything is gone tomorrow." He held up a thirty-five millimeter camera with flash attachment; then in a low whisper he added. "The Chief Inspector is pissed that I forgot to leave the camera when we first came onto the scene while I left for the castle. He could have remembered as well but that's how it works. It's always the underling who gets blamed." He laughed and poked Ron in the ribs. "Isn't that true lad at school as well? I bet that Professor bosses you around like no one's business."

Ron played along. "Oh you don't know half of it. You should have seen him in Italy when we were doing the research there. I had to climb this huge statue and almost got killed. I tell you I almost shit myself on that one and there he was in Rome getting all the credit."

Sargent Carrick had no clue as to what Ron was talking about, nor for that matter did Ron. He was mixing up a variety of events to make it sound good for the ears of the disgruntled policeman who was past forty and still not a Detective in rank. He nevertheless shook his head with empathy, slapped Ron on the ass and told him to get back to the car park never noticing the instamatic camera in Ron's front pocket but certainly having felt it when it slammed into his groin area in the collision. Ron was off and the Sargent was laughing as he thought that the lad must have had a boner when they collided. He wistfully remembered those days of his youth when any little thought of his girlfriend would do that to him. "Ah, to be a young lad again, hard and virile."

From the parking lot the Chief Inspector and everyone else could see the flashes from the camera. It appeared like tiny quick lightning bolts in quick succession across the ruins. "Well at least we may have something to go by but it would have been better if he had done that while we were still in the light of day."

It was done; the moonlight shimmered over the ancient ruins. The blood splattered chancel stone glistened as if the life force spread across it could tell a story of its own about the events of that night. In truth that story would be of ancient times and a Lady in Black who was connected to those days.

CHAPTER FOUR

A High King and Chief Inspector

The ambulance having gone off to a small hospital in Drogheda on the east coast with the body of the Lady in Black now known to be Lady Devorgilla MacMurrough, the Marquess now led the Chief Inspector and his new guests to the entrance doors of Slane Castle. The two police cars and the Trinity College Van had pulled directly in front of its main doors. Up the four steps to the large double oak doors he was about to open it when it was swung open. There stood the Chief Butler, Shamus Sweeney.

"Your Lordship, I am so pleased to see you. The curator returned not long after you left. He is quite disturbed after his ordeal."

"Good Lord man, what ordeal," the Marquess turned to the Chief Inspector. "Chief Inspector, it appears that we have yet another issue for the man of whom he speaks is also my guest. He is the Curator of the Dublin Museum, Mr. Hugh O'Neill." He then addressed his guests from the Trinity College Van. "I am terribly sorry about this situation. Please come in and we shall see that you are all made comfortable. Unfortunately we only have Shamus on duty this evening."

The butler led the Marquess and his guests into the library. Upon entering the young Earl, Henry stood just beyond the door and approached his father. "Mr. O'Neill, he just sits there on that chair looking out the window. I think he's frightened of something…"

"Or perhaps someone but who could that be, he just got here." The Marquess had turned to speak with the Chief Inspector but he had already slipped away. Next to him was Ron. "Oh, I do apologize; this is all so shocking an evening."

"Yes sir, it's been quite the day. If I may, who is that man?"

"That's Mr. Hugh O'Neill the Curator of the Dublin Museum

Chief Inspector O'Connor had already pulled up one of the chairs from the reading table and sat next to the curator. "I am Chief Inspector Rory O'Connor, I was told that you are Hugh O'Neill of the Dublin Museum."

The blank stare of O'Neill's eyes suddenly got a bit of a spark. He turned his head and smiled. "Yes, that's true, but it's the curator of the Antiquities Building which includes the High Kings of Ireland and that Chief Inspector is who you must be named after, the last High King that is."

"Aye, you've got me there sir. My Mom thought it was a name fit for me but I don't think so, we're not descendants of the High King of that I am sure."

"Indeed, but with that ruddy complexion with those red cheeks and hair to match not to mention that warrior build which you're trying to hide under that coat, I'd say I could make a wax copy of you and place it beside the artefacts we have from his reign."

"Well be that as it may, I am just a police detective and we have a bit of a problem on our hands at the moment."

O'Neill turned to take in the crowd of young people around the reading table, the Marquess talking to Shamus and Henry who was speaking with Ron. "So it appears sir, but though they are young people, I have a feeling that they aren't friends of the young Earl."

"And there you would be correct Mr. O'Neill. They are research assistants to some Oxford Professor on an expedition to find artefacts which I might add would be right up your alley, so to speak."

"Oxford you say, that wouldn't be Professor Andrew Pettigrew, by any chance?"

"And sure that would be his name but how did you know? That young man with the slicked back dark hair and bloody shirt who is speaking with the young Earl just gave it to me."

"Bloody shirt, did I hear you correctly?" O'Neil was beginning to re-enter reality.

"Aye sir, that you did, in fact that is why I am here with the Marquess, these young people and speaking with you. There has been a death at the Mellifont ruins. That young man with blood on his shirt was with the victim when she died…"

"Oh my God… she? Did you say the victim was a woman?"

"True, I did say 'she' but why is that important to you?"

"Oh no reason but I was to meet a woman at the Mellifont ruins this evening but I got lost, me who lives just twenty minutes from here in Dublin." O'Neill brushed his fingers through his hair and straightened his tie. "I'm a mess to be sure and confused over all of this."

"To be sure, it's embarrassing to lose your way in your own neighborhood so to speak. But that brings me to my questions. First, who is this woman whom you were to meet? And second, where have you been between these last two hours?"

"I see, you think I am a suspect. The truth as I mentioned is that I was lost between here and the Hill of Tara where I watched the sun setting. And as for the woman, may I ask if her name is Devorgilla MacMurrough?"

Ron was trying to be polite to the young Earl but in the process he was leading him toward the Chief Inspector trying to overhear their conversation. This brought him to the newly arrived display case with its coverings still on the floor with the ropes which had tied the blanket over it. "This is a lovely piece, Henry, what's being displayed?"

"That's part of what I think the Lady Devorgilla was interested in, you see she asked to see the ancient maps my father has in our collection."

Ron's feigned interest became intently real. "Are you saying that these are original maps; Maps of what?"

"I don't know exactly, I'm just beginning to study about our family history and how we are involved in Irish history in these parts. But since the Lady was interested in finding a connection between her family and Mellifont I'd think they are of the last High King's territory, the Kingdom of Rory O'Connor."

"Was she an O'Connor then like the Chief Inspector?"

"That's the question; she said her name was Devorgilla Mac Murrough not O'Connor. And I know this; she carries an ancient name as well. The original Devorgilla was a sponsor of the building of Mellifont Abbey."

Ron's head began to spin; between half listening to the teen aged Earl and the questions which were being asked by the Chief Inspector, a lot of information was coming in and he was making connections. He recalled what the Lady in Black said to him as she died and pushed the paper into his hand, 'the library,' that's where some kind of connection could be found. And here he stood in a Castle Library with the curator of the Dublin Museum which was connected to the Trinity College Library where Professor Pettigrew was meeting with the Dean of Antiquities or so he thought.

In reality, Professor Pettigrew sat quite alone in the vast Library of Trinity College once again perusing the documents he had spread out across the long wooden table. These he had brought from the Vatican Archives. What he needed was the input of Drumond Shannon, Dean of Antiquities. When the chapel bells began to sound the chimes of the ten o'clock evening hour, he was certain he had been stood up, but why? It seemed the Dean was quite interested in hearing about his find in the archives.

The Grandfather clock in the reception hall of Slane Castle was also chiming out the 10:00 p.m. hour when the Chief Inspector made his announcement as a pounding on the castle's front door echoed into the library.

"Shamus, do see to the door. I can't imagine who could be at our door at this hour."

"Yes your Lordship," with that the butler left the library.

Susan leaned into Jan's ear. "Your brother is up to something, I just know it. Look at him being all sweet and interested in what that teenager Lord, or whatever he is, has to say."

"I don't know Susan, look at him. The kid is opening the display case for him."

Bob couldn't resist making a comment. "Oh no, you know what that means. That mind is forming a plan and I think we're involved in it."

Shamus opened the door to find a distinguished looking elderly gentleman on the top step. The lantern above him hung from a narrow archway but square not of the Romanesque type with a curve. It was quite in keeping with the medieval design of the castle. The light illuminated his face which sprouted a gray and black beard. He removed his cap revealing salt and pepper thinning hair. His hazel color eyes had wrinkle crinkles at their sides giving him a distinguished look rather than an old man appearance. He held a brief case under one arm and an umbrella hung over his other arm. In all the butler took him to be an Irish gentleman in a tweed suit with black overcoat which wasn't needed for it was a mild night.

"Good evening sir, the Castle is closed for the evening." Shamus decided to treat him like a wandering tourist.

"My good man, please announce that Professor Drumond Shannon, the Dean of Antiquities of Trinity College, is here on important business."

"Sir, it's after ten, could this not wait? The Marquess is with his guests."

"No it cannot wait. I must see Ron De Cenza and his comrades immediately."

Totally befuddled now, Shamus invited the gentleman into the castle, asking him to wait. "I shall announce you sir, please have a seat there." He walked away hurriedly, wondering how a Dublin professor would even know the group of American and Italian young people. He went to the Marquess rather than Ron. "Sir, the Dean of Antiquities from Trinity College was at the door; he waits in the reception hall."

"Shamus, it's past ten, I can't receive anyone else."

"That's the point sir, he's asked to see those young people not you."

"Well then, that's interesting. We should ask the Chief Inspector as to the proper course to take." As he walked toward the detective he patted Ron's shoulder as he stooped over peering into the display case. "This concerns you and your friends; I believe you should come with me."

Hugh O'Neill was elaborating on his being lost not more than twenty minutes from where they sat. He appeared mortified that he lost his bearings but resigned to understand that O'Connor had to ask his questions and whereabouts. "You see, I didn't know this woman at all. She had contacted me at the Museum by phone and offered information which would be of interest to the Antiquities department, so naturally I agreed to meet her at Mellifont especially when she gave me her name. I immediately contacted the Marquess and requested to visit his collection which seemed so important to this Lady Devorgilla. Her name alone resounds of ancient history of Ireland as you may know."

The Marquess came in at the end of his statement. "That's quite true Chief Inspector. Lady Devorgilla MacMurrough was the name the Lady used in introducing herself to me which resulted in an invitation to be my guest. You do understand the importance of that name in these parts I'm sure."

"I see," responded the Chief Inspector, who racked his brain thinking why that name was important like his own was. Before he could continue his questioning however, the Marquess told him about the unexpected visitor.

"Chief Inspector, the Dean of Antiquities, a Professor Drumond Shannon has arrived at the castle and has requested to speak with this young man," he placed his hand on Ron's shoulder and then removed it when Ron looked into his eyes with absolute amazement.

"Sir, I know that name, so does each of my friends. Professor Pettigrew with whom we came to Ireland for the research was to meet with him this very night. In fact that's why we're here in the first place. He gave us time off to 'explore and have fun,' as he put it."

"Am I to assume then that none of you know why he has made his way to the castle so late in the evening?"

Ron assured him that he or his friends had no clue as to why he would come to the castle. With that assurance, the Chief Inspector suggested that Ron go out with him to meet the gentleman. He, the Chief Inspector would decide whether or not to involve anyone else before he was brought into the Library. O'Neill was told to go to the reading table and sit with those already there. The curator did so with reluctance as he knew the Dean personally, yet he chose to not mention that relationship.

Shamus opened the library door and the American seminarian and the Chief Inspector of the Garda entered the Reception Hall. Seated on a rather plain wooden chair, though being almost fondled by the man in the tweed suit and unbuttoned overcoat was the Dean of Antiquities. O'Connor paused to watch the man stroke the wood of the chair. He held onto Ron to stay with him. It was not more than a few seconds before the Dean noticed the two standing a few feet from him. He immediately stopped his examination of the chair and stood. Seeing two, one of whom he knew could not be part of Pettigrew's assistants and obviously quite Irish he spoke to the slim, dark haired young man whose stare seemed to penetrate to the Dean's very soul.

"Ah, then you must be Ron De Cenza who Professor Pettigrew says is the leader of his pack of assistants. I'd guess it to be you from his description of this slender, wiry dark hair and wide eyed youth who had a keen mind for investigating a situation; of course I can't yet tell if ye are the keen mind part as yet."

Ron was at a loss for words but managed to get out that yes he was who he said he was but not their leader just one of them and then added, "Sir, we thought you were at a meeting with Professor Pettigrew."

"And so that would be true were it not for a series of events which has led me here," he paused to give a once over to the flaming red hair middle aged man standing next to Ron. "I am presuming here that you sir must have something to do with the Garda outside."

"Am I that obvious Professor Shannon? But yes, I am Chief Inspector Rory O'Connor and like Ron here, I am wondering as to what has brought you out to Slane Castle when you were to meet with their mentor?"

"Aye, that would be the truth you'd be speaking. As you can tell from your entrance into this grand hall and seeing me stroking this fine chair, I am interested in all things from antiquity and that is why I am amazed to have been seated on this chair. Whether or not anyone including the Marquess realizes, this chair I am sure dates back to the time of the High Irish Kings, the very last one of whom if I'm not mistaken you have been named for. In any case I will address this priceless item with His Lordship in good time, but as for your question…"

"Yes sir, as to that question, what brings you here at this time of night?"

The Dean stopped his caressing of the chair, turned and spoke with a sense of urgency and almost excitement. He walked across to the middle of the Hall under the crystal chandelier and looked about the art displaying the history of Ireland and the Conyngham family of which Marquess Fredrick was head. "My, it's no wonder this castle has attracted so many people to come for a tour. I would say that such visits are beginning to rival that of the Trinity College Library and we have the Books of Kells on display."

Ron couldn't take what he saw to be a protraction from answering the Chief Inspector's question. He walked up to the Dean. "Sir, this is like a museum for sure but why aren't you with Professor Pettigrew, is he ill?" He was of course having a flashback in his mind about the attack on the banks of the Tiber River in Rome, an attack which almost killed him and which was witnessed by him and Bob.

"Not at all, not at all," he began; with his thick Irish brogue being emphasized. "It's that I received a call from the Dublin Museum…"

"Mr. Hugh O'Neill, why he's here at this very moment," Ron spoke out of turn and O'Connor was not pleased.

"Is he now, well then his assistant, a Miss Tulley I believe, was correct."

The Chief Inspector placed his hand on Ron's shoulder so as to let him know that he was to keep his mouth shut. "This is getting a bit foggy sir; now you say you are here to see a Mr. O'Neill and yet this young man and his friends have informed me that you were to meet with a Professor Andrew Pettigrew at Trinity College."

The Dean placed his cap on the ancient chair as if he were laying the crown of ancient Ireland onto it. "And sure that is a true statement, however as I said I received a call from Hugh's assistant just before Professor Pettigrew was due to arrive. She informed me that plans were changed and that we were to meet here at Slane Castle with Professor Pettigrew instead."

The Grandfather clock across the hall from where they stood was now sounding the eleven o'clock evening hour as the Dean finished speaking. They all paused and listened to the chimes counting the hour. O'Connor checked his pocket watch and ran his fingers through his thick carrot top head of hair. Ron seeing the confusion growing and the impatience also asked if he could speak.

"Yes, do go ahead," responded O'Connor.

"Dean Shannon, I am Ron De Cenza one of Professor Pettigrew's assistants on his project. We are only here at Slane Castle because of a wrong exit being taken and events which followed. At no time did the Professor tell any of us that your meeting was to be changed. He I am quite sure is at Trinity College right now even at this late hour wondering where you are."

"Then lad I am quite befuddled. Why am I here?"

Ron's eyes virtually popped from his head as he realized that a sham had been played on the Dean, if indeed it was one presuming he was telling the truth. "Chief Inspector, please let us go back to Trinity College right now. I fear that Professor Pettigrew is in grave danger. If we leave now we should be there in less than thirty minutes." He turned to go for the door of the Library. "You don't understand, back in Rome he almost died because of what he discovered."

"Lad, is it that serious then?"

"It is sir; we must get to Trinity College."

"Now let's just keep calm. I shall call Dublin and have a patrol sent to Trinity College; where is the Professor?"

"He's in the Library not the part with the Book of Kells, the reading room."

The Chief Inspector opened the library door for Ron and motioned to the Dean to follow him in, "We shall all go to Dublin. It's best anyway given that this would be a grave imposition on His Lordship to have all of you here in the Castle given that tomorrow is a tourist visitation day."

Ron ran to his friends seated around the table while O'Neill as soon as he saw Dean Shannon came to him.

O'Connor called for Sargent Carrick. "Get hold of Dublin immediately, tell them to get to the Trinity College Library and seek a Professor Andrew Pettigrew and insure that he is safe." He then turned his attention to the startled Lord Conygham, the Marquess. "Your Lordship, news has come to our attention which requires us to return to Dublin tonight. We thank you for your hospitality and shall be returning in the morning to Mellifont, then to Drogheda Hospital to see to the remains of the woman called the Lady Devorgilla by you. We may also need your further assistance. When does the last tour group leave the Castle?"

"Henry knows this better than me," he called to his son speaking with Ron and his friends. They had already learned that the tour group would arrive at ten in the morning and most would be gone by noon.

Then the castle would be open from one in the afternoon until three for non-reservation visitors.

As this took place O'Neill approached Dean Shannon. "Good Lord! Drumond what brings you here to Slane Castle at this hour?"

The Dean observing the growing panic in the room was taken aback for the moment, then gathering his wits about him spoke. "Why, your Miss Tulley called to say that I should meet you here at the castle no matter how late. It sounded urgent so I said that I would leave as soon as I met with a Professor Pettigrew."

"But that is who these young people are working for, why on earth would she tell you to leave and not meet with him?"

"That I'm afraid is a mystery to me; but one thing more. When I offered to come after meeting with Pettigrew, she said that the Professor had already been contacted and would meet with me tomorrow instead. So here I am and am greeted by the police and that young man with a blood stained shirt. What has happened Hugh?"

Around the reading table, panic was indeed growing.

"Holy shit Ron, first a murder and now the Professor is in danger again," Bob was beside himself.

"Let's not get crazy. The Chief Inspector is allowing us to return to Trinity College now. The Sargent is having a car go there as I speak and look for Professor Pettigrew," Ron turned to Alessandro. "Can you get us back to Trinity in the dark?"

"That shouldn't be a problem; it's just the highway and a couple of streets by the Liffey River."

"Good, as soon as we get the okay, we'll get out of here. That Lady in Black tried to tell me something and we have to figure out why and what it was all about. Whatever it is, I think it's connected to this library and that piece of paper she gave me with her last breath."

"Ronnie, what paper? Oh my God, what are you hiding from the Chief Inspector?" Susan placed her arm around Jan to calm her.

"Quiet down Sis, it's nothing…at least I don't know yet. I haven't even looked at it. But say nothing about it; got it?" Silently he was kicking himself for letting out that tidbit of information.

The girls sat back down as Susan looked into those cocoa brown eyes of the one she cared for but could not express. She saw the worry for them but also the spark of excitement that the game was afoot as he would say to quote Sherlock Holmes. "You cannot keep information from the Chief Inspector, Ron come to your senses."

"Not now Susan, it's going to be fine. I will just help him out a bit and then when we know something…"

Bob interrupted, "Know what? Let them catch the murderer."

"It's not just about the murder Bob, it's about whatever that paper in your satchel leads us to and what may be in this library. I took photos of those maps in that new display case."

"Oh Christ, this is Rome all over again, we can't keep doing this."

"Listen Bob, all of you, are you with me or not. I'll understand honestly I will. But please say nothing until we know something."

"I'm with you," Susan rose, "but you must promise not to do something crazy like on that statue in Italy."

"Well, I…well I'll try, how's that?"

Before he finished speaking all his friends were standing and waiting to hear the next step. That next step was to get to Trinity Library where he was confident that they would have a dark room to process film and get the photos he took of the scene of the crime and of those maps in that display case developed.

Hugh O'Neill was just telling Dean Shannon that he had been contacted by a woman calling herself Devorgilla MacMurrough. The Dean seemed shocked more by the name than anything else. "Yes, I know, it's the name of the woman whose elopement with Dermot MacMurrough led to the invasion of Ireland by the Normans from England."

"It's more than that Hugh; she is the one who donated the gold for the building of Mellifont Abbey by St. Malachy."

At that point Sargent Carrick ran into the library as Ron was passing the Curator and Dean having overheard their conversation. He wanted permission from the Chief Inspector to leave.

"Sir, Dublin Garda is on the way to Trinity College Library. They will inform us by car radio as to what they find."

"Excellent," O'Connor turned to the Marquess. "Sir, I thank you for your patience and hospitality in this gruesome incident but we shall return tomorrow as I said." He then turned to call out to Ron and the others and was face to face with the American lad. "Good, tell your friends that we are leaving for Dublin. You shall follow us in that van of yours. We shall gather at the library if what you suspect has happened. If not we shall then set a time for tomorrow. All of you will have to return to Mellifont with me. And do nothing with that shirt, it is evidence. As soon as you are able you are to remove it and hand it over to me for examination."

The young Lord Henry hearing this approached them. "Chief Inspector, sir, in our gift shop we have shirts and things. Would that be of help to you?"

"Good man, someone should have thought of that earlier. Yes, that would be most helpful." O'Connor sized Ron with his eyes, "I'd say a men's small would do, eh lad?"

"I thought that I was a medium," Ron replied slightly embarrassed as he fancied himself to be a medium or so he hoped that eating in Italy as he did might have filled him out a bit more.

"Is that so, on what planet would that be lad, you are a men's small. Lord Henry, make that a sweatshirt, it's getting chilly outside."

With that being said, Ron and the young Henry walked toward the gift shop. Susan and Jan followed to make sure he got the sweatshirt and not a short sleeve souvenir shirt which they felt would be too light weight for nighttime. Ron on the other hand was answering the teen's questions about the comment he made concerning the Professor being attacked in Rome and how he was saved. He also managed to slip in that a men's medium might do just fine.

Library of Trinity College, Dublin Ireland

CHAPTER FIVE

WHO'S MISSING?

By the time that Grandfather clock of Slane Castle, which would have seemed quite at home at Balmoral Castle during Queen Victoria's reign rather than 20th Century Ireland, chimed the eleven o'clock hour a certain assistant curator had paid a visit to Trinity College Library. Given her credentials she had been given admittance and entered the Library. There she had found Professor Pettigrew spreading out his notes and documents regarding what he found in the Vatican Archives.

Andrew Pettigrew if nothing else was certainly an intense man who not yet forty was already a Professor at Oxford University. He was also the discoverer of priceless Renaissance art long forgotten in a hidden tunnel under the Vatican along with his assistant Dominic Fontana, who was now with Ron and company to help him on a new venture into the antiquities of Ireland. Typically British some would say he favored tweed suits, an umbrella and a cap which matched his suit. Actually he felt quite at home in the Irish climate after his long stay in the Mediterranean heat of the previous summer into early fall. Standing rather tall along the lines of the Swiss Guard Andreas Berne, he had to bend quite low over the table to study once again the documents he had brought with him after procuring permission to do so from Cardinal Doretti who oversaw the Antiquities Office of the Vatican which included the Archives.

Those recessed hazel eyes were so focused that he never heard the footsteps which approached him from the main entrance leading from the courtyard side of the Library. When the hand touched his shoulder, it just about made him jump out of his skin.

"Excuse me, are you Professor Pettigrew?"

"Oh my goodness," Pettigrew swung around. "Young lady you gave me quite the start."

"Do forgive me, but Professor Shannon has been delayed and I was instructed to inform you that he would not be joining you this evening. Rather, he will reschedule tomorrow."

"Oh, that is disappointing," Pettigrew paused, glanced at the documents which were now being perused by the young woman who he guessed to be near his age. Quickly he began to gather up his papers. "Do forgive me, however this work is just in its early stages and…well Professor Shannon has not yet seen them. Are you his assistant?"

"Heavens no, no one could work with Drumond Shannon that closely. He's quite the curmudgeon if you understand my meaning."

Pettigrew smiled as he thought that in not too many years from now people would probably be saying the same thing about him. "I do understand. Then who are you, he made no mention of staff." He continued to place his papers into a brown leather brief case after he first placed them into a plastic folder.

"Of course, I am Bridget Tulley the assistant curator of the Dublin Museum's Department of Antiquities."

"I am pleased to meet you; however I am still rather confused. The Dublin Museum is on my list to visit but the name of the person with whom I was to schedule a meeting is that of a Mr. Hugh O'Neill. In fact it was Professor Shannon who was to arrange for that meeting."

"That is most odd indeed, however you are in luck. I can arrange for that meeting as Mr. O'Neill is my superior. If you would be most kind and follow me to the car park, I shall retrieve my calendar and arrange for it right now."

"Certainly, let me just tidy up here and get my things organized. So you say that you work with Mr. O'Neill but why are you here on behalf of Professor Shannon?" he zipped up the brief case and was ready to go still oblivious to her pandering and effort to catch what was on those documents he had placed into his bag.

Bridget flipped her knitted woolen shawl with its green and black pattern so frequently seen on kilts about her shoulders. Then she placed her hands under her long black hair and pulled it over the shawl. She smiled and what could be termed none other than batting her long lashes with those blue eyes giving a grand contrast, beckoned him to follow her. He innocently did so. As they traversed the courtyard which ran alongside the library wall with its huge long windows, he questioned her about the weather and such.

"I've been away in Italy for so long that I've forgotten that even in May, the nights can be cool and damp. Do you expect rain?"

She let the conversation stray to weather. "No, just cool but tomorrow that's another story."

They arrived at the wrought iron gates leading into the streets of Dublin. There a guard was posted. Miss Tulley identified herself and asked if he would open the gate for them. Before he did so he asked Pettigrew to open his brief case as no items may leave the College Campus which may be the property of the Library.

"We once had a scare with fellows trying to steal the "Book of Kells" would you believe. Turned out to be a prank of the students but everything must now be checked."

Pettigrew was apprehensive about showing the contents of his brief case. Even if the guard had no historical background for antiquities there would be no doubt that the documents were quite old. He didn't want them to be handled.

"Well my good man, there's no need to fuss over the contents of this brief case I assure you. I am Professor Andrew Pettigrew from Oxford working with Dean Drumond Shannon here at Trinity. In any case I needn't bring them off campus as I am staying here this evening. Why don't you just hold onto my brief case and I shall be back in a moment to collect it," he pulled the strap over his head and handed the brief case to the guard who placed the leather strap over his shoulder with a pat.

"Yes sir that I will do; keep it safe for you."

"We'll be…well I'll be right back." Pettigrew never saw the soft skin of Miss Tulley suddenly becoming aglow with crimson coloring in her cheeks. There was no moonlight in Dublin to shine on her face.

"Are you sure that you should leave such a valuable find with him?" They briskly walked to the car park.

A light began to dawn on Pettigrew and all because of her use of the word "find." How would she know the papers were valuable let alone considered a find of importance? "I think he's armed from what could be seen under that uniform jacket. And I'll get back right after you schedule me."

They continued their journey across the street to find her car.

Traveling along the N2 back to Dublin, Alessandro was following the Chief Inspector's Car and was followed by Professor Shannon's car with Hugh O'Neill in it. O'Connor felt that since O'Neill would be returning in the morning for sure that he could leave his car at the castle. They were followed by another squad car. It made for quite the sight though given the time, traffic was rather sparse.

Ron was delighted that they were finally without police presence and could speak freely about what had happened at Mellifont to him. His sister again sitting next to the driver Alessandro, up front got up on her knees and pointed out their being unobserved.

"Okay Ronnie, what's going on here? No one is around to hear us."

Bob sat quietly in the back seat with Susan on one side and Dominic on the other. He was clutching onto his satchel as if his life were dependent on its safety. All ears wanted to hear what Ron meant about some paper being in Bob's pack. Andreas sitting next to Ron echoed his sister's question.

"Right, so here goes. First Bob hand me your satchel, Jan see if there's a flashlight in the glove compartment. Finally everyone has to swear not to reveal anything to the Chief Inspector until we have proof that whatever the Lady in Black gave me would actually help solve her murder."

There was only one questioning voice in that van and it came from Ron's sidekick, his Tonto, his Watson, his best friend. Bob feared that the Chief Inspector was all business and so keen on solving the murder that such a move by them would be withholding evidence. "You see how he strokes that red beard of his, almost with a look of how am I going to get you. I tell you he's more like a Mr. Hyde not a sweet Leprechaunish detective."

"Stop it Bob, you're scaring the girls."

"Hush your mouth Ron De Cenza," a miffed Susan cut in, "we're not frightened by a Chief Inspector not after what we handled in Italy last year." She turned into her Southern belle mode, "Why honey child, I'll just butter him up and melt him down to sweetness." She leaned over the seat and stroked Ron's cheek with her dainty long fingers with nails of red.

The guys roared but not Ron. He was too jealous and she hadn't even done anything as yet to anyone of the Garda. He just grabbed hold of Bob's satchel and began to open it. "I don't know what the fuss is about anyway. We did a lot more than this in Italy and New York. The worse scenario is that we have something that could show motive for the murder probably not who did it."

"Holy shit Ron, do you hear yourself, that's withholding evidence for sure." Bob grabbed hold of Dominic's arm. "Listen, if Susan can't charm the Chief Inspector maybe he's like you and…"

"What? What the hell do you mean someone like me," Dominic was a bit irritated knowing full well what Bob meant.

"I'm sorry. I just thought if Susan can do it so could you if it came to that. I didn't mean to insult you."

"Va bene, it's okay Bob, I know what you meant. It just frosts me that people think just because Andreas and I are gay that we would just flirt with any guy who comes along. I'll do it, if it's for the good of our cause."Dominic patted Bob's shoulder in a heroic gesture with dramatic flare.

"No way in hell Dominic, I'll do it. I can back it up with force if necessary," said the Swiss Guard Andreas.

Ron was fuming. "Forget it, all of you; no one will do anything like that because it won't be necessary and it doesn't work, or have you forgotten about Brother Michael back in Wisconsin and how we almost failed because of that sex shit we couldn't follow through on."

"You're right; we almost got screwed on that quite literally. Just open the satchel and see what the Lady gave you. Sorry girls for that commentary."

"I have no idea what you're talking about Bob, so don't worry." And indeed Jan was not part of what happened at the Abbey in Wisconsin when Ron and Bob first entered the Seminary. "Here's the flashlight Ron."

Andreas took hold of it and held it up and over the leather bag. Ron opened it gently and reached in. He pulled out a sheet of paper yellowing with age and still moist with the blood of the victim though it was a sticky substance now. "Who has a piece of Kleenex?"

Susan got some tissue from her purse and handed it to Ron.

He lightly dabbed the paper now laying on the side of the satchel with the glaring light shining down on it. "It's some kind of poem. This is what she must have been reading when she got hit by that rock. On top of the page is like a title of something, Lebor Gabala Erenn."

"Hold on Ron, I think I've heard that name before," Susan took out her little Ireland book with Irish language vocabulary and Irish history notes. She began to page through it. "Here it is, what you said is translated as 'The Book of the Taking of Ireland.' It says it's a book of poetry and history of Ireland from creation to the middle ages."

"Great the first thing we need to do when we get back is to get a copy of that book. We'll see where this poem was taken from and maybe that will help us understand what the Lady was doing or looking for. Andreas, you and Dominic can do that while the girls go find where Professor Pettigrew is and Bob and I look for a dark room," Ron pulled the instamatic camera from his pocket. "I took pictures of the crime scene and those maps in that castle display case."

"Ron you do realize that it will be almost midnight when we get back?"

"Yes Bob, I do but I also think that's the best time as there shouldn't be anyone around to bother us." Ron turned over the paper and blotted the still moist areas on it with the Kleenex tissue. "This side seems to be a list of some kind, notes on what she may have done or planned to do I'm thinking."

"What about me, or doesn't the driver have a chore?"

"Sorry Alessandro, why don't you go with my sister and Susan?"

A broad smile crossed the young Count's face as he glanced at Jan next to him. "Va bene…I mean okay."

There was no feigned shyness in return, she returned the smile and gave him a gentle jab in the ribs. "Stop the nonsense young man," she began in a whisper as she leaned into him, "we have work to do."

Ron was already back to his focus on the paper and reading off the list as the van rolled along the N2 and into Dublin proper. The very first note struck him as it made him recall what he photographed in Mellifont. "Listen to this; the first line has two names but it's clear that they are the same."

"Well go on Honey Child, what is the name?" Susan leaned over to the middle seat from the back. Her breath could be felt on the back of his neck and the scent of Chanel #5 filled his senses.

Ordinarily he would have given her a glare but not this night. He was in game mode. "Sure sweetie anything you say but first let me just say that you smell really good."

"Ronnie De Cenza, you stop that right now." Jan had come to Susan's aide and not to that of her brother. "What does it say?"

"Spoiled sport, okay we all know the name Devorgilla as that of the Lady in Black and that her last name is MacMurrough according to her Passport, but according to this that name is also 'Derbforgaill' so that must be the Irish spelling."

"But what's that got to do with anything?"

"Elementary my dear Susan; I took a picture of the stone on which the Lady died. That's because it had letters carved into it but worn down. The blood filled in the crevices and may reveal what it says on that stone. I think it will tell us that The Lady in Black has the same name as whoever is buried under that stone in the ruins of Mellifont."

"So then she has a connection to the Mellifont Abbey in some way but why would someone kill her for that?" asked a bewildered Bob.

"Maybe it was some ancestor buried there."

"That Andreas is exactly why she wrote this, I'm sure of it. She is connected to the Devorgilla who must be buried under that stone and I think she wanted to prove that in some way. But that wouldn't answer the more important question which is why would someone want her dead because she has an ancient relative?" Ron read on down the list. "Maybe this will tell us on that point. She wrote here that St. Malachy was the Monk who arranged for the building of Mellifont Abbey and that a Devorgilla spelled in Irish gave funds of gold and gifts of a chalice and altar linens for the chapel."

Susan was busily paging through her introduction to Irish history and language book after she sat herself back down between Andreas and Dominic. "Listen to this everyone; the book has a section on this other book which you guys," she gave a glance to the Swiss Guard and Pettigrew's original assistant from Oxford, "which you are looking for in the Trinity Library."

"Great, then we should get more answers in the Lebor Gabbala Erenn. Only we need to find it first," observed Andreas.

"Well then this might help. There are two versions; the one we know of and another one which is called Tadgh O'Neachtain, but I can't pronounce it right."

"Well then we shall look for them both, right Andreas?"

"Sure, we'll split up once we get there; I'll go to the English catalog and Dominic, you can go to the Irish one where that title will certainly be listed."

The wheels were turning again as Ron studied the list of notes. "I hope that the books you find will help us to learn more about these two things, she jotted down under the gift list. The one says 'Our Lady's Well' and the other the St. Erc's Hermitage Well."

"What does a well have to do with murdering that poor woman?"

"Maybe nothing Bob, but it will give us an idea perhaps as to why this Lady Devorgilla was roaming these ruins. What was she looking for?" Alessandro said as he followed the Chief Inspector's car exiting the N2 and began to follow the Liffey River route again toward Trinity College.

"Well let's just think of what we just learned, one that she gave gold so that the Abbey could be built, two St. Malachy got the gold and the gifts so he's involved in some way and three, after eight centuries those altar cloths are long gone and disintegrated, the gold was spent as soon as the saint got it so that the abbey could be built. So that would leave the chalice. I say she was planning on discovering the whereabouts of that Holy Vessel and that folks provides us with motive. Someone else wants that Chalice bad enough to kill for it."

"Ronnie, that's like that Signore Aventino guy who wanted to steal the art which Dominic and the Professor discovered all over again."

"Not to worry sis, we're not climbing up any huge statues but maybe we'll have to dig down."

"Well that does it; I'm clueless at this point."

Behind them, Drumond Shannon and Hugh O'Neill were engaged in a similar conversation as they now entered the more populated area near the college. The lights of the city made it sparkle like those on a Christmas tree. Given the hour, the streets were empty of people as the shops had closed for the evening and traffic was almost non-existent. The Dean of Antiquities was rather poetic as he observed how still and eerie the city was at night.

"Almost as if we are going back in time when the ancients first came and settled this land." Then he said something which struck the reflective Curator of the Dublin Museum. "Perhaps that Lady in Black was really Lady Devorgilla come back from the 12th Century with a message, but what could that message be I wonder?"

"I can easily tell you Drumond. It's that you have let a harrowing day and this empty city get to you. There is no spirit in Mellifont. The poor woman got herself killed and I…"

The Dean interrupted. "Hugh, what are you saying? How did she get herself killed?"

"That's the problem, I don't know how but I think I may know why."

"Good grief man, you must tell that Chief Inspector before he finds out and suspects you."

"Drumond, why would he suspect me?"

"He suspects everyone, I would presume and you were out lost at the Hill of Tara or some such place when this murder took place. And now you're telling me that you may know why such a crime took place." The van in front of them turned off Aston Quay and onto Westmoreland Street. The Dean was duty bound to follow though he felt they should have continued to D'Olier Street. In any case it distracted them for a moment, but only for that moment. "Now where were we…ah yes you were going to be a suspect."

"Stop it Drumond, I was lost that's all's to it."

"Hmmm, sounds fishy to me; here you are the Curator of Dublin Museum and you get lost not twenty minutes from your home. And then there is that poor woman whom I have a feeling you knew."

O'Neill was now a bundle of nerves and the Dean could see the sweat forming on his brow on a rather cool night. The lights of the city glistened in the droplets the curator tried to wipe away with his handkerchief. "It looks bad doesn't it? But truly, I did not know this woman even though…" he paused for suddenly he didn't know if he should share the rest of his story.

The pause was just long enough to realize that they were entering the Gates into the grounds of Trinity College.

"Ah, Hugh, we shall talk later as I am sure this Rory O'Connor Chief Inspector will need to speak with us once again. Imagine such a name, the last of the High Kings of Ireland for a policeman. What is this country coming to?"

Hugh O'Neill was saved from his own words and he knew it. "So it seems; and you'd be right about him wanting to speak with us once more. He said that we should all meet him in the Library. I presume you have the keys."

"Of course, let's not disappoint the Chief Inspector who thinks he's a king." Drumond Shannon laughed throwing his head back as he did so thus almost hitting the college van in front of him. They jerked to a quick stop.

Inside the van Ron was continuing to read off the list on that page given to him by the Lady in Black as she died. "So who knows anything about this St. Erc's Hermitage place?"

Except for Alessandro, no one had ever visited Ireland; they were ignorant of its history. He received only grunts and shrugging shoulders in reply to his question. That is until Susan pulled out her eyewitness Tour book. They had stopped right in front of the statue of Edmond Burke at the Main Entrance as she did so. Several Garda officers were waiting at the gate. With them was the Chief Inspector and Sargent Carrick. They were being given instructions to take the van and the Dean's car to the parking area as its occupants would need to go with him to the Library.

"There is a something about that place in my tour book; I remember the strange name when I looked up Slane Castle. It must be near it." Susan flipped through the pages.

"Good, but not now; it seems that we are being beckoned by the Chief Inspector." Ron opened the side door and jumped out. "Now listen up everyone; no one is to mention this paper or what I read from it. Just stick to what happened in the Mellifont ruins."

The seven gathered at the side of the van as O'Neill and Shannon came up to them from their car. "Well now, here we all are," began the Dean. "Now tell me which of you killed the poor woman?"

A pall of horror fell upon them. Their faces if they could be seen properly in the moonlight night were chalk white. The idea that such a prominent person of the College would even think of them as possible murderers was shocking. They became frozen if not in fear certainly from disbelief.

Drumond Shannon threw his head back and then had to adjust his cap as a twinkle of mischief sparked in his eyes as he winked at Ron. "Take a breath ladies and gentlemen; I am only jesting at your expense. Here comes the Chief Inspector."

Susan pulled on Ron's arm. "Well I never heard of such meanness. He's probably the murderer not one of us."

"Shush, he'll hear you."

"Let him, the old goat is rude."

The Chief Inspector approached them. "Good we are all here. Now we shall not make this a long evening for it's quite late, as it is. We shall enter here and turn right at Library Square where the bell tower is. The Library will be opened by Dean Shannon, just a few questions will follow and then we shall get some rest."

No one said a word; they just nodded their understanding.

"Well then, let's be on our way." The Chief inspector looked up onto the star studded sky. "It's fortunate that we have such a pleasant night. Perhaps the evidence will not be washed away by a stray shower. That is back at Mellifont of course." He handed the plastic bag with the blood stained shirt taken off Ron to Sargent Carrick.

He led the entourage into Parliament square. On the opposite side of the square was the Campanile. Standing gloriously 98 feet tall, it was an imposing site. Bob remarked that it reminded him of the height of the huge statue back in Italy. He expressed hope that they would not have to do any of that sort of thing on the bell tower.

"Don't be a worry wart Bob," began Ron. "In any case I don't think any of us is about to play at being the Hunchback of Notre Dame." Just as he spoke the bells of the tower chimed out the one o'clock hour.

Jan was holding onto the arm of Alessandro as they shuffled along the gravel path toward the library. "I think that I would appreciate those pretty chimes if it was one in the afternoon and not in the morning."

He drew her in closer. "It's almost over Jan. After tomorrow, hopefully our part will be done."

"You don't know my brother very well despite our little experience in Italy together if you think that. That Paper with its list will spark that brain of his and tomorrow when that Chief Inspector guy is done with us, we will be looking for the St. Erc's Hermitage. I just know it. He said that the Lady told him about a library when she died. Well, here's the Trinity Library in front of us. We already know it houses hundreds of ancient books. Then there is the library at Slane Castle with those maps he photographed. And I'm thinking he expects to find ruins of a library at that Hermitage place."

"You are his sister all right. I am tired already and the day hasn't even started."

"Oh yes it has my dear Count of Pianore. Remember it's already one in the morning."

O'Neill and O'Connor flanked Dean Shannon as he unlocked the library doors. He entered first to flip a few switches and illuminated the vast interior of what is called the Long Room. "Chief Inspector where would you like us to gather, you have two hundred and ten feet of space from end to end to choose from."

The Chief Inspector ignored the sarcasm. "We shall just gather in the first alcove for a short time sir." With that he ordered his Sargent to follow at the rear of the line and the others behind him. At the marble bust of Jonathan Swift he turned. "This will do fine; hopefully our travels tomorrow will not mirror Gulliver's Travels and this sordid incident will come to an end." He smiled at the Dean and Curator with satisfaction that he was a literate man as well as a policeman.

Across the way in stall P was the pure white marble bust of William Conyngham Plunket and Ron noticed it. He held back and pulled on Bob's arm. "Do not forget to tell Andreas and Dominic to look in that stall. That guy has the same name of the Marquess back at Slane Castle not to mention the family name of Saint Oliver Plunkett."

Gathered between the high shelves of books in the Swift Stall, the Chief Inspector laid out his plans for what he now called potential suspects. The outrage first came from the Dean and followed by the Curator Hugh O'Neill. The seven from America and Italy already knew what they would be up to and decided to remain as stoic as was possible.

"I do apologize Dean Shannon and Curator O'Neill, however it is my duty to follow the evidence and that simply tells me this; first Mr. O'Neill is unaccounted for during the time of the murder, second Dean Shannon mysteriously shows up at the castle also without verification of where he had come from and of course you young men and women. One of you actually held the murder weapon, the rock which crushed the Lady Devorgilla's skull…"

There was a gasp of horror as the scene came to life for them once more. They could no longer remain silent. "Chief Inspector, my brother just went to her rescue and tackled the man in black and the guys simply chased the actual murderer into the parking lot."

"So you have said back at Mellifont, however, where is this person whom you call a man but no one can identify? Until we verify your story, all of you are either perpetrators of a crime or witnesses of one. Do not fear we shall find out the truth." O'Connor stroked his vibrant red beard as if accomplishing something but what that was in the minds of the now potential suspects was not known. "And that brings me to what shall take place later today. We shall meet here at nine in the morning and travel back to Mellifont and if necessary to Slane Castle. Once there you shall demonstrate to me the events as you say happened. As for the Dean and Curator, you shall verify your whereabouts before coming to Slane Castle. Now then I believe the hour is late and we all need some rest. Thank you for your time, my men will be posted here at the college through the night for your safety."

Ron glanced at Andreas and Dominic. How would they manage to get back into the library and check out books which address what was on that list if the Garda was about? How would he and Bob get to the dark room and develop the film?

As they walked out of the author Jonathon Swift stall not a word was spoken, only a glance at Stall P and a nod from Ron to Andreas could be detected should anyone have bothered to watch their departure. However O'Connor was still speaking with Dean Shannon and the Curator Hugh O'Neill. His words to them were quite different as one had questions about his whereabouts still unanswered and the elder of them had only a story about a phone call which directed him to come to the castle. Also neither of them lived on campus so the issue as to whether to allow them to return to their homes or arrange for rooms at the college was now being presented to the learned scholars.

"Gentlemen, it's been a long night and I'm sure we all wish to get home. However that is a concern of mine."

The elder of the two, Dean Shannon, responded. "Chief Inspector, simply send one of the Garda to watch our home. In that manner, we shall not attempt to escape if indeed I for one would even think of doing that at my age. Come let us be reasonable here. I am no young student like those who just left and my colleague here is certainly beyond sleeping in a dorm room."

"The esteemed Dean is quite correct Chief Inspector. Why would we, who've done nothing but get lost or…" O'Neill paused because he didn't know what to say about Shannon's sudden appearance at the castle without incriminating his assistant, Bridget Tulley. "Drumond, I am at a loss for words."

"That's understandable Hugh given that it was your assistant who called to direct me to Slane Castle in the first place. This we talked about earlier, if you recall, with the Chief inspector."

His effort to protect failed. The Chief Inspector knew of Bridget Tulley, his assistant curator no matter what was said.

"We already know about this Miss Tulley. However she hasn't been found as yet and that brings me to the next question Mr. O'Neill. I presume that you could get me her home address, is that right?"

"Of course, Chief Inspector, I have it right here in fact." O'Neill pulled from his inside suit coat pocket a small brown leather bound booklet. By the look on O'Connor's face it was clear what he was thinking. "Let me assure you this is not that infamous usually black book with names and contacts for ladies. I use this to list people like the Dean there; Professor Pettigrew is even in here as are other research people and of course the employees of the Museum which includes Miss Tulley." He began to page through it. "Ah, here it is, Bridget Tulley. You'll find her apartment to be across from St. Stephen's Green North near Dawson Street. In fact it's called the Dawson Street apartments. It's only a couple of blocks from the Museum, quite convenient."

"I thank you sir, and now may I have that pad. All your people may have to be contacted during the investigation, quite routine I assure you."

On the green of Library Square Ron was leading the group toward the dorm area near the main gate at Parliament Square. A tall man in a guard's uniform was about to pass them when Ron noticed the leather brief case which he was carrying under his arm. There was no doubt as to who owned it in his mind as he noticed its worn leather, and the Union Jack Flag tag of the United Kingdom hanging from its handles. He gave a tug on Bob's sleeve and pointed.

"Holy Shit, what's that guy doing with Professor Pettigrew's brief case?"

"No clue, spread the word to the others, I'm going to follow him." Ron waved off the others and ran to catch up with the guard. None of them paid the slightest attention to him as Bob had to corral them around him and explain what they saw. They gathered under the arch of the Bell Tower deciding who would go as back up for Ron.

"Let's not get crazy here; Ron will just ask him about the brief case and that will be that. He'll meet us at the dorms. The guy is a guard and we all saw him when we came through the gates."

"Dorms Bob, really and then how will Jan and I find out what's going on. We'll wait right here and…wait a minute, maybe this guard is a fake, then what? Oh my God, Ron could be in danger." Susan was genuinely concerned as she pulled on Bob's arms.

"Okay, okay, I didn't think of that…"

"Why not, you're supposed to be Watson or whatever aren't you? Get your ass going to protect Ron. Andreas go with him. We'll wait here and go talk to that guard now at the gate to see if the one you saw is legitimate."

"Here we go again, that boyfriend of yours never can let a day go by unless he gets involved in a situation."

"He's not my boyfriend…"

"Sure, we all know he's going to become a priest and must swear off such entanglements." Andreas grinned then grabbed hold of Bob; gave him a slight shove to get a move on. They began to sprint across the green. By the time Ron came into sight, Bob was already huffing and puffing.

At the main gate, Susan, Jan, Alessandro and Dominic surrounded the guard on duty. They soon found out that the guard with the brief case was indeed one and just relieved of his shift. Most importantly was the info that he was bringing a brief case given to him quite a while ago to the security office.

"He told me that a Professor Pettigrew gave him the bag and that if he should return to tell him that it would be at the Security Office," the Guard, who was actually around their age and rather green at his work seemed uneasy as they closed in on him.

Susan sought to relieve him of such anxiety. "Well honey child, I do declare that you've been so helpful." She stroked his cheek with a tickling rhythm which made him blush. "You see, we are the Professor's assistants and well we haven't seen him all day and it's one in the morning."

Holding his hand to his cheek, "That's quite understandable Miss. I'm sure your Professor's things will be quite safe until his return."

"Well sweetie, with such a strong lad as you guarding the campus, we are sure of that." She turned away, signaled the others to follow her and strolled back toward the Bell Tower.

On the other side of the green Ron watched the guard approach a lighted doorway at the end of the Old Library Building from which they had just left. There was a glass pane on the top half and gold lettering which read, "Security Office" across the frosted glass. He stooped behind a large rock until the guard entered and then made his move. In the silence of the green long void of students and tourists rushing about to classes or into the display area of the Library he felt quite alone. That is until a rather strong hand plopped on his shoulder, the left one so as to avoid that old injury from the gun shot.

He jumped up, "Shit Andreas you scared me half to death." He glared at Bob. "I told you to get them to the dorms."

"Well Susan was worried that this guy might be a fake and that…"

Andreas stepped in, "What he's trying to say is that your girlfriend was worried about you, so here we are."

"Once and for all, Susan is not my girlfriend. She's just a good friend."

"Right, just like Dominic and I are just good friends. Get a life Ron, she cares for you."

"Kiss my ass, the both of you. I can't take this, I'm too tired and we have to meet that Chief Inspector in the morning."

"So why should I be included in this. I didn't say Susan was your girlfriend," said the offended Bob.

With head bowed, Ron placed his arms around each of the guys. "I'm sorry. I think it's been a long day and night for that matter. I can't think straight…"

Andreas laughed, "Oh Ronnie, what are you saying?"

Suddenly the dawn of what Andreas just said hit Ron. "That's not what I meant and you know it." He pushed himself away from the two and stomped off back toward the Bell Tower.

Catching up with him, Andreas apologized. "Amico, I was just trying to lighten up the situation that's all."

"I'm just shit faced Andreas that's all; too much to think about." He turned to Bob. "Come on Watson, we have a lot to do and we need to get some sleep before it all begins. The Professor's brief case will be safe for now." With his arms over their shoulders once again, off they strode into the still of the night as the bells sounded the half hour chimes.

Bell Tower, Trinity College

CHAPTER SIX

SEARCHING FOR PETTIGREW

After escorting the girls to the women's dorm, the guys crossed the green once again and entered the men's dorm. It was decided that all would meet under the Bell Tower at 8:30 a.m. and then go to the Library as a group to meet with the Chief Inspector. Dragging from fatigue the guys climbed up the stairs to the third floor of the dorm. Once again Alessandro would be alone as the rooms only had two beds. This time however, Andreas and Dominic invited him to stay with them as the two of them could squeeze into the same bed. They waited for some kind of shocked reply but the young Count didn't even give a glance to Ron or Bob who were his former roommates when he felt insecure about being alone while they had time to discuss what was to be done to catch a thief. But that was back in Italy. Now in Ireland they had to find a murderer and solve the mystery of what connected this Devorgilla MacMurrough of eight hundred years ago and the one who died in Mellifont.

"Luckily for us that the term is over and rooms opened up," commented Dominic as he opened the door which led to the hallway.

They didn't have to walk but a few steps when they stood in front of Room 301. "Thank God, we don't have to go all the way across the building," Bob looked at the number knowing that he and Ron would be in Room 303 next door to the Professor. "I just want to go to sleep."

"And so we shall pal," observed Ron as he gave the knob on Room 301 a turn. "Holy shit, it's not locked. Why would Professor Pettigrew not lock his door after all that happened to him in Italy?" he peeked inside as the others now crowded behind him pushing the door further open.

"Well look at this! Some room for college kids."

"This isn't what our room will be like, I'm sure. They call this the Floor Monitor's Room but really it's a suite. See over there," Ron pointed to the end of the bed just visible beyond an archway which led from a sitting area which had a sofa, some chairs, a desk with chair and a bureau and book case. "This even has its own bathroom."

"Well that's sure a cool job to have," Alessandro paused as he pushed himself higher while pressing down on Ron's shoulders. "But look at this place, I don't mean how fancy it is for a college dorm room but that nothing in here would indicate that Professor Pettigrew was here were it not for that suitcase on the chair by the desk."

"Hey, you're right. Where the hell is our Professor?"

"I'm too tired to think Dominic; let's just go to bed."

Now that comment by Andreas did bring on a wide eyed response without words across the face of Alessandro. "So you guys aren't planning like sleeping naked or doing something are you?"

"I am offended by that amico. What do you think we are some kind of sex maniacs?" A slight grin showing just a little bit of teeth followed.

"Oh Madonna mia, I am so sorry Andreas. I didn't mean you'd be having sex or whatever you guys do…oh shit, I mean…"

A slap on the young Count's back and a hearty laugh followed. "I'm just joshing amico, you don't have to worry. Dominic and I are too tired to frolic in the sack tonight."

Ron having heard enough walked into the room. "Are you three finished talking about sex. You think that was the only important thing in the world. For Christ's sake get a grip and focus on what we're not seeing in here."

Bob turned around to face the others behind him, all still in the doorway. "He's just tired and cranky, ignore him."

"It's okay Bob but I must say that he protests too much and doesn't laugh enough about such things. And that tells me that there's more to what's going on inside him." Andreas walked past Bob and patted him on his shoulder. "So Ron, speaking of sex, I remembered something." He swung his arm over Ron's shoulders.

Ron threw his arm off of him and glared. "Really, now you're going to shock me about your sexual exploits with Dominic. Well I have you know that I had a girlfriend back in Chicago and she and I…"

"What the hell are you saying Ron? You never told me that you did it with that Jewish girl in our Biology class."

"Well just Fuck you Bob, fuck all of you…that's not what I was going to say. Get your heads out of the gutter. I was trying to say that she and I had a relationship and I even touched her boobs, so there."

Andreas flung himself across the untouched bed, while the other guys stood like statues in shock that they had obviously touched a sore spot. "So the boy has a dick and wants to be a man."

Ron exploded and threw himself on top of Andreas. The guys began to shout for them to stop as they wrestled and fell off the bed onto the oak floorboards. In an instant Andreas had thrown Ron off and now straddled him while holding his arms down. "Really Ron, do you think that you could get the better of a Swiss Guard. Just because we are the world's smallest army doesn't mean that we aren't well trained soldiers."

"Get off me, asshole…okay I'm sorry, I don't know what's wrong with me these days." Ron's eyes began to glisten as tears filled them.

Andreas jumped off of him and pulled him to his feet. "I'm sorry too. I shouldn't have teased you. I think we're all just tired with all of this murder stuff and the Professor not being here…"

"The Professor, we have forgotten about him."

Ron went up to Bob and then each of the guys giving them a hug with an apology. He saved Andreas for last. "So what's this thing that you remember about sex and the Professor?"

The Swiss Guard sat down on the now destroyed bedding. "Just this, as we left the gate, that young kid of a guard mentioned that he was told that the Professor left the grounds with a woman."

The remaining guys exclaimed, "A woman."

Andreas smiled. "Looks like someone else wants to be a man tonight."

"Ooh la la," exclaimed the others except for Ron. He stood stoically.

"Stop your shit. It's the Professor. He probably had to go explore some kind of…"

"Yeah Ron, explore all right and it's not a library or museum," Alessandro noted.

Ron gave up the pretense of protecting the Professor's honor. "Well whatever he's doing, it's obvious that he's not coming back here tonight, even for his brief case. So let's get some sleep before we fall down."

"Well I for one am staying right here. Now that we've unmade the bed, we might as well use it. Alessandro you can have the sofa while Dominic and I share this comfy bed."

The decision was made and Bob dragged Ron out of the room and into Room 303. There they found two twin beds separated by a night stand with a lamp and a small desk on each side of the room. Their suitcases had been placed on top of the desks. As the bells of the Campanile Tower rang out the two o'clock morning hour, they had all shed their clothes save for underpants and crawled into bed.

Mother Nature had been quite kind to these amateur sleuths and the Chief Inspector and his Garda officers. The night sky remained bright with moon glow and brilliant stars. That light shone through the window over the bed on which Andreas and Dominic lay tangled in sheets, their bare legs hanging out and arms grasping not each other but the edge of the sheet and blanket pulling them up to their necks which accounted for their legs being exposed. On the sofa Alessandro was already lost in a dream about Ron's sister, Jan. her short midnight like cropped hair blowing in the breeze as they stood arm in arm amongst the Mellifont ruins where they strolled oblivious to their friends screaming around a flat rock on which a dead body lay. The fog rolled in to shroud the body while the two of them almost floated into the sanctuary ruins as he tenderly placed his arm around her waist and brought her closer to his tall sleek frame. Jan looked up into his smooth smiling face accentuated by those long lashes and brows which were more of a De Cenza family trait but it was a dream and so it was allowed. They walked down a rocky hill until Alessandro flung her around and hugged her tightly placing a kiss on her ruby red lips. Sweat poured off his brow on that sofa while a smile bright and broad crossed his face.

That same moonlight filtered into room 303 through the panes of a small wooden framed window over the nightstand between the beds on which Bob and Ron lay. The world did not exist to either of them so lost were they in sleep until the moaning of Ron could be heard if anyone was about and awake to hear it that is.

"Watson, I think I have solved the case."

"Already Sherlock, it's only been a day."

"I know but then I am so bright, the top of my class, the most revered of all detectives, the most…"

"The biggest asshole in the land; yes I know how you feel about yourself."

"Watson, how can you say that? You cut me into my heart which is full of love this night."

"What do you know of love Sherlock? You never had a woman. You are a boy at heart playing games of which you show your superiority to your closest friends."

Ron stirred. Sweat poured off his brow as well but it wasn't from a feeling of pleasure but one of regret and heartache. In his deepest thoughts covered in a mist of a dream, his soul felt burdened as he twisted and turned in the wee morning hours before sunrise.

"I tell you Watson that I do know love. I love you my dearest friend don't I?"

"Do you Sherlock? You overlook me at every turn. You even fight with that Swiss Guard instead of me your dearest friend."

"Why Watson, are you jealous of our new friends?"

"Don't be coy with me, I know you too well. Of course I'm jealous. It used to be just the two of us and then came along Susan and now these others."

"Ah Susan Liguri, so poetic a name, isn't it Watson? Her breasts reach out to me to fondle. Her eyes twinkle with invitation to take hold of her and squeeze her tightly in an embrace, her lips so pink and soft pucker up to receive my kiss which would allow my manhood to rise to the occasion."

The moaning became louder. Bob thought he heard something and popped up in his bed. "Ron, is that you? Are you sick?"

There was no answer just a pleasurable moaning as Ron turned into his sheets like a caterpillar creating a cocoon.

"Oh shit, I need to get my own room." Bob made the Sign of the Cross and snuggled back down and was off in his own dream world where he was Sherlock and Ron was Watson.

As those dreams unfolded in those young minds not more than six blocks from where they dreamed, Professor Pettigrew was opening his eyes to find the face of Bridget Tulley not more than a couple of inches away from his own. Her ruby red lips were moist and inviting. Those he could see quite clearly and yet the room was still a blurry vision. He was dazed and confused. Those lips broke into a smile with closed mouth. He could feel fingers tickling his chest hair and moving down toward his manhood ever so slowly. It was then that he realized as had Adam in the Garden of Eden, that he was naked. He blinked over and over again in an effort to clear his vision. From the lace covered window across the room a faint light which was not that of the moon but of the sun, began to filter into the bedroom. It was a bedroom to be sure as he now realized he lay upon silk sheets which were cool and shimmering in the fading glow of the embers in the fireplace and the sunlight making its way into the room. He looked about as the hand now played with his belly button which was very close to a still sensitive wound on his side from a knife attack on the banks of the Tiber River back in Rome in early fall of the previous year. It was pleasurable, that he could not deny but it was disconcerting at the same time.

"Oh my Lord, Miss Tulley what's happening here?" He pulled up the smooth sheet as best he could to verify that he was indeed nude under it. "Oh my, oh…Miss Tulley please, Oh God help me should Mr. O'Neill ever find out that…"

She made no sounds save to hum and then with an "aha", she clinched her fingers around his aroused manhood and squeezed. It was no longer pleasurable. He pushed away from her only to plummet off the side of the four poster bed which was set quite high above the oak floorboards. By the time he hit the pink shag area carpet below, he was deflating in more ways than one. The shy Professor was still a young man for being in such a position at Oxford University and already distinguished in his research of the Renaissance Era and now venturing into the Medieval age in Ireland. Hence the worry about scandal and offending his sponsor on this research venture, Hugh O'Neill, the Curator of the Dublin Museum.

Having no fig leaves handy, he pulled at the corner of the sheet and pulled it with some difficulty down from the bed only to have Miss Tulley coming with it, stopping herself just over the edge with her bare breasts just above his head. He gasped in wonder and awe and soon fell into despair and panic.

"Miss Tulley, I am so sorry about this but you must understand that I didn't mean for this to happen, not that you're not most attractive." He tried to force a smile but failed, rather a look of fear like a rabbit cornered by a fox with eyes wide and trying to find a way out of his mess.

The woman smiled again and then pulled the sheet back to cover herself as she slid back so that only her head hung over the edge of the bed. The move once again showed his shame. Pettigrew pulled at the shag carpet's fringe and pulled it up to cover his loins.

She finally spoke with a sweet high voice punctuated with a thick brogue. "My dear Professor that's not what you said as we tasted the wine before we…"

"What! I don't recall being together. We had a lovely walk across St. Stephen's Green and then onto a street when something happened. My head hurts, here," he pointed to the back of his thickly covered disheveled head of coal colored hair.

The room was coming into focus as he looked about for something more substantial with which to cover his nakedness. He took in its Victorian Era décor with the pink netting cascading from each of the four poles of the Four Poster Bed above him. "Did I fall or something?"

"Or something," her long fingers with ruby painted nails to match her lips ruffled through his locks as to twist it even more than it was. Her long blond hair, slightly wavy fell about her shoulders as she did so.

"You have pretty hair, it shines so nicely." He couldn't believe that he was talking like one of his young assistants. "I mean this is all too disconcerting." He quivered as she stroked his cheek.

"Dear, dear Professor, it seems that you needed quite a bit of the drink of Bacchus to bring up your courage to lay with me." She pointed down to his manhood now covered with strands of shag carpeting and then lightly touched his cheek as she pulled away to wrap the sheet about her and kneel up on the bed.

"But I assure you that I rarely imbibe in such a fashion as to lose memory of what took place. I am quite the teetotaler actually."

"I am sure that you are…" her words were interrupted by the sound of a bell. It seemed to alert her. "And that bell my dear Professor means that you should get dressed."

"I don't understand."

"Let me allow you some dignity and modesty." She slipped off the other side of the bed and wrapped a pink silk robe about her, turning her head just as he came up to his knees to see her tying the cord about her waist. "As I said Professor, get dressed for in about sixty seconds a man shall appear at my door and take you from this place where you attacked me last night…" She then pulled on a cord hanging at the side of the bed, the type which in the 19th Century called servants up to the living quarters.

"This can't be happening," Pettigrew jumped up grabbing the released sheet no longer being used by the woman, who now watched him wrap it about his waist and search the room for his clothes. "Attack, I would never do such a thing, you must be mistaken. I may have desired to kiss you and hold you but without your consent it would have gone no further, not with me."

"Is that so my dear Professor? Well your manhood was certainly saying otherwise last night and now you can't even get it up."

He found his clothes neatly hanging over a desk chair under the window through which the new day's sunlight was now streaming. "Who is this man? I can't believe this; I mean why would you do such a thing like this Miss Tulley?" There was a pounding on the door as he zipped up his pants and tucked in his white button down collar shirt. Then grabbing hold of his shoes under the chair, he tried to get them on as she walked slowly to the door. "Please Miss Tulley, let me at least finish dressing."

She pulled down the robe off one shoulder and ran her fingers through her long blond hair so as to make it appear as if she was in a struggle. "Thank God, you're here; there he is. It was all I could do to escape his clutches. See, his undergarments are still there on the floor. It was all too horrible." She swooned and the burly man caught her in his arms. He lifted her up into his arms and placed her gently onto the sofa, the very one where the table in front of it held the Pinot Noir wine bottle and two Waterford crystal stemware glasses still half filled with wine.

"You get your ass here or I'll make what you did seem like a picnic before I get through with you," demanded the big man.

Pettigrew backed away from the archway leading into the bedroom area. He stumbled over the irons for stoking the fireplace now almost completely gone out. Taking hold of the poker he lifted it up and held it out. "I didn't do anything. I woke up here with her like that well not like that; she and I were naked, that part is true. But nothing happened that I can recall."

"So you want to play rough do you," the man with the green and brown patched work cap slipped his hand into his inside coat pocket. "Now you were saying?"

Pettigrew was looking into the barrel of a gun. He knew it was over. He dropped the stoking iron onto the shag carpet. The thud made him shudder. "I am willingly going with you officer. I'll explain everything at the station."

"That's a good lad. Now come here and sit nice and calm." He pulled the desk chair to the archway just far enough so that Pettigrew could see Miss Tulley lying on the sofa unconscious. "That's it, now don't you move."

"What are you going to do officer? I am not resisting arrest. Shouldn't you be seeing to the wellbeing of Miss Tulley?"

The rather large fellow pulled a nylon scarf hanging off the mirror of the dressing table. "This is just to make sure lad, that's all." He tied the scarf like a gag around the Professor's mouth. "Now just keep quiet or I'll have to shove it down your throat."

Before Pettigrew could react, the man took hold of his hands and wrapped a rope about them which he pulled off his belt. "Now we'll just go peacefully and no one will get hurt." He placed the gun into Pettigrew's ribs and pulled him up off the chair. "Turn around and walk nice and calm to the staircase not the elevator." Opening the door, he checked for other residents and then pulled the Professor into the hallway.

As soon as the man closed the door behind them, the woman on the sofa sat up and pulled on her hair. She took off the blond wig and walked into the bedroom. Seeing the stoker on the floor, she took it and jabbed the embers of the logs. A slight flame burst up. She then threw the wig onto it. The flames flashed brighter and higher. She placed the irons strewn about where they should be and then pulled the cords off the drapes of the living room windows. "These will do just fine, but that ass took my scarf," she mumbled. "Damn you Fitz, why the hell…" she found another in the drawers of the bureau. First she tied it about her mouth. Then she walked into the closet. There she realized that the silk robe could be identified. She quickly found her old chenille cotton robe so comfy when the weather turned really chilly. There would be no alluring quality to it. But what to do with the silk robe; she began to get panicky as time seemed to fly by. She stuffed it into a suitcase which was already packed for her planned trip. She hadn't realized where she would be going but now after pulling information from the Professor, she had a pretty good idea and it coincided with where her boss was. Taking the drapery cords which she then pre-tied so that they could be pulled tightly around her feet and hands she managed to pull the closet door shut. Falling to the floor which allowed the robe to reveal just enough of what she wasn't wearing, she waited for salvation in the darkness. It was a darkness reflecting that of her own soul as her plot seemed to be working. She sat with thoughts of what the Professor had shared with her about why he had come to Ireland.

The usually demure Professor was no match for this wrestler type of man who would be so comfortable performing in a ring where he could pounce on his opponent with a vengeance. It was pointless to struggle. Down the five flights of stairs, the Professor was dragged. Finally he managed to hang on the hand railing in one of his efforts to take hold of it and free himself from the grasp of the giant of a man. The attempt was just enough to put them both off balance. They tumbled against the wall bounced off of it and rolled down the stairs. People began to appear out of their doorways wondering what was going on. A voice called out for the Garda to be called. The door of the stairway entrance opened and men appeared with their wives behind them. They shouted. The thug had no choice; it was either him or the Professor being caught. He called back to the voices.

"This man tried to rape Miss Tulley in Apartment 520."

The Professor, gagged, couldn't respond but he could and did kick his captor in the balls. As he doubled over, he made a run for it down the remaining flight of stairs and out onto Dawson Street. A Garda car with lights twirling and siren blasting was pulling up to the front of the Apartment building. Sunrise had turned into an unusually bright day but he managed to stay in the shadows of the buildings out of sight. While the police were being swarmed over by the residents of the building, Pettigrew made his way up to Nassau Street on the way to Trinity College. The man called Fitz managed to get outside before the Garda entered. He ran toward the Shelbourne Hotel on the north side of St. Stephen's Green which was in the opposite direction from that route taken by the Professor and in the direction of where he had parked his car. It was in that grand hotel that the plans for what had just happened were concocted.

The diversion of the residents had given Tulley just enough time to appear as a defiled woman who was captured and robbed. Finally hearing the noise of residents and Garda entering her apartment she kicked on the door of the closet.

The closet door swung open and two male officers stood in its framework. They stood stunned as her bare legs leading upwards and the top of her breasts were the first things they saw. The taller one of the two came to his senses and bent over to pull down the gag.

"Thank God, I am saved." Again she swooned into a false faint.

"Cormack, get that female officer up here immediately." Officer Kilbourne told his partner and then gently closed the open robe and lifted the woman up and onto the sofa. He noticed as he did so the wine bottle, one half full glass and one empty one, not knowing that the other had just become empty when Tulley gulped down the contents just before she gagged herself.

Turning onto Grafton Street, Pettigrew managed to stay in the brush and trees lining the outside buildings of the College until he neared the main entrance where Grafton St. and the College Green met. He now had no choice but to present himself to the guard on duty. Haggard looking and in disarray he stood before yet another young guard earning money to help pay for his college tuition.

"Where is the other guard?"

"Other guard sir, I'm the only one here."

"You don't understand, last night I left my brief case with the guard on duty. I need it back." He pulled out a twig from his hair.

"And what is your name sir, if I may ask?"

"I am Professor Andrew Pettigrew of Oxford University here to meet with Dean Shannon."

"Aye, that is the name given to me to be sure, but I must see some identification before I can do anything else; you do understand." The guard decided that he should be thorough as this unshaven man before him with clothes which hadn't seen an iron and a shirt open and not tucked gave him more of an appearance of one who had just come from a charity ward.

Pettigrew pulled out his passport from the inside suit coat pocket and flashed it before the young guard.

"It seems to be in order sir. You will find your brief case in the Security Office on the right side of the Bell Tower."

"You have been most kind, thank you." With that the Professor entered the campus and made his way toward the Bell Tower just as it began to chime out the eighth hour of the morning.

Those same chimes could be heard through the slightly open windows of the dorms. In the women's dorm, Jan and Susan were already up and dressed.

"God help me Jan, but I almost messed up my pledge to not test your brother and leave him to God."

"You don't have to tell me; everyone saw you google eye my brother's belly button of all things."

Susan sat on the foot of the narrow bed and looked over to Jan who was on the desk chair tying up her sneakers. "Today, I am going for comfort and not style or professional assistant to our missing Professor; hence the blue jeans, comfortable cotton top and the Loyola University, Rome sweatshirt. Do I look passable?"

"You look just fine for Count Alessandro, who can't keep his eyes off you. But listen to me; you don't have the focus of your brother do you? Anyway, I am distressed can't you see that?"

Jan got up and sat herself down next to Susan. "Now listen to me, first, I'll ignore the focus statement and secondly, I did hear you loud and clear. But you're telling the wrong person. You need to tell Ronnie about how you feel and then maybe he won't be doing what he's been doing to you."

"You mean like what I usually do, teasing and flirting but with me as the target."

"Exactly, now if you ask me, he's testing himself. So you have two choices. First, let him go on with his silly test of whatever and secondly tell him how you feel thus bringing the whole thing out in the open. Then he can face the truth of the matter and perhaps come to a decision not based on what's between his legs. Trust me, that's what this test is all about; I know my brother and guys in general. He's in love but doesn't know it; so he thinks its lust because he thinks he's a stud. Like anyone would think my brother is a stud..."

"Well I think he's a stud; he's so cute and so well formed and..."

"Knock it off, he's my brother. He's skinny and handsome in a boyish way not like Alessandro, who is handsome in a manly way. You know, broad and filled out."

"Indeed, your Count of Pianore is a good five or six years older than Ron, so it figures he's more filled out. Anyway, I think Ron is cute just as he is; like a model for a Michelangelo statue."

"Well maybe for the Bacchus statue he carved but as for the David, that is all about Alessandro."

"I agree, he's not the warrior David, but he is like one of those statues called the slaves, all innocent and alluring and writhing in anguish over life and death and..."

"Oh my God, you do have it bad." Jan pulled Susan close to her. "Listen sister, it's time to tell him the truth about your feelings. Let him choose between God and you."

"Easier said than done; I'll think about it but first I am going to change into something very similar to what you're wearing which couldn't possibly be alluring to him. I think I'll put my hair in a ponytail, your brother likes the over the shoulder free fall look, so that should deter him."

Across the green in the men's dorm, the bells hadn't caused a stir in the guys, either in the Professor's room or room 303 where Ron and Bob lay dead to the world. It wasn't until the eighth bell had rung and the hymn of the day was being played that Bob popped straight up in the bed. He looked over to Ron with his head under the pillow and heard a faint moaning sound from his best pal in the world.

"Oh Lord, here we go again." He picked up the pillow and threw it. "Ron, get your ass up. That Chief Inspector wants us to report to him." He jumped out of bed and ran about gathering his clothes.

A head peeked out from under the pillow. "What's biting your ass this morning pal?"

Bob hadn't a chance to answer, as he was at the door about to run off to the bathroom down the hall when the knob began to turn and then the sound of mettle inserted into the lock. Ron had heard it too. He jumped from the bed and joined Bob at the door. "Hand me that Bible on the table, just in case."

They stood there in their tight white Jockeys poised to pounce, Bible ready to slam on the intruder's head. Whoever was trying to get in could not; the key in the lock didn't work. A pounding on the door followed.

"Let's get a grip on this Watson, maybe someone just has the wrong room. We're just on edge that's all." Ron handed the Bible to Bob and unlocked the door from his side and slowly pulled it open.

Professor Pettigrew fell forward into his arms. They both collapsed onto the bare wood floor with a thud. On top of Ron, looking into his wide dark eyes were the azure blue eyes of the frightened Professor. "Do forgive me Mr. De Cenza, I thought that I was at the door of my room."

Bob was now pulling him off his friend and onto his feet. "Sir, what on earth; what's happened. Your room is next door, 301; this is 303." He walked him to the desk chair and sat him down.

From the floor Ron sat up and watched as Bob took over the situation, fetching the Professor a glass of water from the sink's faucet in their room and checking his head for a wound after being told that someone or something hit him. "There's just a little blood and quite a bump back here sir. Should I call for a doctor?"

"There isn't time; I must get my brief case before…" the Professor looked about as if he was being spied upon.

Ron stood and walked to him. "Sir, no one is here but Bob and me. Are you sure that you're okay?"

The Professor realizing that the lads where standing there in their underwear became embarrassed, "I do apologize for all of this. Perhaps you'd like to put on some pants. I think I've seen enough nakedness this day."

The lads looked at each other. "Who would have thought?" Bob softly spoke.

The comment meant only for Ron was heard. "Oh lads, you have me wrong there. I just escaped from a man true but it was a woman who stripped me and had her way with me or so I think. I am quite confused on that part. In any case you are quite safe with me."

"Oh shit…a woman took advantage of you; I mean how awful…and who was this woman, sir?"

"Mr. Wentz, she's none other than the assistant to the Curator of the Dublin Museum, a Miss Bridget Tulley, I believe she told me that was her name." He ignored Bob's obvious excitement in voicing the question.

Ron was pulling up his jeans watching his pal get all riled up over what he envisioned had happened. "Bob, get your ass covered. It's indecent to stand here in front of the poor man like that." It worked Bob ran to the wardrobe and pulled out a pair of jeans.

"So sorry Professor, it's just that I never heard of a woman doing that to a man."

"That's quite all right, I am not quite sure what the 'doing that' is frankly. I just woke up in a bed with a naked lady and found myself to be likewise in that state."

"Well whatever happened you sure look like it's been quite the night. Why don't I take you to your room and then we'll get cleaned up and dressed properly and try to figure all of this out, before that Chief Inspector gets here," Ron looked at the Mickey Mouse watch on his wrist. "Wow, not much time; he wants us at nine. Can you stand?" Ron took hold of the Professor's arm to assist.

"I'm just shaken up and my head hurts but I'll be fine not like what happened back on the Tiber in Rome right gentlemen?" with that he looked down his open shirt. "I think I may have spoken too soon."

"Shit, that changes things; maybe you should lie down and I'll call a doctor."

"There's no time, may I call you Ron?"

"Of course sir…"

"And you can call me Bob, sir."

"You are most kind. If you would just get me a wet cold cloth please and if you don't mind, I'll lay on the bed for a bit until my head stops spinning." Pettigrew sat on the bed behind him.

As Bob wet the hand towel at the sink, Ron tucked his pillow and the one thrown at him under the Professor's head. "There, now let me check that wound, if you don't mind. We have a first aid kit and I can put a bandage on it, if it's not too bad."

Pettigrew unbuckled his belt. "Please be aware that I am not wearing any underwear."

"Holy shit, Professor, who would have thought that you would go commando," Bob handed the cloth to Ron who gave him a look of disbelief in what he just said.

The Professor returned a smile; telling them that it was not done intentionally but that he was in a rather big hurry to escape and had no time to fully dress. "So you see, I had to run here to the college, couldn't get into the Security Office and came to what I thought was my room."

After placing the cloth on the back of the Professor's head, Ron told Bob to fetch the kit. He unzipped the pants and pulled them down slightly. At the top of the scar blood was forming. "Well the good news is that it doesn't appear to be a severe break. I'll put some iodine on it and bandage it. Then we'll go tell the guys, who by the way are sleeping in your room because we have had quite the night as well to get out and dressed. Will you be all right?"

"What happened? Where are the girls?"

"Everyone is fine including Jan and Susan, so don't worry," Ron began.

"We are to meet with the Chief Inspector shortly to review the murder that's all."

"For shit's sake Bob can't you ever keep that mouth of yours shut. We'll tell you everything sir, but for now take these two aspirin while we get cleaned up and get the other guys."

Chaos ensued as the guys were roused and told that the Professor was injured in escaping from a woman who called herself the Assistant Curator of the Dublin Museum. Bob quickly added that the woman and the Professor were naked in bed.

CHAPTER SEVEN

THE MISSING BRIEF CASE

By 8:55 a.m. the Professor rushed along the edge of the Library Green with the lads toward the Security Office. Upon arriving they found Susan and Jan administering aid to a young man in a guard's uniform sprawled out across the steps leading into the office. The glass of the door was shattered and the door itself was ajar.

The red plastic First Aid Kit was being held by Jan as Susan wrapped a gauze strip around the guard's head. Given the early hour of the morning and no classes as the spring session had ended while the summer classes had not yet begun, the green was literally empty of people. The lads ran to the girls to offer assistance with Alessandro going directly to Jan and offering to hold the kit for her. She readily handed it over after pulling out the tape which would be used to fasten the gauze wrapping.

"Here let me help you Susan," Ron took hold of her hand to retrieve the bandage. "I kind of have some experience with wounds and the like after what happened back in Rome."

"Ron De Cenza, I do not need your help. I'm just wrapping this guy's head…"

"My name is Pierce Dawson if you don't mind. I'm a student and part time guard like most around the campus." The guard who was about the same age as Ron, around twenty seemed a bit peeved about being ignored as the two touched hands which changed the entire focus onto them and not their patient.

The Professor after the initial shock of seeing the results of an attack not unlike what happened to him ran to the shattered door. Bob seeing that he was about to enter without the slightest hesitation as to who might still be inside the office ran up to him and became his backup.

"Professor, we'll just stick with you just in case."

"Thanks Bob, but if I think what happened actually did occur then I'm afraid we're too late. Whoever did this was seeking my brief case and what it contained, of that I am quite confident." He pushed open the door slightly more and squeezed through the opening. "I thought it would be safe here overnight and after what happened to me, I..."

Bob placed his hand on the professor's shoulder. "It's okay, whatever we find, we'll deal with it. After Rome, how bad can this be?" He cracked a smile as they entered.

The morning light was streaming into the office from not only the doorway but also a long window on the outer wall. It was in shambles as the contents of whatever was being held in the cubicles along the back wall from where they stood were tossed about the room.

At the same time this was taking place Chief Inspector Rory O'Connor was walking through the arch of the Bell Tower with several of his officers. He immediately noticed the commotion taking place off to the right of the green and sent Sargent Carrick to check it out. He and the others made their way to what was called the Long Room of the Library Building.

Running toward the group of young people he thought to be students up to no good, Carrick soon took notice of the broken glass in the door behind them. He also recognized the lads and lasses gathered around the guard as those he had seen at Slane Castle. Besides Bob, also missing were Andreas and Dominic who had been sent to the Library Alcoves to search for the books they needed which had accounts about the last High King of Ireland, the original Rory O'Connor and the establishment of Mellifont Abbey as well as the poems of the ancients revolving around Irish Mythology and early Christianity. If Ron was correct in his thought, if those books could be found, there would be a connection to that which the Professor had discovered in the Vatican Archives about St. Malachy and the establishment of his Abbey at Mellifont.

Inside the Alcove between the marble bust of Jonathon Swift and William Conygham Plunket were Andreas and Dominic frantically looking for the Lebor Gabbala Erenn and the Tadgh O'Neachtain version of it. Dominic had his hand on the 1745 edition of the latter book when they heard footsteps. He grabbed the centuries old text and shoved it under his sweatshirt and into his belt. They peeked out from behind the fine example of such sculpture by Peter Scheesmaker as if they were little kids sneaking out of a naughty movie theater. Reacting as if they were soon to be caught, they hurried as far as they could to the back end of the alcove lined with original works covering centuries of history. As they huddled together knowing full well where those footsteps would lead which would be to the alcove directly opposite of them for that's where the Chief Inspector had told them to meet him at nine in the morning. It was the one where the bust of the Roman Orator, Cicero was located. Above them the light coming from the window at their backs illuminated another ancient text. It was the Lebor Gabbala Erenn. Andreas' eyes focused on its gold lettering on the spine. He reached for it and slipped it off the shelf just above his head.

The Footsteps became louder, echoing throughout the 210 foot long hall off the vaulted 19th Century ceiling. They decided that they could do nothing to avoid detection so rather than being in a position of being caught they decided to simply appear. As soon as the sound of leather on wood came closer, out walked Andreas with the book he had taken from the shelf open and reading from one of its poems of the ancient days.

"As he set his right foot upon Ireland, Amorgen Ghuingel spoke…

Iam Wind on Sea, I am Ocean wave, I am Roar of the Sea, I am Bull of Seven Fights, I am Vulture on Cliff, I am Dewdrop, I am Fairest of Flowers, I am Boar for Boldness, I am Salmon in Pool, I am Lake on Plain, I am a Mountain in a Man, I am a Word of Skill, I am the Point of a Weapon, I am God who fashioneth Fire for a giver of inspiration. Who smootheth the ruggedness of a mountain? Who is He who announceth the age of the Moon? And who the place where falleth the sunset?"

Feigning ignorance of the Chief Inspector's presence in the hall, Andreas walked right into him, still reading. "Madonna mia, Chief Inspector, I am so sorry." He reached out his hand to catch O'Connor as he tumbled backwards into two officers, none too pleased to see their boss being smacked into and thrown almost to the ground were it not for them.

Dominic ran to O'Connor and pulled him up off his officers and steadied him on his feet. "Mi dispiacere Chief Inspector."

"What, I don't understand your language sir."

"I said that I was sorry, sir. We were so enthralled with this book of poems that we didn't even notice you."

"Indeed, well, it's nice to see that you have an interest in Irish Literature. What are you reading Mr. Berne?"

Andreas held up the book and read its title, "Lebor Gabala Erenn, The Book of the Taking of Ireland. It's really quite interesting almost like our mythology."

"Is that so, well I can tell you this much from that book; the Irish can trace their roots back to Noah, whose daughter came to escape the flood or so the story goes," replied the proud Chief Inspector.

"That's quite the recommendation; I do look forward to the reading of it. Now then are Dominic and I too early for our meeting?"

O'Connor thrown completely off kilter looked the tall blond Swiss Guard up and down. "And may I ask why you two are here right on-time while I see no others about?" He paused to emphasize that the bells were ringing out the hour.

Andreas gave a quick glace to Dominic and nodded as if he had something up his sleeve. And that he did, as he turned the focus from them. "Sir, I can only guess as we left to come and explore this beautiful place but perhaps you haven't heard. Our Professor came to us this very morning…"

O'Connor stiffened and readied himself to give orders to his officers. He cut off Andreas in mid-sentence. "And you chose not to share this with me; where is he now? The entire Garda is out looking for his body for now we thought him to be a victim of foul play."

Dominic took over with an award winning performance. "Foul play! God help us. You think that Professor Pettigrew has a…" he thought hard looking for a good English language police type word, "a target on his back." He reeled backwards into Andreas with his hand up on his forehead, imitating the scene from an old movie, "Gone with the Wind." "Andreas, everyone who knows the Professor also knows that I am his research assistant that means they'll come to get me too."

He collapsed forcing Andreas to catch him but not wanting to show that they had a 'thing' going on between them, he just softened his fall to the bare floor. Holding him by his shoulders he lowered him while Dominic opened one eye with a squint to give him a look of not appreciating the lack of concern. The attempted cover-up of their 'thing' didn't work. O'Connor looked down at the handsome dark Italian on the floor and then up to his officers and winked.

"Ahem, Mr. Berne you may take Mr. Fontana to a chair where we shall meet as soon as your friends arrive." Then he instructed his officers to look for Sargent Carrick. "Perhaps that commotion was more than students up to pranks?"

No sooner had his question been asked than the thunder of many running across a wooden floor reached their ears. At the far end of the Long Room came running the lads and lasses. They were accompanied by Sargent Carrick with Professor Pettigrew on one side of him and the bandaged guard on the other. Ron screeched to a halt as the scene of Dominic now seated on the floor under the bust of Jonathon Swift with Andreas now on one knee hovering over him and the Chief Inspector and officers forming a backdrop clearly came into view. He held up his arms to stop the others, but not the Sargent. He passed through them with the Professor and Guard.

As they approached, Dominic decided to continue his act. He jumped to his feet and ran to the Professor, throwing his arms around him. "You're alive, you're alive…"

The British in Pettigrew kicked in as he looked into his research assistant's eyes incredulously. "Of course I'm alive. Dominic you just saw me not an hour ago."

What the Professor hadn't picked up on, Ron did and ran to them. "Oh Professor, Dominic is just distraught after all that we learned about how you were kidnapped and, well stripped and taken advantage of.

Now Dominic, let the Chief Inspector get filled in." Ron pulled the now embarrassed assistant off the neck of his boss. "There now, just go sit over there by Andreas and let the Chief Inspector do his job."

Chief Inspector O'Connor stroked the gruff beard on his chin, raising an eyebrow as he heard the tantalizing highlights. He wondered why the fuss, after all this man they called Professor was mature enough to have an affair, why was that so shocking. It was the attack part of the story which he decided to focus upon. He began by stating the obvious.

"Professor Pettigrew, I presume…"

"Quite so, you'll forgive my assistant. He and all here had thought that I was a victim of foul play."

"But sir," the Chief Inspector moved to Ron and placed his arm over his shoulder. "This young man has said that you were just that. Was he exaggerating your…shall I say encounter and subsequent, ah…abuse?"

Ron squirmed to break away from the clutching of O'Connor. He let him do so as he walked up to the now red faced Professor. Once again his entire body shuddered as he approached with those piercing eyes taking in his every attribute. He could almost read the thoughts of the Chief Inspector who was thinking, "How could such a young virile looking man and obviously fit one at that could be taken advantage of by that woman referred to." He broke his hypnotic stare on the Professor and glanced back at Ron. The Sherlock in Ron was now acting more like a stool pigeon who gave out too much information and O'Connor could sense the change in posture and confidence. He strode back toward Ron as the eyes of all were now watching this unnerving of their friend and the Professor as if they were at a tennis match.

The Professor took matters into his own hands quite literally. He cut in front of O'Connor and in what an astonished Ron could only respond with those big shocked cocoa brown eyes stood frozen as the Professor placed his arm around him and pulled him close.

"Ron here, like all those who I'm told you called for questioning are just concerned over my well-being after what happened in Rome last fall, but that's not important…"

O'Connor coughed as if to indicate that everything about this Professor may be important, but he let his words stay unspoken as Pettigrew continued what he thought was getting Ron and the others out of the spotlight of suspicion. He waved his arm high in a gesture that he should proceed; the unbuttoned suit coat spread apart revealing the handle of a pistol tucked in a holster concealed by the jacket.

All eyes now zeroed in on that weapon as Pettigrew continued with a glance at Susan and Jan which caused him to get red in the face. But he continued his statement, "Now then as for the situation Ron alluded to, I regret to say that I am quite embarrassed by it all as having taken place. Something did happen not more than six blocks from this college campus in the Dawson Street apartments."

The Chief Inspector now had his arms folded across his chest with one hand again stroking his beard. It was his intent to demonstrate no emotion or even a keenness to hear the siliceous details of being stripped by a woman and so forth. Rather, he was deciding how to react with some sensitivity to an awkward situation being addressed in the presence of the young people especially the two lasses.

The morning light was creating streams of beams into the long hall from the windows high above them. One of those sunbeams struck the bust of Cicero, the great Roman Orator. O'Connor took that as a sign. "Sargent Carrick, please take these young people to that table in the Cicero alcove. From them get their statements and that of this injured security guard as well as to how he came to get that gash on his head."

Carrick corralled the others and led them across the hall into the Cicero alcove. That is all except for Ron who was still being held onto rather uncomfortably by the Professor who smiled at him one of those comforting ones so as not to worry that all will be well. They waited for their instructions from the Chief Inspector and got it.

"Now then, perhaps we should take a stroll down the long hall so as not to disturb the Sargent in his statement gathering." O'Connor directed the two onto the shiny oak flooring and walked them to the Jonathon Swift alcove. "Now isn't this convenient…there's a table in this one but we aren't here to speak of far off places with little people are we?" He waited for no answer. "Do be seated and make yourselves comfortable as possible on these stodgy wooden chairs and tell me exactly what happened to you Professor and you Ron as to what you and your friends were doing at the

Security Office when you were supposed to meet me here." He took a seat across the table from them and took out a small pad on which to jot notes and in doing so once again revealed the gun which unnerved both the Professor and Ron.

Nevertheless, Ron took the proverbial bull by the horns and decided to speak first which he thought would give Pettigrew a bit more time to put together his embarrassing story so as to reveal only that which was necessary.

"Sir, if you don't mind may I begin for I think you will soon see that the two incidents are not related so let me fill you in on the meeting with you part of your question."

By the time the tenth hour of the morning was being announced by the Bell Tower chimes, Sargent Carrick had concluded his collection of statements and was sending the Security Guard off to the medical facility with a uniform officer. Leaving the remaining officer with the lads and lasses, he searched for O'Connor, finding him on the far end of the Long Hall. A slight hand motion from the Chief Inspector alerted Carrick to remain silent as the Professor was finishing up his story.

"And that Chief Inspector is what happened. She said that she was the Assistant Curator of the Dublin Museum. She seemed to know who I was, and that I had a meeting scheduled with Dean Drumond Shannon and later with her boss, the Curator Hugh O'Neil. I'm afraid that's all I really remember until I woke up in her bed in a rather compromising manner."

O"Connor stirred away from the part of his waking up in her bed and focused on his brief case. "But Professor, how do you relate the theft of your property here on campus with what appears to be a seduction perhaps to blackmail you at a later date? You said that you thought you had some wine, could you have been drugged?"

"That sir, I don't remember. I don't even recall taking any of the wine in her apartment though there were two glasses filled on the coffee table when that big man took hold of me."

"I see," O'Connor looked into Ron's eyes. "You said the two were not related but it appears young man that the missing brief case is not just a theft but perhaps part of what this woman had hoped to steal in the first place. When the Security Guard was given the Professor's brief case it put as you Americans would say a monkey wrench into her plan."

Playing along, Ron agreed. "Yes sir, so it seems. But we guys and the girls had no idea that it would be connected to the abuse situation as we didn't even know about that…ah we just were on our way to meet you when the commotion drew our attention."

Sargent Carrick stood silently waiting for an opportune moment to announce the conclusion of his task but suddenly intrigued to overhear something which connected to what he had been told. O'Connor from the corner of his eye realized his presence. He didn't respond to Ron's statement but spoke to Carrick.

"Did all go well Sargent?"

"Yes sir, all the statements have been taken. That lad Bob Wentz in his may have answered the issue over a connection as you just stated. It seems that the Professor's brief case and nothing else was stolen from the Security Office."

O'Connor rose from his chair and stood there for a moment. One could almost hear the machinations of his brain churning and integrating what he was just told with that which the Professor and Ron had just told him. He was not alone for Ron was now connecting all of that to the murder at Mellifont Abbey.

After a prolonged silence the Chief Inspector spoke. "I see, get the forensic team to that office and search for fingerprints." Carrick turned to leave. "One more thing; see if a disturbance has been reported at the Dawson Street apartments."

"Sir, I can answer that second part right now. A radio message was just received regarding a woman found bound and gagged in a closet at those apartments."

The Professor interrupted. "Chief Inspector, was it apartment number 520?"

The Sargent confirmed that to be the number.

"Sir, that's the apartment where I found myself earlier this morning. I am sure there was only that woman with blond hair in bed with me," he coughed and took a deep breath…"and then that burly man who attacked me and from whom I ran. There is one way to make sure that's the place," he added. "I ran after the muscle bound oaf in shall I say a disheveled state. If you find underwear on the floor by the bed then you will know, oh and socks too the paisley print kind with my school colors which are…"

"Thank you Professor but we shall make sure it's the place right now."

The machinations went into high gear in two brains at that moment as Ron and the Chief Inspector arrived to a similar approach. Ron jumped up from his chair and slowly made his way toward O'Connor now at the Professor's side with Carrick just behind them. "Chief Inspector, I think we should go to the apartment and see it for ourselves. Don't give time for the woman they found to alter anything in the apartment."

"Get to it Carrick, release those young people and have a car brought here for us. Good thinking young man and you say that you're preparing for the priesthood? Interesting…"

The sound of thunder on the oak floorboards echoed through the Library as Carrick ran to the officer ordering as he ran to get a squad car immediately brought to the Library. "Ladies and Gentlemen, you are free to go," Carrick announced as he stood before the young people who hadn't a clue as to what was taking place. "But stay on Campus; we will still be going to Slane Castle and Mellifont Abbey but just later."

As he ran off, the group spilled out into the wide aisle between the rows of reading tables. Ron and the Professor were walking toward them with the Chief Inspector between them.

Bob's crystal blue eyes just about leapt from their sockets. He grabbed hold of Jan and Susan. "Oh my Lord, the Chief Inspector is holding onto them. What could they have said to get them arrested?"

Before anyone could get further upset by the sight, the three stood before them and O'Connor laid out what was about to take place.

"We will be taking the Professor to the scene where the situation took place regarding a certain woman. All of you are to remain here until we are ready to leave for Slane Castle."

Bob needed clarification. "But the Sargent said we just had to stay on campus not here in the Library."

Ron shot him a grin which said, keep it up. I need time to think."

"It's already approaching eleven and we haven't had breakfast. Can't we go to Stephen's Green there's this nice American Café and…"

"Mr. Wentz, I said that you are to remain here meaning on Campus. We do not know who tried to abduct the Professor and if anyone is still around and saw you they may make a connection and get to you. By now the entire city has probably learned about the Dawson Street incident and the theft here at Trinity College. That means your little group is also known."

"Well, I guess I get your point, but perhaps we can order lunch and have it delivered."

"Why can't you just go to the college cafeteria?"

"Oh, of course, it's still open then, I get it. That will do just fine." Bob was pleased with himself.

"That being settled we shall return after lunch, so everyone be sure to eat. I don't want anyone wasting away to nothing over a little crime like a stolen brief case and a woman found bound and gagged in a closet."

Bob feigned embarrassment while the others thanked O'Connor for worrying about their health.

"Chief Inspector, before you go may I suggest that the Professor not be alone. Shouldn't his assistant Dominic or even I accompany him just in case the scene makes him upset."

"There will be a team of forensic people there, my officers, and myself; he will be perfectly safe."

"It's not the safety part of which I am speaking sir, it's you know that scene with the clues lying about the floor and so forth."

The dawn came upon the Chief Inspector as a flood of images of underwear, used bedding, victim in the closet and so forth came to mind. "I see your point Ron. Professor is it your wish to be accompanied?"

The Professor had not known Ron for all those months since the attack on him in Rome and the subsequent developments without realizing that the young man had something up his sleeve. "Yes Chief Inspector that would be most comforting given the situation. Perhaps both Ron and Dominic would make themselves available."

The issue was settled leaving both Susan and Bob a bit disgruntled that Ron had suggested Dominic instead of them, his sidekick and the one who got his synapses firing in that brain of his. Jan didn't care so long as Alessandro was there with her. That left Andreas the odd man out but he had the ancient books which had some kind of connection to whatever brought the attack on the Professor in the first place not to mention the murder in Mellifont. Ron took the Swiss Guard aside after recalling that he had those Irish History books.

"Andreas, get everyone to read over those books you found. Look for anything which might refer to Mellifont Abbey or what's on that paper in Bob's satchel." He then turned to seek out Dean Drummond and Hugh O'Neil knowing full well that just seconds before O'Connor arrived with them that they had slipped out of the Library once the Sargent dismissed them after ordering everyone to stay on campus. Bob had given him a shrug of shoulders as he pointed to the chairs where they had been seated. "Chief Inspector, where are Dean Drummond and Mr. O'Neil?"

Sargent Carrick answered his question. "It's fine sir, they weren't needed any longer and decided to get some lunch. Seeing that the interviews were finished I didn't see the need to retain them here not knowing that you were coming."

"Gosh Bob they had the same idea as you; why don't you and the guys take the girls to the cafeteria and join them. Perhaps they can help you read some Irish poetry or something."

"An excellent suggestion Ron," O'Connor addressed the group, "do go and when we return from this little side trip, we'll leave for Slane Castle," with that he left the smiling troupe of investigators with Ron, Dominic and the Professor.

Alone around that table, they just stood for a moment and then called for Andreas to produce the books. From under his shirt he pulled out the "Lebor Erenn Gabbala" and opened its fine pages. "This is the book I found, there by you Susan is where Dominic was seated, look on the chair, I think you'll find something if I'm not mistaken."

She did as he directed and there was the "Tadgh O'Neachtain" version. "Why Andreas wasn't your little ole friend just so sneaky as to slip this little book out of sight right in front of the Chief Inspector," she laughed. "So let's get started boys, we have work to do."

A loud pounding on the table brought their attention to the far end. Bob stood with arms folded across his chest. "I thought we were going to do this in the cafeteria; so did the Chief Inspector."

Susan immediately closed the book she had taken off the chair and scurried up to Bob, patting him on the cheek. "Watson is right; we should have lunch to keep up our strength. Come along boys, Jan you too."

CHAPTER EIGHT

THE DECEPTION

Outside on Dawson Street a small crowd had gathered as the police presence had cordoned off the entrance into the Apartment Building thus creating some interest in the neighborhood which is usually just full of tourists. Sargent Carrick flashed his badge as he crossed over the crime scene ribbon. "Chief Inspector O'Connor is here to interview the victim; is she still inside?"

Entering and going up the wooden staircase Pettigrew pointed out the spot where he fought with the burly man whom he thought the woman called Fitz. There wasn't much to see, just wood railing and stairs with a small light fixture on the white plaster wall under which Ron noticed a glistening silvery object. Purposefully lagging behind the others he stooped down to get a better look. It was an embroidered patch with threads still attached to it as if it had been ripped off whatever it once was attached. Some of those threads were silver and gold and picked up the light. After a quick glance he pocketed it wondering if the Coat of Arms was from a school, club or some other type of organization.

The Chief Inspector and the Sargent were standing in the doorway when he caught up to them. Dominic turned to him, "Madonna Mia is the Inspector angry. Look who beat us here."

Peering between the shoulders of the two detectives Ron saw Dean Drummond speaking with the female officer watching over the victim and Mr. O'Neil seated on a sofa with Bridget Tulley, still in her chenille bathrobe. He also noticed the half full and empty wine glasses on the coffee table in front of the Curator and his assistant as well as a crystal decanter with some wine still visible in it. It was a red wine not that such would mean much.

O'Connor having brought himself under control took a step forward into the apartment in direct line with the sofa and the police officer with Shannon Drummond to the side of it. "Gentlemen, I thought you were told to stay on the college campus."

Hugh O'Neil jumped to his feet and without hesitation offered the explanation that they presumed such a direction was aimed at the young people as they lived off campus. "In any case, I could not just sit around while not knowing what had happened to my assistant, Miss Tulley. Oh, Chief Inspector may I present Miss Bridget Tulley."

"How do you do Miss Tulley. I am Chief Inspector Rory O'Connor and this is Sargent Carrick. I regret this inconvenience after all you've been through but it is imperative that we try to discern everything that occurred here from last night to the time that the Professor was accosted by the burly man named Fitz, I believe."

She daintily rose to her feet and pulled on the fluffy cord to make sure it was tightly fitted. "Thank you Chief Inspector…Rory O'Connor did you say as in the last High King of Ireland?"

O'Connor smiled with some flushness appearing on his cheeks. "Yes Miss, however there is no relation of that I am sure. Now as to what happened here, would you mind sharing the events with us? Perhaps you would prefer to be seated at the table. But first I should like to introduce you to the man who says you took him to this apartment last evening from Trinity College. This is Professor Andrew Pettigrew and his assistant Dominic Fontana and Ron De Cenza, part of his research team."

The assistant curator's eyes grew wide as she looked at Pettigrew. "I never saw this man in my life sir."

Before the Chief Inspector could respond Pettigrew spoke. "She's correct sir, I never saw this woman. The Miss Tulley who came to get me from the library had blond hair and this woman has long coal black hair and her eyes, I thought they were green and this woman has a hazel coloring but I may be wrong on that given that it was dark and I was upset when awakening to find myself in bed with that other woman."

Hugh O'Neil rose to place his arm around his assistant. "My good man, hasn't she been through enough. At least allow her to get dressed and then interview her."

Drummond echoed his concurrence to the suggestion.

O'Connor apologized for the insensitivity and directed that Officer Colleen Frawley accompany the assistant curator to her bedroom to refresh herself. Once they had gone, he suggested that the others take a seat around the dining table while he and the Sargent looked about the apartment while the Professor filled them in on what he could remember of his time in it. They obviously could not go into the bedroom to find the clues as he called the underwear and socks. The Professor stood at the bedroom door as Pettigrew instead of telling what he remembered walked through what he did once outside of the bedroom area.

He ended up at the entrance door to the apartment for it was there that the burly man came through and attacked him. "I just don't understand what happened to that woman. She didn't accompany Fitz, he is the one who had the gun and forced me to go with him. Once I was able to get away on that staircase, I made my way back to the college and eventually to my room. I don't know where this Fitz person went or where that woman disappeared to as I was quite frightened and just wanted to get away from it all."

While the Professor spoke Ron slipped off the chair at the table and moved slowly to the fireplace as all eyes were on Pettigrew's reenactment. One of the pokers was on the bricks of the hearth and not in its stand with the others. Stuck on the end of it were some blond fibers he thought. He bent down to check it out and realized that they were hairs, rather long bleached ones. As he did so he saw others in the dying embers in the fireplace. They were singed and not totally burned. Leaving the ones on the poker alone, he pulled some of those in the fireplace out and slipped them into his pocket.

"Mr. De Cenza don't touch anything get back to the table. The forensic people will soon be here to check for prints and evidence like blood."

Pettigrew froze in place by the sofa just as he was about to explain how the woman lay on it and taunted him in his nakedness to dress before the burly man arrived to take him away. "Blood, Inspector, they will find my blood right here for I fought with the Fitz person. I got in a few good swings so his blood may also be somewhere around here, otherwise there was no injury which brought forth blood."

"So then Professor, are you telling me that they will find no blood in the bedroom?"

"Quite right, I fell off the bed and twisted in the sheet to cover my embarrassment but the wound on my side wasn't bleeding, at least I don't think so."

"Professor I was not talking only about blood. Will they find other types of evidence from the body shall I say?"

"Oh my, I understand all too clearly. That sir, I don't know for I can't remember anything about what happened in that bed until I awoke to find that woman next to me nude."

"So then we really don't know if you were abused as Ron and the others have said or if you raped some poor girl or if nothing at all happened because you were knocked out…"

"That's it sir, the wine; have your people check out the wine. It's the last thing I remember after we arrived in this apartment. She said that she would get more comfortable and offered me some wine."

"I will surely direct them to do so. Now as for the rest of you; we shall begin with the Curator and then the Dean. Mr. O'Neil you seemed quite friendly with Miss Tulley when I came into this apartment."

"Don't be ridiculous sir I am just worried about her that's all. Good heavens I am twenty years older than her at least."

"It wouldn't be the first time that an older man would be what the Americans call a sugar daddy to a young woman." His comment fell flat and O'Neil was upset as was Drummond who protested that such behavior was not in the make-up of the curator that he knew.

"And I would agree with that because Miss Tulley was not the woman who seduced the Professor," began Ron as he pointed to the poker lying on the bricks of the hearth. "There are long blond hairs on that and in the fireplace you will find half burned hairs perhaps from a wig and certainly not those of Miss Tulley who has raven black hair. Someone other than the Professor and Miss Tulley and that burly man was in this apartment." He had decided that the Curator needed saving at least for the moment because of what was in the Professor's brief case that he could verify if found.

Just as Ron finished his analysis, the bedroom door opened and out stepped Miss Tulley dressed in a plaid skirt below the knee, a white blouse with a jacket which matched the pattern on the skirt. "You will forgive me but Mr. O'Neil is not my sugar daddy or anyone else's for that matter. He is too innocent and kind."

O'Neil didn't know whether to be offended or pleased to be made out to be a fifty plus year old virgin wimp. He sat silently at the table with his head in his hands and Drummond patting his back.

"In any case I would have heard something from inside that closet which adjoins my bedroom if there was anything which made noise like a fight or whatever. I'm afraid all was silent as I sat tied up in the darkness." She ran her fingers through her coal-like hair as if to emphasize that she couldn't be that blond hair woman who seduced the Professor."

The gesture was not lost on Dominic who gave an eye to Ron. He began mimicking her and ran his fingers through his dark hair which came over his ears if it wasn't sleeked back with hair cream. Ron nodded understanding. No one was suggesting that Miss Tulley could have been the one in the wig because of being found bound and gagged in the closet. They simply assumed that she was a victim of a break-in so that her apartment could be used to lure the Professor in with his brief case but were only half successful. Ron now began to visualize her in another role but at the moment could not prove anything so kept his thoughts to himself.

The Chief Inspector continued his investigation by escorting the Professor into Miss Tulley's bedroom to identify what he called the clues. As he did so, Pettigrew almost seemed elated thought Ron as he shot out a grin to Dominic. Perhaps somewhere deep inside after being made out to be some kind of who knows what, he was wishing that something did happen on that night of which he had no memory.

As this side trip and kidnapping of the Professor continued on Dawson Street, back in the Trinity College Cafeteria the rest of Ron's crew surrounded one of the reading tables on which lay the two books which

Dominic and Andreas had found. Susan was carefully paging through the *Lebor Gabbala Erenn* with Jan looking for any poem or narrative which had any connection to those words on that note which the dead woman passed onto Ron. That bloodstained note was laid out flat on the table above the text so that Andreas and Alessandro could refer to it as they paged through the other ancient text of stories compiled in the 18th century, the *Tadgh O'Nechtain*. Page after page they carefully looked for that poem printed on the bloodstained paper which had been slipped to Ron as the Lady in Black died.

"This is crazy, it's just a poem. Even if we find it, what will that mean?"

Susan looked at Ron's sister not quite knowing how to respond. "Well Jan, it would at least confirm that the lady knew of these books and that just maybe something was in them which could help us understand why she was in the ruins in the first place."

"I doubt it but okay if you say it will help…"

"What are you doubting, Sis?"

The heads glued to those pages on the ancient books popped up to find Dominic and Ron standing at the entrance to the alcove.

"Ronnie, good you're back. I was just saying that what good is that poem on the note…"

"Ah, well sister dear it's not so much the poem as what's written in her hand on the other side of that note that may be of help to finding a motive for her murder." Ron had cut her off which she wasn't too pleased about.

He walked to her and Susan while Dominic made his way to the side of Andreas. Placing his hand over that of the Swiss Guard, he cast a weak smile so as not to embarrass him given that Alessandro was on the other side of him. All eyes then turned to Ron as he reached into his pocket and pulled out the piece of hair. "First things first," he began. "I found this in the fireplace of the Assistant Curator's apartment. It's from a wig I think as there's a woven base on the end of it. It was obviously part of a larger piece which had been burned. See the singe area here at the end." He placed the fragment down on the table. "Now all we need to do is find out who that wig belonged to."

"Well that's obvious, it belonged to the assistant curator; after all it was in her apartment."

Ron shot Susan a look of "no kidding" but chose to point out that Miss Tulley was found bound in a closet and therefore whoever did that could have been in a disguise to lure the Professor to that apartment in order to get something from him.

"Sure, she wanted sex," Jan blushed as the word left her lips. "I mean, he said he was naked in her bed and everything…"

"Really Jan, Professor Pettigrew? If you saw him and heard Miss Tulley as Dominic and I did, I think that wasn't the lure at all. It had to be something else."

"I agree," chimed in Dominic. "You should have seen Pettigrew's face, all red… so how do you put it…ah cute like a boy on his first date."

Bob who had remained in the background rather silent as he was still upset that Ron took Dominic and not him finally spoke. "That's it Dominic, just like Ron when he first met Susan…"

Suddenly the alcove was filled with silence. Could it be that Ron's Tonto, his Watson actually said what he said and so casually? No one dared to speak or giggle or anything but gasp and that was stifled. Ron literally jumped onto the table and flung himself onto Bob on the other side. They tumbled to the wooden floor with a bang. Bob in horror as to what he had said offered no resistance. Ron straddled him pinning him down. His large cocoa brown eyes were aflame with hurt and embarrassment.

"It's okay, take a swing at me, I deserve it Ron."

His best buddy trembled with what he had done just by jumping off the table onto him let alone the thought of striking his best pal in the world. Ron bent over so as to be close to Bob's ear. "Why did you have to say that of all things?"

He pushed himself away from Bob and jumped to his feet. Andreas ran to him and not knowing the meaning of the remark took hold of Ron and pulled him toward another table. Bob lay on the floor, a glistening tear drop perched itself on the corner of his azure blue eyes. He did not move except to use the sleeve of his shirt to wipe that drop away. Jan held onto Susan in shock that her brother would do such a thing to Bob of all people. Sure they would argue and pound on each other but it was more in jest not this…this attack. Dominic and Alessandro were lifting Bob up to his feet but not with his cooperation. He just wanted to sulk in his self-pity.

Across from the table with almost empty trays which contained remains of Shepherd Pie, Andreas was trying to understand this explosion within Ron which brought on such a response. "Amico, this is not like you. Bob is like what Dominic is to me, how could you do such a thing to him over a red face comment?"

Ron looked into those eyes filled with confusion wanting to say that he and Bob were not like he and Dominic in that way but thought better of it. He understood the meaning which he tried to convey, one of brotherhood and friendship, one of brothers from different mothers. Once he began to think in that manner and not of the sexual innuendo, he slumped into Andreas. "Oh shit, I just attacked my best friend in the world over something so stupid."

"Stupido, I would agree…"

Ron straightened up and turned looking out the window toward the library. "You know there's a marble bust of the Roman Orator Cicero in that Library. He attacked his best friend too and lost him forever. I can't let that happen. But you need to understand something Andreas. Would you mind if I shared that something with you?"

"Of course Ron, I am here for you." Andreas placed his hand on the shoulder of his new friend and guided him closer to the windows of the cafeteria now almost void of all people even the cooks.

As they stood gazing out the large panes of glass in the window next to each other, Ron began. "You need to know that I am not upset over a comment about blushing as on a first date. I let the actual event of what happened to me when I first met Susan consume me…you see I didn't only blush, I…" he couldn't get his words out. How would a Swiss Guard take such a story, especially one who was gay? Nevertheless he continued. "You know what sometimes happens to a guy at night when he's dreaming?"

Andreas suppressed a smile. "As a boy first coming into manhood, yes I understand."

The comment didn't make Ron feel a bit better as he was not a boy coming into manhood when what he was about to share happened to him. In fact it wasn't a dream but a real event with Susan and he was almost nineteen at the time not just entering puberty. "Well what Bob was talking about wasn't a dream, I actually…you know, ejaculated all over myself when Susan and I first met in the Abbey."

"Madonna mia Ron, you had the sex in an Abbey?" Andreas made the Sign of the Cross.

"No, no that's the whole issue here. We didn't have sex, I came and made a mess all over myself and all she did was…well it wasn't having sex, she just made eyes at me and lifted her skirt and placed herself over me but we were standing and I got all excited and aroused and then it happened and I ran away."

Andreas took hold of Ron's hands. "Ah so you love Susan so much that you wanted to be one with her. That is a beautiful story not one of shame to me."

"That's the whole point Andreas. I am studying for the priesthood and I have these feelings but that's not why I got upset it's worse than that. I just came from that Assistant Curator's apartment where the Professor reacted something like I just did, though not so aggressively, he's British after all and quite in control of himself and he's old, like thirty-eight or something. And I noticed Mr. O'Neil too. He seemed to be turning red in the face too. And I thought, good God, he's in his fifties and still hasn't known anything about love. Well when Bob said that and he's mentioned it before but this time I was thinking about how Pettigrew and O'Neil were probably feeling the same way. Here Pettigrew was seduced and obviously didn't do a thing. I don't want to not know love not just the sex part but love, do you understand?"

"I do understand Ron. It's different with me, of course, since my love is for a man but what we feel is the same and what I wanted in life is not unlike what you desire, to find love and experience all of it. That's what happened when I first met him during his excavation work in the Vatican. There was that something which caused the attraction, the desire the pull to be together. I think I'm embarrassing you, no?"

He was but Ron lied. "No not at all, go on. I think I am beginning to get the message." That latter part was not a lie.

"Here's what I see. Almost every day I must work amongst the priests and those who seek to become one. I see the struggle some of them have with the sex and the love being absent from their lives. Some of them handle it with prayer and commitment, others not so much. I see how Susan looks at you and how that makes you nervous, uneasy. I think that you are having a struggle amico, a struggle to do what is expected of you and a desire to fulfill a calling. At the same time, I see that spark that attraction which pulls you away from that calling to another way of life. Do I make sense to you?"

"Well that's the whole point Andreas and Bob knows that to be true. He also knows that I am testing myself so when he said that it all came crashing down on me and I couldn't handle it. I lashed out to my, as you say amico, friend. I need to go to him pronto." Ron jumped to his feet and embraced the Swiss Guard. "You're one hell of a guy, Dominic is lucky to have you."

"And now you make me to do the bushing."

Together they returned to the center of the cafeteria. Bob was surrounded by the others but no one was talking. Tonto was just sitting on a chair with his head in his hands. As soon as they saw Ron and Andreas they slipped away to leave Bob alone which allowed Ron a clear path to walk up to Bob. He knelt in front of him and took hold of his arms, lowering them and looking into his reddened eyes. "Did I hurt you?"

Bob looked into those cow-like eyes also reddened but for him with regret and sorrow. "Really, of course you hurt me but not in the way you think. Do you think that skinny body of yours could do anything but bounce off this," he puffed out his chest to make himself appear even larger than he was. He tried to crack a smile.

Ron returned that same effort. "Well, I acted like an asshole and I'm sorry. Can you forgive me?"

"Of course, I forgave you already from the time you landed on top of me. I knew that I had touched a sore spot but it was too late to do anything about it. Tonto betrayed the Lone Ranger pal and that's a fact."

"No way pal; the Lone Ranger is the guilty one because he knew the truth of why he was disguising himself with the mask of religion and the call to a vocation. I need to remove that mask right now and be who I am, a confused guy searching for meaning in my life."

"But you knew that already Ron didn't you?"

"Kind of, but it was all about the sexual attraction stuff which is still there but now thanks to Andreas I have a better understanding that what I seek is the meaning of love. Whether that means with a woman or the Church is what I must discover."

"Holy cow that must have been one hell of a talk; we tried to listen but couldn't hear a thing. But for now on your sidekick will be there for you and you had best choose me next time."

"Holy shit man you mean this is all about being jealous of Dominic coming with me and the Chief Inspector?"

Bob lowered his head and admitted that it was. Ron grabbed hold of him. "You're such an asshole. I had to do that for the Professor's sake not because I prefer him over you. Are we good here?" He tightened his embrace.

"Always pal..."

"Oh Jan look at them, isn't that just so cute. It makes you want to cry." Tears were streaking down Susan's cheeks as she spoke for she too was beginning to understand the struggle Ron was dealing with and that wasn't far different than hers and that promise to his sister not to tempt him away from his calling.

The touching moment when friendships were solidified and emotions were fraught with that tinge of joy mixed with sorrow which comes from understanding one's struggle came to an abrupt end. The Chief Inspector and his Sargent came clumping across the stone floor of the cafeteria with the Professor, Dean Drumond Shannon and the Curator Hugh O'Neil.

Ron and Bob split into soldier like stances side by side as their voices were recognized. As they were standing at the center of the cavernous eating area they awaited O'Connor's arrival. And arrive he did with his entourage which Ron immediately noticed was absent of one important person and so he posed a question.

"Sir, glad to see all of you but where is Miss Tulley?"

O'Connor was not too pleased that the first statement out of his group of material witnesses would be about Bridget Tulley. He pulled on his beard, more like rubbing it as if thinking about the words; no more than words rather how much information should he share. He decided to actually present his thoughts on what happened on Dawson St, at Trinity

College and Mellifont Abbey. Inviting everyone to have a seat he placed on the end of the table a plastic bag. In that bag were the strands of hair taken from the iron poker which Ron had pointed out in Miss Tulley's apartment.

"It appears that the young man from the States has asked a question which implies something else. May I just point out that at this time all we have is hair strands as you see in this bag. There doesn't seem to be a connection between what happened to Miss Tulley and what happened to the Woman in Mellifont Abbey ruins. The Curator has every confidence in his assistant who I might point out was found gagged and bound in a closet. Thus she has been given time to compose herself and rest after her traumatic encounter with whoever these hairs match, if indeed it was even the person who tied her up. Now let us talk about Professor Pettigrew's brief case taken in the apparent robbery."

As the Chief Inspector eyed each of those whom he first met just a day ago over the murder scene, Ron noticed the blood stained note still lying on the table slightly stuck under one of the ancient books. He glanced at Susan who was standing nearest to where that book lay. She placed her purse on top of the book and managed to pull that book toward her and in doing so the note as well. He nodded she nodded back as the Chief Inspector was going on about the timetable for departure back to the murder scene at Mellifont. The note was unobtrusively inserted into Susan's purse as she placed the long strap holding the Italian leather bag over her shoulder. With a pat on the bag she shot a smile of accomplishment to Ron.

Miss Tulley in the meantime was indeed composing herself but not in her apartment. She left shortly after the last of the police presence departed and was riding with the man she called Fitz who bungled the capture of the Professor. While she gave him a tongue lashing for his incompetence, he just smiled. He knew who had stolen the Professor's brief case and wasn't about to share that information until the price was right. True he had bungled the capture but also the theft of the Professor's brief case from the Trinity College Security office in the wee hours of the morning, or so Bridget Tulley thought. In point of fact, he simply arrived at the security office after the theft had occurred.

"Are you quite through with the drama Miss Tulley?" Fitz asked with his voice losing patience.

"How dare you speak to me that way; you're nothing but a thug hired to do a simple task and failed miserably. Just get us to Drogheda hospital morgue before that Chief Inspector or that kid finds out anything. I need to confirm that the woman killed at Mellifont was the one who spoke with O'Neil."

"And then what? Who cares if she spoke with him?"

"You are quite dull aren't you? Well my bumbling man who should have been able to overpower that wimp of a Professor, if she is the one then our cause may not be totally lost. It would mean that O'Neil knows something that we need to know if we are to find it."

"He's your boss, just ask him or maybe let me get to him. I won't fail if you send me after him."

"All in good time my man. Why threaten or place ourselves in jeopardy when he or perhaps those research assistants of the Professor can lead us to what we seek?"

"And exactly what is that thing we seek which would make you create this whole scene of high drama?"

"Let me just say that it will make us rich."

"Christ almighty, don't tell me this is all about some old piece of shit?"

"Piece of shit you say; how ignorant you are. This is about history, civilization…"

"And money, let's not forget that missy…it's all about the money."

Bridget Tulley folded her arms across her chest and mumbled something about ignorance but said nothing more lest she lose the muscle she needed to gain the prize. Fitz continued driving along the N2 which would take them to Slane where he would turn to head to Drogheda. Dancing in his brain, the one Tulley thought he didn't have, he was already spending his cut and also thinking of a way to get even for being called a failure.

Also on the N2 heading toward Slane was the Chief Inspector in the lead car with Sargent Carrick, the Curator O'Neil and the Dean Drumond Shannon. Following them was the Trinity College van filled with the Professor, Ron and company which was followed by a black Fiat containing a couple of uniform officers of the Garda.

In the back seat of that van Ron, Bob and Susan were once again reading the note handed to Ron by the dying woman in black. Only this time they were not concentrating on the poem but a list of words hastily written as if someone, perhaps the woman called Devorgilla herself, wanted to create a check list of some kind.

CHAPTER NINE

THE LIST

The Trinity College van made its way along the N2 highway from Dublin towards Slane. It was sandwiched in by the Chief Inspector's car and another Garda squad car behind it. Though disconcerting to be as it were in custody by the police, it was affording Ron and his cohorts the opportunity to finally study that bloody note squeezed into his hands in the ruins of Mellifont Abbey. The material witnesses as Rory O'Connor, the Chief Inspector called them were bouncing off the terms on each other as Ron read each one with a pause after each was announced.

"The Malachy Chalice," Ron paused. "What do we know about this?"

"Obviously it's a holy vessel for mass," noted Bob who was tucked in between his pal and Susan so as not to have those two next to each other.

"That's true," observed Dominic, "however it's the name Malachy which is important because that relates to the work of Professor Pettigrew which is in that brief case stolen from the Trinity College Security room."

Dominic, of course, would be the most familiar with the contents of the professor's brief case as he was his assistant on the research surrounding the find in the Vatican archives.

Susan perked up realizing that very fact about Dominic's familiarity with the Professor's work. "Listen Dominic, you need to remember more than that. The Professor was about to share what he discovered with that Dean at Trinity who never showed up for their meeting. All of us had some type of understanding that his work with you found some documents.

Only you and Ron however really had that information shared with you; and only you actually helped to put it all together. So honey child it's time to search inside that pretty head of yours and think."

Andreas smiled leaned over toward Dominic and whispered. "Well she's sure right about the good looking part."

"Stop it, not here…with all these people."

"Who are you calling people Mr. Fontana? If we're not your friends what are we after all we've been through?" Susan was giving more of a show for dramatic effect than actually being hurt by the statement.

"Madonna mia Susan, if you please…I did not mean it that way. I only meant that you know like when you and Ron are near each other and sparks fly. It's embarrassing, no?"

She had been put in her place and didn't like it; especially the reference to the sparks between she and Ron. But she decided to handle it southern style to conceal her true feelings. "Well bless your little ole heart but there are no sparks dear boy, only respect for his calling from above," dripping the southern accent she firmly added. "And don't you forget that in the future. There is nothing going on here between me and that holy Joe who is conveniently ignoring everything we are saying."

Jan climbed up on her knees in the front seat and watched her brother's face. He was studying the note and writing on a small pad of paper with head bowed and total separation from the banter in the van. At least that is what he wanted everyone to think and she knew it. Sure he wanted to start to put the pieces to what the connections were between the theft of the Professor's brief case, the murder in Mellifont ruins and what happened in Miss Tulley's apartment. Still understanding that she could tell when he was truly zoned out. She was thinking of being back home in Oak Park Illinois when he would use that to separate himself from what was going on about him when she would watch the late night show and he hating it would put himself in another world. And then she thought of his fake disengagement as when the entire De Cenza family showed up to his going away to the seminary party and making a fuss over him which he ignored by feigning to be working on packing. Since his bedroom was right off the living room with a glass door as once it had been used as a sun room, everyone could still see him and she saw that he was packing and repacking the same things.

She called out, "Ronnie, pay attention. This is important."

"Huh, what the hell…Jan what's so important is this note. The Chief Inspector doesn't see a connection between the brief case theft and the murder let alone what happened to the Professor in Miss Tulley's apartment. We have to help him out."

"Oh Ronnie, you are so frustrating," she pounded the back of the seat. "The sparks are also important and you know it."

Utter silence followed her statement. Ron was furious and Bob could feel the tension building up in his pal's demeanor. Susan was so tightly squeezed in that she couldn't even slide down and try to be unobtrusive. Her baby blue Capri pants so tightly fitted and revealing just the top of her ankle where the white socks ended and before the hem of the pants began did not go unnoticed by Ron, no matter how hard he tried to focus on the note. She pulled as best she could on her white rain jacket to cover the matching blue cotton blouse which had a bit of a plunging neckline as the buttons were not all being used. All that Ron noticed was the tiny gold cross daintily hanging just above that last unused button. All eyes were on Ron except for those of Alessandro, who was driving but he could clearly see his American friend's reaction in the rear view mirror.

The ball point pen was lowered and then attached to the page he was writing on with the clip. Ron shoved very gently the note under the pen to keep it in place. He looked up and scanned all those eyes including the dark ones like his own in that mirror. Then he looked right into those of his sister. "Jan De Cenza, the only sparks flying around here is what I just figured out on this note while trying to remember the Professor's research."

It worked. Everyone began to speak at once and rattle off questions as to what Ron had figured out. Even Susan was relieved that the focus was off she and Ron and back onto the mystery. She pushed on Bob who crushed into Ron and forced herself to sit up straight, her long crimson hair falling about her shoulders like a waterfall. Her pale face with those ruby red lips and sparkling green eyes catching the sunshine filtering through the windows did not go unnoticed by the sleuth taking control of what had been an awkward situation. Even his sister couldn't figure out if what was going on was a ploy to divert attention from the sparks comment and the truth of a discovery he had figured out.

"Hold your horses will you guys. I can't say that I've come up with the murderer but here's what I believe is the connection. Dominic you get ready to back me up on the historical parts and artistic worth of this Malachy Chalice." His big cocoa brown eyes leapt from one set of eyes to another as his focus bore into them to build up wonder and excitement. "Now here's what we know. This note was given to me with the last breath of the lady in Mellifont. It's safe to conclude that she used the poem for some reason perhaps to place herself into some type of spiritual state. It's also reasonable to think that this list on the back was made by her for some reason and that wasn't to stimulate her memory but to leave clues in the event something happened to her. I believe that the Lady Devorgilla knew that her search would bring danger and yet she kept her search a secret even to the Earl of Slane Castle. She wanted to confer or share her thoughts with an expert and that brings in the Curator of Dublin Museum, Hugh O'Neil. He went to Slane Castle as well and was lost, so he says, when the murder took place."

"Oh my God, Sherlock…are you saying that the Curator killed that woman over some research?" Bob's amply proportioned body shook.

"Easy does it pal," Ron patted the shoulder of his buddy. "Maybe, we cannot discount it at this time, so we must all be careful of what we say around him even if the Professor trusts him. I mean look at what happened to him because he trusted some girl he didn't even know who lured him into shall I say a rather scandalous situation."

"Oh my Lord in heaven, Ronnie; he was thrilled that some cutie wanted to have sex with him who never had a relationship with anyone who wasn't dead over a couple of centuries let alone one who expressed interest in his trinket hunting"

"And you my dear sister should get your head out of the gutter. We are talking about the Professor who almost got killed over ancient trinkets if you remember what happened last fall in Rome. So let me get back to my thoughts."

"Well I was just saying…"

"Jan, maybe you should let your brother get on with it. We are only about ten minutes from Slane," Alessandro suggested as he pointed to a sign alongside the road listing the town and Mellifont and the exit for Drogehda if one was to take that route east to it.

She smiled back at him, leaned over and kissed his cheek. "You are so cute when you think you're protecting me even if it's from my own brother's wrath."

The tender moment ending, Ron continued noting the time frame announced by Alessandro. "Are we done here? Okay, now the Malachy Chalice is something mentioned in the research in the Professor's brief case, is that not so Dominic?"

"Si…I mean yes it was a major find for it was created by Saint Malachy for the Abbey called Mellifont which he was instrumental in having built in the year of our Lord 1142. He brought Monks trained by Saint Bernard some of whom were Irish but some were French from Saint Bernard's Abbey. By 1157 the Abbey was completed. Is that what you meant Ron?"

"Exactly, good job on the history lesson. Well like any building project then and now people need money to pay for its construction. Saint Malachy got his from the King of Ulster one called Muirchertach Ua Lochlainn. He gave gold and cattle to help finance the project. The land itself however came from the Donnachadh Ua Cearbhaill who was King of Airghala. You see back then Ireland was a series of little Kingdoms each with its own King and the High King having some authority over them in a loose confederation. Anyway, now the Saint had the land, stone and the money. As for the livestock, it was used to continue to fund the project and support the Abbey once it was operating."

"So what's all of this have to do with the murder, the Professor being assaulted and his brief case being stolen?" asked Bob.

Ron went on to explain that the connection was between the original Lady Devorgilla who donated a golden chalice and altar cloths for the Abbey chapel. That chalice became known as the Malachy Chalice and became the Holy Grail of Ireland as it was revered for centuries as coming from the Saint himself. When the Abbey was first dissolved by King Henry VIII in 1539; that Chalice was never found. So it never got placed in the treasury of the king."

"So what happened to the Malachy Chalice?"

"Good question Andreas, that's where we come in and I believe what the Lady in Black also known as Lady Devorgilla comes in. I think she was following information which if confirmed by the Curator O'Neil would lead her to finding the chalice. The question is would O'Neil really be able to confirm anything other than it had once existed and secondly who would want to kill her over something lost for centuries. While the Chief Inspector seeks to find the murderer, we need to find the chalice and who's after it and when that is done we shall know who the murderer is."

"I don't know Ronnie; this sounds like an impossible task not to mention that it's dangerous."

Ron became very quiet as he saw in his sister's eyes worry but then a slight grin crossed his lips and a twinkle shined in those big eyes. "Really sis' as in capturing a guy who tried to steal works of art from the Vatican or how about the attempted heist of the Pieta in New York at the World's Fair and…"

"I get it Ronnie, but let me be clear about two things. First, I wasn't involved in the World's Fair plot or the murder at the Wisconsin Abbey so I was in blissful ignorance. Secondly, I was a firsthand witness to you almost getting killed last fall in Italy so I know what this investigation around the Chief Inspector may actually cause. I don't think I like it very much."

A sudden jerk of the van tumbled Jan into Alessandro as he turned onto the ramp leading off the highway toward Slane Castle. He came to an abrupt stop on the side of the road. Planting a kiss gently on her lips he promised to keep her and her brother safe.

"Now you just listen to me you Count of Pianore, just who the heck do you think you are kissing me in front of all these people? I'll let you know when it's okay to…well I will let you know and that's that." Jan tried to be irritated but as she said these things she snuggled up to him and then she pulled him to herself. "And I say let's try that again."

The hoots and hollers resounding in the van came to an abrupt halt when Sargent Carrick knocked on the window of the driver's side of the van. "Young man, roll down that window."

Alessandro dutifully did so.

"And what do you think you're doing pulling off the roadway? Get this van back on the road and follow us."

"Yes sir, but as you saw, we were having a moment and…"

"The Chief Inspector doesn't like moments like this so get your ass back on the road or one of the officers will take over if you're too distracted."

Through this exchange Ron just smiled and leaned back into the seat while concealing the notepad. He was delighted that the focus was off him and Susan for a change. Once they were following the Garda, he resumed his thoughts on the Chalice while giving no recognition as to what just happened.

"Listen up; we don't have much time to execute a plan. Once we're at the castle we have to find a way to get into the Earl's library and look at those maps. The photos I took aren't very good. We need to find out if they show this place listed here on her note. Where and what is St. Erc's Hermitage? That is the question we need an answer to. We already know of Mellifont Abbey ruins, and that's a crime scene. Next on the list is the word 'Library' but which library because next to the word she wrote Erc, Slane and Beaulieu House which so far no one has mentioned."

While all of this was being discussed in the Trinity College van along that very same side road simply labeled as N51 a black Fiat containing Fitz and Bridget Tulley made its way through the town of Slane and onward toward Drogheda on the eastern shore of Ireland on the Irish Sea. Fitz as she called him was white knuckled on the steering wheel trying to control his excitement over the deception they had pulled off on the Chief Inspector. She was pleased with herself as she patted the Professor's brief case lying across her lap. By the time anyone realized that she was not recouping after the trauma of an assault, she would be connecting the dots which would lead her to a discovery bringing her wealth beyond her imagination. Once she verified that the dead woman in Drogheda was the same one she saw in Dublin when she first attempted to see the Curator O'Neil, she would then use the information in the brief case to lead her to the lost Malachy Chalice or so she thought. Only she had seen the Lady in Black as O'Neil was in Connaught studying of all things a small stone bridge which had been used in an American movie starring John Wayne and Maureen O'Hara titled, "The Quiet Man." O'Neil loved that film.

For him it was a holiday adventure requiring little thought and certainly at the time no idea that still within Ireland a treasure such as the Malachy Chalice could still be in existence.

She flipped up the flap of the brief case and peered into it. Then pulling out a couple of pages she suddenly gasped and then screamed a bloody curse on the Professor and whoever wrote what was on those pages. "Oh *feck*; this can't be happening not now."

"Christ Miss Tulley what's wrong now?"

"Oh nothing at all; just that these are written in Latin and I don't speak or read Latin."

"Ah feck that screws us royally," he laughed thinking he had made a humorous analogy.

She wasn't having it. "Shut your fowl mouth; this will hold us up for God only knows how long. We will need to improvise." She rifled through the pages still in the brief case. "Oh wait a second, this one is written in long hand in English. We're not at a total loss Fitz. Obviously it's not an ancient text with the details we need if we are to find that chalice before that Chief Inspector adds two and two together or those so called assistants to that Professor figure out what we've got."

"So does that mean we don't have to go look at a dead body?"

"You're such a child Fitz. Of course we must go; if for no other reason than to lure the Chief Inspector to Drogheda hospital when they report someone came to identify the body."

Bridget Tulley had her plan working already. She would present herself as the niece of the murdered woman. Once again she would disguise herself, this time with a chestnut brown wig and a very sophisticated tweed suit with a white silk blouse. The frumpy suit would hide most of her curves and such. Whoever reported to the Chief Inspector would be doing so mainly about facial features which she was already altering by removing all signs of make-up. She then placed a set of sunglasses on which she would say were needed to rest her strained eyes from the flowing tears since the learning of her Aunt's death.

It was late morning as the Trinity van with its police escort slowly rolled along the gravel driveway circling around the expansive lush green lawn now almost dry of its dewdrops given that the sun had come out and promised a fair day. Suddenly between the lead Garda car and the van a sheep scampered across the driveway followed by a distraught young man who was none other than the Earl of Mount Charles' son whom they had met on the night of the murder. Alessandro screeched to a halt. The black Fiat behind them with the Professor, Dean and Curator had no choice but to stop as well. Sargent Carrick looking in his rear view mirror once again began to curse.

"Son of a Bitch but those kids have stopped again, Chief Inspector."

O'Connor was not too pleased as he checked his watch knowing that much ground had to be covered in the daylight hours. "Just stop the car." He stuck out his head from the back seat of the car. "Good Christ, there's some kid chasing a sheep around the driveway, no wonder they had to stop. Sargent call the officers out of the cars and get that sheep so that we may proceed."

Sargent Carrick jumped out of the car along with a uniform officer as the Chief Inspector stepped out and began to wave to Alessandro in the driver's seat of the van. He received no response, so he ran toward the van while the other officers ran after the sheep thinking where there is one more are soon to follow.

"Oh Dio Mio, the Chief Inspector; he is coming towards us. Ron what do we do now?"

"Calm down everyone, it's just Henry the Earl's son chasing that sheep for God only knows why. Let's get out and meet the Chief Inspector."

Jan quickly folded the map they were using for navigation and exited then opened the side door of the van to let the others out. Alessandro jumped down from his seat just as the Chief Inspector arrived.

"Listen here young man I have had about enough of these shenanigans from you and your friends." As he spoke the others gathered around the young Count of Pianore, Ron being grateful that for a change it was not him being called out.

"Mi dispiacere Chief Inspector but the boy and that sheep they came right in front of us and I had to stop."

"Yes, yes, but as you can see they are off onto the lawn area if you drove slowly you would not have harmed them. Now we shall all walk to the Castle and leave our vehicles where they are; am I clear about this…" he paused. "Where is your leader? Ron De Cenza you shall walk with me."

Whispering to his pal, Bob, he placed the note from the Lady in Black back into his satchel, he then peeked out from behind the others who had formed a human wall just so that he could hide the note. "Here I am Chief Inspector." He just about skipped around the group to meet O'Connor. "Now then, what's happening sir?"

"You tell me young man. That boy and that sheep seem to have halted our progress."

"Well sir, isn't that Henry, the Earl's son? I don't think Alessandro would have been received with any courtesy if he had hit him."

"Don't be sassy with me Mr. De Cenza. I can see the problem just not why you felt compelled to stop. In any case we shall walk the remainder of the way. You shall walk with me and the others may follow." He had said that loudly enough for all to hear. "And you Mr. Wentz may inform the Professor, Dean and Curator that we shall be walking and that they should follow along."

Bob turned to leave, throwing his satchel strap around his neck and patting the leather bag. As he did so out from behind the rear of the van stepped Professor Pettigrew and company.

"Ah good, Gentlemen, we shall walk the rest of the way; God forbid that we should run over that sheep…"

"Or the Earl's son, sir; that would also be a problem, wouldn't you agree?" added the Professor with the slightest grin.

O'Connor's face was turning a lovely shade of red as he wanted to shake Ron so badly so as to force him to reveal the actual reason they pulled off to the side of the road earlier and now using a sheep and a boy to stop once again when they clearly didn't present a threat. He did not give in to his baser instincts and simply ordered everyone, which was now a small platoon of people to follow him to the castle.

As O'Connor led his material witnesses and assorted people of culture to the castle entrance not more than six miles away two figures made their way down the stark corridor leading them to the morgue of Drogheda Hospital. Bridget Tulley was now dressed in a black tweed suit consisting of a tightly fitted skirt, white blouse and wool jacket. Covering her now brown hair was a small pill box hat with a fine netting which created a veil covering her face. The veil was constantly becoming stuck on the sunglasses that she wore for good measure.

Accompanying her was her thug, Fitz who being a rather large burley man who was more comfortable pounding on another human being rather than playing at being a mourner for the loss of a loved one, was noticeably uncomfortable. He kept pulling at his black tie saying that it was strangling him. Tulley had given in and allowed him to simply wear a white shirt with the tie and no suit coat.

"There's the Coroner's office now stop your fidgeting and just follow my lead." She knocked on the glass window on the upper half of the door and entered.

Behind a typical unadorned wooden desk of no particular interest as far as furnishings were concerned sat a woman not much older than she, that being not yet thirty. She looked up at the bereft woman behind the veil and then at the huge man next to her who was pulling down on his tie.

"Good day to you; may I be of help?"

Tulley glanced at the metal name plate on the desk. "My dear Miss Clancy, I am here to see my Aunt just brought in but a couple of days ago." She pulled out a linen handkerchief from a small purse dangling off her left arm. Dabbing under the sunglasses, she continued. "I am her only family. The poor dear was all I had as family." She leaned into Fitz, who finally took the hint and placed his arm around her after a jab with her elbow into his side.

"Oh, I am terribly sorry Madam, do have a seat. Now what did you say was the name of your aunt?"

"I didn't but you certainly would remember it as she was the last of a great line of an ancient noble family." Tulley paused as she wasn't sure as to whether or not that name connecting her to the 12th Century nobleman Dermot MacMurrough was legitimate.

"Oh my dear madam, you must be referring to the grand dame of our hospital. Never has there been such excitement as the night she was brought in. Poor thing…oh of course it was a tragedy you understand…"

"Tulley now seated lifted her head and cracked a smile. "Yes quite a blow to me and all who knew her."

"Well, still we could not be shall I say be moved by the privilege to host even in death such a noble woman who met her maker in such a ghastly manner. Imagine how we felt…" Nancy Clancy made her way around the desk to kneel beside the grieving Tulley as Fitz stepped back grateful not to be involved in the scene of drama. "And now to meet the Lady Devorgilla's niece herself why it's just such an honor…"

Tulley patted the young woman's hand. "You are too kind. But now I must identify her."

Nancy Clancy rose and tried to become professional though finding it most difficult. She first walked to a wardrobe closet and opened its doors. Hanging inside was the dress of the Lady in Black murdered in Mellifont. "I am so relieved that we might actually call our guest Lady Devorgilla. We have her dress here, certainly you will want it to transport her home and for the funeral perhaps." She pulled out the still blood stained dress and the broad rim hat with torn and blood saturated veil. Seeing the condition of the hat, she quickly placed it back on the shelf. "I am so sorry for being so careless madam."

Tulley rose quite slowly so as not to appear overly interested in seeing the dress. She moved to Clancy still holding the dress. "Oh isn't it a lovely frock. She so loved to play the role of the dowager but where is her purse? Surely the contents would have verified her name for you." She clung to the dress gripping it tightly as she felt she had jumped into asking about the accessories too quickly.

"Why there was no purse Madam….what did you say your name was?"

"I didn't. Then what are you saying that she was robbed and then…oh my killed." Tulley swooned backwards and with her free hand motioned for Fitz to come to her. He ran over and feigned to catch her.

"Oh my, let me get you some water." Clancy ran to the opposite side of the office and poured some water from a metal pitcher into a glass. "Here you go, just take a sip it will help."

"You are too kind. Now you were saying something about my Aunt's purse…"

"Yes, I was trying to explain that there wasn't one because the police kept it for evidence or some such thing I'd presume."

"Then this is all there is, her dress and hat?"

"Yes madam and one more thing which I forgot to mention." Clancy went back to the counter where she had fetched the glass of water. In a glass next to the pitcher was a red rose, slightly damaged. "The Lady Devorgilla came to us with this resting in her hands. I was told that a young man…I think his name was Ron De Cenza or some Italian sounding name but he's American so I don't exactly know, but in any case he placed this rose in her hands I am told. Perhaps you would like us to send it with her to wherever the funeral will be." She shook the drops of water off the stem and handed the rose to Tulley.

"That is so sweet…ouch," Tulley tossed the rose aside while losing her veneer of sweetness as she spoke in her true voice. "What the fu…"

Clancy stooped to retrieve it as Tulley rubbed her finger, curbed her obscenity and brought herself under control over a slight pinch to her pale smooth skin still unbroken and no blood issuing forth. "I guess there's still a thorn left on the stem." She managed to scrap off the lonely thorn and attempted to return it to Tulley.

"Well that's quite obvious… no thanks, just keep it with dear Aunty." She returned to a somber speech pattern.

"And that we shall do Miss. And now, where shall we send your Aunt? The police would need to know as her movement will not be permitted until the investigation is completed."

Bridget Tulley could not possibly answer such a question. She began to squirm trying to hide her discomfort by returning to the wardrobe closet and once again holding the black dress as she thought of a reply. It shook in her hands but Clancy saw this as grief and emotion. Fitz seeing her meltdown grabbed hold of the dress and tried to save the day.

"Just put her back in this dress, our mortuary people will be contacting you once the police have done their work which we hope will be soon for that murderer should pay for what was done to poor Miss Tulley's beloved Aunty." Fitz handed the dress to Miss Clancy. "And now if you would be so kind as to have us view…" he didn't quite know how to say what had to be said without seeming callous. Luckily he didn't have to finish his request.

"Oh, you wish to see our Lady Devorgilla."

As soon as Clancy had used the lady's name as she did an illumination like the proverbial light bulb shining brightly filled Tulley's thoughts. She calmly took the dress back from Fitz and spread it out on the desk. "She did so love the mystery of exploring the old ways."

"Then she was a woman of quite a reputation in the history of our people, is that it?"

Tulley never lifted her head as she answered while continuing to adjust the lace overlay of the dress just so. The lovely innocent assistant to the Medical Examiner was playing right into her hands. "Oh quite so my dear Miss Clancy; hadn't you wondered as to why she was in the ruins of Mellifont Abbey alone save for the one…" she paused to add a dramatic moment.

"Oh my dear Miss Tulley." Clancy placed her arm over the shoulders of the Assistant Curator as Fitz once again moved into the shadows of the corner of the office; he being quite proud that he had saved the day. "Now then, do have a seat. Would you like some tea?"

"You are too kind. However, we have so much to do as you may have surmised. I think it best that I say my farewell to dear Aunty."

"Of course, I understand about arrangements and so forth. Do follow me. The Medical Examiner is not here but I can show you to the viewing area. Just sign this form to verify your request." She opened a file and pulled out the paper.

Tulley had no intention of placing her actual name on anything. "Glory be, but I am feeling weak in the knee." She held onto the arm of the chair and slipped into it slowly. "I think that tea would be a good idea if you don't mind."

"Not at all not at all; I shall go fetch it." With that being said Clancy exited through the glass paneled door and was soon out of sight down the hallway.

"Now what Miss Tulley?" Fitz was bending over her and she wasn't too pleased at his close proximity.

She pushed him out of her face and jumped to her feet. "Now we get out of here before she returns. We can't sign this form with other names as you've slipped up by saying my actual name. In any case look here, Devorgilla MacMurrough. She's listed with an ancient noble name. She really did think that she was the descendant of the benefactress of Mellifont Abbey. Now keep a watch for her."

Tulley ran through a door on the opposite side of the room from which Clancy had left. Immediately she found herself in the morgue area. It was a small stark looking room with an examination table in the center and along the far wall four stainless steel doors around three feet by three feet is size. Behind each was a slide out tray on which the body of a deceased person could be placed. On the desk just next to the door through which she entered was a folder with the name of the Lady in Black printed on it. A chart hung on the white plaster wall above the desk. It listed names and the compartment number the body was in and date of arrival. There were only two names. After glancing at the file and noting date of death and condition of the body, she ran to compartment number two. Swinging open the heavy door a blast of cold air hit her in the face as she pulled out the tray. Lifting the white cotton sheet off the head of the body she easily recognized the lady as the very one who had come to the museum to seek out Curator O'Neil. She shoved the tray back in, forgetting to recover the face of the victim. Running back into the office she grabbed hold of Fitz's arm.

"Come on, let's get out of here. It's her all right no doubt about it."

Walking slowly down the corridor just as the two ran out the main doors was Miss Clancy carefully holding a tray with three cups and a pot of tea. "Oh the poor dear, just couldn't face seeing her dear Aunty I suppose." She continued her intended way and entered the office area. She would not waste the tea and have a bit for herself. When she entered however, she noticed nothing unusual save that the Morgue Door was ajar. She called out. "Doctor O'Donnell, have you come back?"

There was no answer of course so she poked her head into the morgue room. Just as she began to close the door her eye caught something amiss. Door number two on the cooling wall was not closed all the way. Mumbling about inefficiency and wondering where the attendants might have gone since they were not in the break room, she decided to save their asses and close the door without a word to O'Donnell. As she placed her hand on the handle she realized that it was the resting area for the Lady in Black. She pulled open the door to have a chat with her and inform the deceased that her niece was just too distraught to come to pay her respects. The uncovered face of the victim was immediately seen. Clancy jumped back.

"Now why would you be uncovered dear lady?" Gently placing the cloth as it should be, Clancy turned to seek out what she thought were incompetent attendants and give them a piece of her mind as to how they should show respect for the deceased, especially one who had been so brutally murdered. She stopped at her desk first with the intention of removing the dress and put it back into the wardrobe closet. The unsigned form was directly next to it. "Why I'll be, if that wasn't what just happened here. Why those two took a peak and didn't even sign the request form…such nerve."

While Nancy Clancy pondered on what to report to Doctor O'Donnell and inevitably the police Bridget Tulley and Fitz sped away on the N51 back toward Slane. At the same time up the gravel driveway another person named after a historic ancient leader led his flock of people to the door of Slane Castle.

Beaulieu House

CHAPTER TEN

BEAULIEU HOUSE

The Chief Inspector had ordered Sargent Carrick and the officers to remove the lone sheep from the driveway. Their efforts were not entirely successful but rather created a follies scene of comedic romping about the lawn and driveway as they unsuccessfully tried to do so when about two dozen of the sheep's family members appeared bleating away as they joined their wandering cousin tinted with blue coloring on his fluffy wool posterior. So now his officers were trying to round-up twenty-five sheep all of whom were scattering along the driveway which made the moving of vehicles unthinkable. O'Connor stood with folded arms and flaring eyes as he watched his team trying to catch the sheep rather than just scooting them off to the side of the driveway. For what seemed to be an interminable amount of time this scene from a bad comedy played out and as it did so Ron huddled with his compatriots.

He had pulled out of his pocket a swatch which he found on the staircase in the Dawson Street apartments when they went to question the Museum Curator's assistant Bridget Tulley. With all that happened since that time the torn cloth was long forgotten.

"Well will you look at this. I forgot all about it." Ron held up the swatch which clearly was part of an embroidered piece illustrating a coat of arms of some kind.

Bob was excited that they might have a clue which the Chief Inspector knew nothing about and then he became concerned. "Oh God almighty

Ron, you didn't give that to O'Connor. What if he arrests you or us for withholding evidence or something?"

"Get a grip Bob, it's only a piece of cloth and probably belonged to one of the tenants at the apartment…"

Professor Pettigrew interrupted Ron as he pulled him to the back of the Trinity College van and out of view from the Chief Inspector who was now barking orders to his officers to get those sheep out of the way. The others quickly followed and along with them the Dean of Antiquities, Drumond Shannon and the Dublin Museum's Curator, Hugh O'Neil.

"Okay this is better. Let me look at that cloth Ron." The Professor held out his hand to receive it. It was left empty.

"I don't think that would be wise sir," replied Ron. "If this is evidence you would then be implicated in hiding it. Here look at it as I hold it up."

Bob was agitated now and envisioning a prison cell with he and a murderer as a cell mate. "So do you think the Chief Inspector would actually arrest us over that torn cloth?"

Susan quieted him down. "Bob, stop it. You're getting everyone upset. If it is a clue Ron will let the Chief Inspector know about it." She patted him on the shoulder and then gave him a squeeze.

"Thanks Susan, I'm okay now."

Professor Pettigrew was relating the story of his escape from the burly man whom he heard being called Fitz, "and when he was shoving me down the staircase I grabbed hold of the railing and he grabbed me to pull me away. I turned to push him off and in the struggle I took hold of his jacket to use it to swing him off of me. That's when something ripped. But I didn't know what, he just ran down the stairs and shouted at the people now coming into the stairwell that I was a rapist. So now I began to chase him and several of those tenants began shouting at me and began to chase me."

Ron became sullen. He was about to place the piece of cloth back into his pocket. "So this is probably nothing more than a school emblem which anyone might have sewn on their jackets. Wait a minute, Dean Shannon is this the coat of arms for Trinity College?" Ron's face began to brighten up once again.

The Dean squeezed through the others in order to get a better look at the embroidery. "I'm afraid not Mr. De Cenza. We do not have blue in our crest."

"But Drumond, don't you know who does? Surely you've seen it on our visits to its library to study its rare editions of Irish History."

"Truly Hugh, what on earth are you talking about? There are a number of Catholic Schools in particular which have blue in their crests, as it symbolizes the Virgin Mary."

"That Drumond is no crest of a school of any kind. That's the crest of Beaulieu House."

"Good heavens man, are you going daft? Why on earth would someone from there be in the Dawson Street apartments?"

"Why indeed, my dear Dean Shannon," commented Professor Pettigrew. "Ron if that is the Coat of Arms for Beaulieu House then you may be holding a clue of sorts."

"Well it's at least a connection to something. But what is Beaulieu House?"

A voice cracking as one who is changing from a boy into a man could be heard coming from behind Dominic and Andreas at the back of the group surrounding the rear of the van. "Oh that's the home of a famous lady race car driver. Her name is Gabriel de Frietas."

All heads turned to see who spoke this bit of news for them. There stood with a sheep in his arms, Henry son of the Marquess. It was the sheep with the blue tint on his rump but not just any sprayed painted blotch. The blue paint was placed in the shape of the letter "H." "I think the Chief Inspector wants you to join him. There's a lot of shouting going on now that the other sheep are gone. This is my special one. I rescued him from being shunned by the herd as he was the runt. So I paint this "H" on his rear end as he grew into the fine specimen he is. Everyone knows that he is my special pet."

The girls quickly made their way to the lad with the sheep in his arms and began to pet it much to its complaining at being touched by someone other than Henry. The lad had to put it down, such a fuss he made. As he scampered off Henry told them about Beaulieu House. "It's a 17th Century Manor House not as old as Slane Castle but it's surrounded by antiquity of the ancient days. Their gardens are famous and are open like ours to visitors on certain days."

"And would today be such a day?" asked Ron.

"Sure it would as all the gardens along the trail of the gardens open on the same day so tourists may go from one to the other. And I know we are opening our gardens today so Beaulieu House should be open as well."

The Earl's son was interrupted when the Chief Inspector tapped the shoulder of Alessandro and told him to step aside as he was blocking his view of the crowd now formed behind the van. "The sheep are away, we may continue," he announced.

Ron shoved the cloth into his pocket. "Chief Inspector we were just getting a lesson of how Henry here saved that sheep and made it his pet."

"Indeed, and of course that story was so interesting that none of you heard my call to join me up front at my car?" O'Connor turned to Henry who stood unflustered and smiled while nodding agreement with Ron's statement. He didn't know why Ron left out a mention of the cloth with the crest but let it go. "Young man, perhaps you may be kind enough to announce us to your father so that we may continue with our investigation of a murder, if that's all right with all of you who are so interested in the history of that sheep."

Dean Shannon chose to speak for all present. "But of course Chief Inspector, do lead on. We will follow like sheep."

There followed stifled laughter but everyone fell in line and followed more like rows of ducklings than a herd of sheep however.

"My dear Drumond, I had no idea that you could be so sarcastic," the amused Hugh O'Neil told the Dean.

"Oh my good man, there is much to learn about me," Drumond Shannon smiled as he adjusted the cap on his head.

Shamus, the Butler of the Castle was standing at the door when the entourage arrived. The commotion was heard inside and the Marquess thought it best to be ready to receive the guests. "His Lordship is waiting in the Library Chief Inspector."

"Thank you and do join our little group there as I have a few questions for you as well."

"I sir, well now how could I be of help?" Shamus stepped aside to let the herd-like group inside.

The Chief Inspector entered the library first and found the Marquess Frederick, Earl of Mount Charles standing next to the trolley table set for tea. "Good morning Chief Inspector, I took the liberty to having tea made for you and your guests. The ride from Dublin so early and all considered..."

"You are most kind Your Lordship," O'Connor turned to his officers first. "Sargent Carrick, arrange the officers at the doors of the castle please and you place yourself at the Library door."

"Yes, sir," and off the Sargent went to assign stations to his officers just as Shamus entered the Library.

"Ah good you are here Shamus," began the Marquess. "Do invite our guests to be seated around the table and serve the tea." He motioned with his arm for the entourage to take a seat at the long reading table in the center of the Library. Those that didn't fit around it sat just behind those that did. Ron made sure he got a seat behind and took Bob with him to do the same so that they sat next to the new display case with the medieval maps.

As Shamus served tea and the Marquess pulled up a chair to be next to the Chief Inspector, O'Connor began his explanation of what was to take place and what was known thus far about the murder of the Lady in Black known now to be a person named Devorgilla MacMurrough. Hugh O'Neil was seated next to the Marquess, then Drumond Shannon and then the Professor with his assistants on what was to have been an archeological research holiday project completing the perimeter around the table with Bob and Ron on the outer rim by the display case which would have a chair for Shamus on the other side of it. The circle was completed with Susan and Jan coming around and being next to the Chief Inspector on his left side which made for an awkward situation for the girls who felt he would be able to detect that they were concealing information about the crime.

Tea and biscuits being served the Chief Inspector, Rory O'Connor rose more for effect than necessity to present the details of the murder, theft of the Professor's brief case, assault on the Professor by the unknown woman, escape of one of the Professor's captors who was also unknown and the Lady in Black. He looked around the table and paused as he watched Shamus take his seat. Then he turned to the Marquess. "Sir, where is your son?"

"Henry? He's only fourteen hardly needed for such a discussion I would think."

"For now we shall agree. However he may have to be questioned later more about what just happened out on your driveway as we arrived."

"Sir, what has my son done?"

"Let us just say that his sheep got away from him and what followed was utter confusion and distraction."

Nervous eyes glanced at each other around that table as all knew what that distraction was all about. Most didn't want to see the young man get into trouble with the law over it, and all remained silent for the moment to see what O'Connor was about to present played out.

The Chief Inspector stroked his crimson beard and watched the growing nervousness of his suspects and material witnesses. "Now then, shall we begin with the murder itself? We all now understand that the Lady in Black is known as Lady Devorgilla MacMurrough which is an ancient Irish name of a woman who caused the Normans to invade Ireland when she went off and married MacMurrough. But that's centuries past and how would that impact on our murder in our time? That we hope to answer as we conclude our investigation, so let me continue." His gaze set upon Ron. "At Mellifont Abbey ruins these young men and women gathered but not intentionally. By their own statements they had gotten off at the wrong exit of the highway N2 and found themselves there or so they say."

Susan could not remain quiet. "Sir, that's exactly what happened."

"And so all of you have said, may I continue?" O'Connor waited for no answer. "All these so called research assistants found themselves in the ruins…"

"Excuse me Chief Inspector, but they are my assistants, every one of them. In fact Dominic Fontana there is an accomplished researcher who helped me discover Renaissance era art long thought to be lost to civilization. And as for the others…"

"Yes, Professor, I did not mean to imply otherwise. Forgive me."

"Well the others saved my life in Rome and also saved the nation of Italy and its historic art work."

"Again, I should be pleased to hear of those details when we have concluded this investigation. Now as I was saying. These assistants were in the ruins of Mellifont Abbey. One of them, Ron De Cenza saw a shadowy figure crossing the stones of the inner chancel of the abbey chapel. He pursued the figure with his friend Bob Wentz. Ron tackled the person he says but he got away. All the others chased the person but were fired upon they said…"

"That's true we had to hit the ground or get shot." Andreas stood like the soldier he was with authority and conviction.

"Yes, Mr. Berne so you have said. But the problem is that the finger prints of Ron De Cenza are the only ones found on the murder weapon which was one of the rocks of the ruins itself." He turned his gaze across the table to look for a reaction in Ron.

Bob could sense the trembling in Ron who was trying to conceal that fear once encountered before. His pal knew only too well what circumstances led to another detective arriving at the wrong conclusion. But what to do, how should he react was the issue gnawing at his inner being. "That's enough of circumstantial evidence," Bob jumped to his feet so fast that Andreas felt compelled to sit down but not the Chief Inspector. "Do you really think that this guy could harm anyone let alone a total stranger who looked like she was praying? Look around this table Chief Inspector. What do you see? Well let me tell you loud and clear. You are looking at friends who would give their lives for each other, friends who would go the extra mile to help one another, friends who love each other so much as to risk their futures. Would any of us do that if we thought one of us could murder someone?"

Ron grabbed hold of his pal's sleeve and pulled him down. He clutched Bob's shoulder and squeezed it as he slowly rose to his feet. Looking down into Bob's flushed face he softly said, "Thanks Tonto but this time the Lone Ranger has to do this on his own." Then he looked straight into those fierce eyes of the detective and into those of each person around that library table. He stopped briefly to stare down those three people who he didn't really know, who certainly were on his personal list. The one closest to him were those of the butler, Shamus. *Could the butler really have done it or was that too easy of a solution* he asked himself. Then he glanced across the table to the Curator, Hugh O'Neil. He was lost for hours not more than twenty minutes from where he lived and ten minutes from the castle he was visiting. Next to him sat the Dean of antiquities who he hadn't even met until after the murder and of whom no one at the table knew except for O'Neil. *Could that nice old guy really be a murderer,* he asked himself.

These inner reflections were disturbed by that commanding deep voice of the Chief Inspector. "Mr. De Cenza, are you rising to say something?"

"Huh, oh…" Ron blinked furiously as if to clear his thoughts. "Yes I am Chief Inspector. I am rising to thank my brother from another mother for coming to my defense, to thank my friends for their support when you first found my prints on the smooth side of that bloody rock. But it's more than that; I would like to say something about this case which needs to be said. See this display case well it contains a map which I believe is what the Lady in Black killed in Mellifont needed to see before she acted on something which we don't know about as yet. I didn't kill anyone and I think you know that. But someone did brutally end the life of the guest of the Marquess; the question is why did that person do so? And one more thing, this map is probably connected to what Professor Pettigrew found in the Vatican archives with Dominic. And now we may never see that connection because those papers have been stolen as they were inside his brief case. Find the brief case and we probably find the murderer."

The Chief Inspector stroked that flaming beard once again and cracked a benevolent smile; then he walked over to Ron and held him by his shoulders looking into those piercing cocoa brown eyes with his emerald green ones. "Good lad, it just so happens that I believe you but needed to hear you say so." He slapped Ron on his back and pulled him to the front of the display case as those around the table melted into puddles of tears and laughs and relief save for those Ron stopped to stare at before he spoke. "Now tell me what do you see on this map which would lead us to the murderer?"

"It's not so much to lead us to a person but to a thing which is the reason the Lady Devorgilla was murdered."

Hugh O'Neil jumped to his feet and ran to the display case. "It can't be; it's only a legend like those in the *Lebor Gabala Erenn*. Tell them Drumond of our talk about St. Malachy and his abbey at Mellifont just last night and our conclusion that there was no evidence of its actual existence."

Drumond Shannon stood but didn't make a move. "Of course you are quite right Hugh, there is no such thing in existence."

"On the contrary gentlemen," Professor Pettigrew rose and walked over to Ron and the Chief Inspector. "Documents which were in my brief case verified the existence of what has come to be called the Malachy Chalice."

O'Neil turned to the Professor at his side. "Yes of course it once existed in some fashion and then it became part of Irish Legend that's what I meant."

"And what I am saying is that there is evidence that the legend is true. The chalice not only existed when the abbey was first built but it survived the dissolution of the abbey by Henry VIII and later its destruction by Oliver Cromwell as he ravaged Ireland," the Professor concluded as he placed his arm over Ron's shoulder. "Now tell us; what does this map tell you."

"I'm afraid I don't quite know as yet…it's just a guess right now." Ron's answer was interrupted by Henry, the son the Marquess running into the Library.

"Father, there is an urgent call for the Chief Inspector from the Hospital Morgue in Drogheda. She sounds quite upset over the body of the Lady Devorgilla."

The Earl excused himself saying that he had been waiting to hear about the family of the Lady Devorgilla so that funeral arrangements could be made. "As she was a guest in my house I felt obligated to help find her some peace and a final resting place."

"Of course your Lordship." O'Connor leaned over to study the ancient map once again. "What are you telling us?"

That question was not to be answered by Ron or anyone else as the Marquess reentered after a brief time and summoned O'Connnor. They stood just outside of the library doorway. "Chief Inspector I think you should speak with this Nancy Clancy. She believes that someone presenting herself as the niece of the dead woman managed to distract her and entered the morgue to view the body. She did so without signing the proper forms or in the presence of the Medical Examiner or staff people."

The room exploded with conversation. Everyone overheard what the Marquess was saying and began to express a theory but Ron stayed at the map and looked into the display case. "Bob, say nothing just listen to me. Remember these three things, one the call refers to a woman. Two, Beaulieu House Library and Three, St. Erc's Hermitage right there on this map." He pointed to the drawing beneath the glass. It's right on the grounds of this castle."

The Professor standing on the other side of Ron hearing this took hold of Ron. He twisted him around to face him. "This is Rome all over again. You cannot place yourself in danger."

"Thank you for your concern Professor but this time is quite different. All we need to do is find evidence in the Beaulieu House Library which supports the theory that the Malachy Chalice still exists. Then we come get this map and look for it. The murderer also wants it and will make himself or herself known and none of us will be in danger because by then the Chief Inspector will be involved."

Silence followed the chattering as now the Chief Inspector had not returned but went to take the call. The girls decided that action was needed. Asking the lad Henry for directions to the bathroom, they left the library and entered the reception hall. In the sitting room opposite the hall they could see O'Connor on the phone with the Marquess standing next to him as well as Sargent Carrick. The officers in uniform being scattered at various entry areas to the castle were not to be seen. Jan and Susan scurried to the staircase which began just past the doorway to where the Chief Inspector was listening and at the same time dictating what the Sargent should be writing down.

"Thank you Miss Clancy. Your diligence to help preserve the integrity of the Hospital is most appreciated. We shall come to the hospital arriving I would say around noon." As he hung up the girls ran back into the library and right up to Ron, Bob and the Professor.

"Ronnie, you need to hear this…"

"Shush Jan, hold that thought." Ron pointed to the drawing of St. Erc's Hermitage again but this time he opened the display case and soon everyone was gathered around him. "Well there it is folks, we just have to figure out how these ruins figure into the death of the Lady Devorgilla."

Standing in the doorway and listening intently was the Chief Inspector. "Is that all you have to do Mr. De Cenza?"

"Shit," Ron mumbled under his breath as he turned to see O'Connor walking up to him and waving those surrounding him to move aside. "Chief Inspector, I didn't see you come in."

"That's not important but the phone call was. Sargent Carrick and I will be leaving for Drogheda Hospital with the Marquess. It seems that someone has to identify the body and…"

"And of course the Earl has seen her alive while none of us did except…"

"Except who Mr. De Cenza?" asked O'Connor.

"Why Sir the murderer of course who else?" Ron replied innocently as he watched the faces of the three who were not with the Professor's research team.

"And me of course Chief Inspector," added Shamus the butler of the castle and one of the three singled out by Ron. "I did catch a glimpse of her while His Lordship welcomed her and I did show her to her room."

"That would be true Chief Inspector," verified the Marquess. "It wasn't until later that Shamus went out to look for Mr. O'Neil who was lost."

"And that would be the time frame in which the Lady Devorgilla was murdered isn't that so."

"Why yes, I suppose that would be the time period," replied the Marquess to O'Connor rather than responding to Ron who asked the question.

"Mr. Sweeney, I would suggest that for the time being you not leave the castle. I will need to speak with you further upon our return. Ladies and Gentlemen, please make yourselves comfortable. I ask this on behalf of the Marquess. We should be back by three this afternoon. At that time we shall continue our discussion, shall I say. Good day to you." That having been said the Chief Inspector turned and waved to Sargent Carrick to follow him.

The Marquess bade them farewell and directing Shamus Sweeney to take care of providing lunch for their guests followed the Chief Inspector across the hall toward the doors.

Shamus followed and closed the Library doors so that he could get to the entrance doors and open them for the Marquess and the Chief Inspector. Sargent Carrick had beaten him to the door and his presence was not needed. He excused himself and said that he would go to the kitchen to see to lunch preparation.

"Well now what do we do?" asked the Dean of Antiquities.

Hugh O'Neil suggested that they should walk about the grounds and think about what the Chief Inspector had presented thus far and perhaps discern what was to come next upon his return. That played right into Ron's hands.

"Great idea sir, we need to get some fresh air." Ron took Bob's arm and pulled him toward the French doors leading out onto a veranda and the gardens. "Well come on girls and guys, let's explore this place."

As the young people swarmed across the veranda, the Dean of Antiquities and Curator of the Dublin Museum were left standing quite alone for even the Professor followed Ron outside.

"Well Hugh, it would seem that we have been abandoned. I for one am exhausted by all of this. I think I shall need to rest for a bit if you don't mind."

"Not at all Drumond, why don't you go up to my room. It's the second door on the right up the stairs. Lie down for a time and I shall peruse this library for something which might distract me from what has been happening and make a few calls to locate my assistant Miss Tulley. I am quite concerned for her wellbeing."

Outside, Ron had gathered everyone around a small fountain in the center of the gardens. He sat on the ledge and was gently wiggling his hand in the basin disturbing the water so as to make small waves. They all watched him in this trance like movement almost mesmerized by it and wondering what was really going on in his head. His sister and Bob both knew that something was up when he became docile and quiet as if off in another world. They were quite correct for suddenly Ron punched the water. It splashed up into his face which didn't bother him in the least.

"Damn if I'm just going to sit here while that murderer sends the Chief Inspector on a wild goose chase to confirm something we all know to be true. Lady Devorgilla or that Lady in Black as we call her whether truly of noble ancestry or not has been murdered and it has to do with her namesake and the Mellifont Abbey's construction by St. Malachy and eventual dissolution by Henry VIII."

"That's my brother, he's on to something. Okay Ronnie what shall we do?"

Ron grabbed hold of Bob and Susan who were standing on either side of him and then called everyone to squeeze in closer just in case one of those uniform officers was about the gardens. "Sis, you know me too well. Okay now here's what I've come up with. Professor let us know if it sounds feasible. Your memory of those papers in your stolen brief case is very important to the plan. Here we go, Bob what was the first thing I told you to remember?"

"Nancy Clancy of the hospital mentioned a woman…"

"Right and we overheard the Chief Inspector mention that a large man was with her at the hospital. Professor, how large was that man who tried to abduct you?"

"He was quite a burly man to be sure. Large body and strong and he carried a gun."

"And yet you managed to get away because he must also be awkward carrying about that large frame and got hold of this bit of cloth with this crest embroidery." Ron took the cloth out of his pocket. "And Mr. O'Neil identified it as that of this place called Beaulieu House. And that brings us to the second point. In that house is a library one mentioned in the Lady in Black's notes. So we must get to that library before Miss Tulley does and that thug Fitz with her."

"Ronnie are you crazy?" screamed out his sister.

"You think Mr. O'Neil's assistant is a murderer," added Susan as she broke away from Ron's hold and looked into his flashing eyes to seek his thoughts.

"Ron," began a confused Professor. "Miss Tulley? The one who lured me from the Trinity Library was not really Miss Tulley. We know that from the police finding the real one tied up in the closet."

"Exactly right Professor and she almost got away with it even with the finding of hair from a wig in the fireplace and stuck on the poker. But there's no denying the size of that guy she called Fitz being there. He's hard to disguise. And it was a woman and a large man that showed up at the hospital morgue. The Chief Inspector will surely figure this out when he gets there but may miss catching them because they are long gone and on their way to where, I wonder."

Naturally everyone had a thought about that most of which led them right back to Slane Castle. Ron however brought them back to Bob's list. The second item was the Beaulieu House Library and he figured that they would have to seek that out once they tried to read the ancient papers in the Professor's brief case. Ron remembered that Dominic mentioned that those papers were written in the language of the Church which was Latin. Because of that, he was convinced that Fitz, given the description of him was not the scholarly type. That wasn't so much for his size as it was for his gruffness and not being too articulate from what the Professor could recall from their interaction. That would leave Miss Tulley the real one who pretended to be another person and then herself afterwards to throw everyone off the track of Fitz who she thought had the Professor in captivity. Whether or not she was classically educated and thus articulate in Latin was a question which needed to be answered.

"So Ron, you're suggesting that this Fitz guy could not translate the ancient documents and maybe this Miss Tulley or her faker could."

"Not exactly Alessandro, I am convinced that Miss Tulley the real one and the fake one are the same person. Therefore she either can or cannot translate them. If she can't and that's a big IF, then we need to get to her at Beaulieu House because in all probability she knows that its library contains ancient texts of Irish History and she would need them to piece together the third part of what Bob is supposed to remember."

"Number three is St. Erc's Hermitage which is right here on the grounds of Slane Castle," Bob proudly announced. "We all saw its location on that old map in the display case."

"Right you are pal. Out of this garden is a natural incline which the lad Henry wants to change into an outdoor amphitheater like in ancient Roman times. And past that are the ruins of St. Erc's Hermitage where if I am correctly remembering what the Professor jotted down in his notes that I read on the plane coming over, we will find the forgotten treasure of Saint Malachy's Chalice."

The professor was reluctant to pour water on this flaming deduction but felt it was necessary to do so. "Ron, that all sounds plausible but there is no way that the Republic of Ireland will allow us to dig up the ruins on what is essentially a hunch."

"And that Professor is why we need to get to Beaulieu House before Miss Tulley and Fitz do as there in one of those ancient texts is the story of the Chalice similar to the one on those ancient documents which you found in the Vatican Archives. Of that I am convinced or why should the Lady in Black have written Beaulieu House in her notes. If we can find it, and if someone can read the ancient Irish it's written in or perhaps the Latin used then we shall know exactly where the Chalice is hidden."

"Ronnie," Susan stroked his cheek gently. "This is a grand idea that you have concocted but it sounds like a gigantic plan which will take time to figure out let alone find the actual Chalice."

Taking her hand, Ron then kissed it as Jan gasped along with every person around that fountain. "Are you saying that you have no faith in me Susan?"

She slipped her hand out of his. "Not at all you silly boy; how can you even think that after all we've been through back at St. Benedict's Abbey in Wisconsin, then the New York World's Fair and just a few months ago in Rome. It's not a lack of faith; it's the lack of time to catch this Miss Tulley and Fitz…"

"And their accomplice in this caper to rob Ireland of its heritage," Ron calmly added.

"Accomplice," yelled Bob, "Nothing like bringing in something from outer field. What makes you think that there are more than two people?"

"I just feel it in my bones I guess. Let's walk to the ruins while I explain. First the Professor is lured away from the Trinity Library by someone calling herself Mr. O'Neil's assistant, one Bridget Tulley. But the security guard stopped them and that threw a monkey wrench in their plans. The professor here gave the guard his brief case which meant someone would now have to steal it. I say Fitz is the culprit there. That would leave Miss Tulley who was busy seducing, pardon my expression, the professor. So who is left to kill the Lady in Black?"

The now red faced professor offered a thought. "But Ron it would have to be someone who understood the value of what was printed on those pages in my brief case or someone who was promised a chunk of money after the revered chalice was found."

"Exactly professor and that would leave us with Mr. O'Neil himself who was lost during the time period when the murder took place, Dean Shannon who was to meet the professor at Trinity Library but never showed but ended up at Slane Castle or the butler, Shamus Sweeney who said he went out to look for Mr. O'Neil. I am leaving out the Marquess and his son from this equation as they would certainly not use the heritage of Ireland to make money…"

"Unless they wanted to spruce up the castle and create that amphitheater, is that too cruel a thought?"

"No Jan, it's not cruel just unlikely. I think we have three suspects and should focus on them." Ron stopped and placed his hands on his sister's shoulders, such a demonstrative gesture not in his wheel house usually. Then he hugged her. "Don't feel badly about accusing the Earl, someone would have to so that he could be eliminated from suspicion. Come on we're almost at the ruins." He placed her hand into that of Alessandro and ran up to Bob and Susan placing himself between them. He would incorporate yet another experiment in love as he explained his theory.

The others joined them; they linked arms and formed a straight line looking at the ruins of St. Erc's Hermitage.

CHAPTER ELEVEN

ST. ERC'S HERMITAGE

Without a word they stood like a platoon of soldiers planning their attack or rather a plan of action to thwart what they knew whoever that Miss Tulley was and her muscle, Fitz were doing would soon impact what they had to do. Ron was confident that there was a third person. As he viewed the huge standing stones marking the grave of St. Erc and scanned possible areas which centuries ago would have afforded the Monks an opportunity to hide their valuables from the King's marauding troops he realized that what they needed to do was an impossible task. That is unless there really was a clue in some ancient text at Beaulieu House or in the Lebor Gabala Erenn which Andreas and Dominic had slipped out of the Trinity College Library or one more possibility. He tightened his grip on the arms of Susan and Bob as an illumination burst worth sending his mind whirling. In the center of the ruins was a large circular formation resembling a large well missing its crossbeams and buckets on a rope which would have been lowered into the well to pull up water for the thriving spiritual community over fifteen hundred years ago and until Cromwell finally destroyed almost anything left of the once envied educational institution in all of Europe.

Ron broke ranks and walked to the other end of the line toward the Professor. "Sir, look in the center of the ruins. What does it appear to be to you?"

Professor Pettigrew, without dropping his hold on Alessandro's arm, hardly had to blink before responding. "Ron that's what's known as St. Erc's well. But as you can see it doesn't function that way and hasn't for centuries. As I recall before Cromwell's troops came to totally destroy the Hermitage School, the monks fled while the local farmers filled the well with stones which would be impossible to remove given the depth of the well. The incoming troops would have no source of water and would have to move on, though obviously they destroyed what was left of the Hermitage.

"Exactly Professor," Ron was getting excited he grabbed hold of him and began to tell a story as he wrapped his arm around his shoulders. "Now everyone come close and envision this."

Jumping onto a protruding rock Ron let go of the Professor and swung his arm horizontally so as to present the whole of the ruins and coming back to the rock filled well.

"Here he goes again guys..."began Bob. "Brace yourselves for a quest."

Ron smiled at his pal who sat next to the rock waiting for that illumination to be revealed. Everyone else closed in surrounding the would-be priest who wasn't quite sure about his vocation. With a dramatic pause Ron began his tale by first bringing them back to the 12th Century when Mellifont Abbey was being built by St. Malachy and the original Lady Devorgilla MacMurrough who gifted the abbey with funds, a gold gem encrusted Chalice and altar linens. "Imagine the joy and celebration as St. Malachy along with his Irish monks and imported French monks finally completed the Abbey's chapel down which we centuries later ran to find the Lady in Black who called herself Lady Devorgilla MacMurrough as well. The stone on which she died is the burial marker of the original lady benefactress of the Abbey. Now jump to the year 1539 during the reign of Henry VIII. He promulgated the dissolution of the Abbeys across his Kingdom. What would you do as a monk who just heard that the King's troops were coming to take over the Abbey?"

"That's a no brainer Ron," answered Dominic who did know of the Abbey's history because of the research he did with the Professor. "They would hide their valuables so that the troops would only find empty stone buildings."

"Possibly, but I think they didn't do that at Mellifont. The Chalice by then had become more than a Holy Vessel, it was the Holy Grail of Ireland. It had become a symbol of Irish heritage if not freedom as Rory O'Connor, the last High King of Ireland had viewed it as that powerful symbol in his failed efforts to keep Ireland free of English rule back in the 12th Century."

"I don't understand where you are going with this tale Ron," began the Professor. "Henry VIII dissolved the abbey as you said in 1539; that's almost four hundred years after it was established."

"Right you are. I'm getting too much into the history and not enough into solving the murder. So let's jump those centuries. Now King Henry did away with these powerful land rich Abbeys to fill his coffers with their wealth. So what did those Cistercian monks of Mellifont Abbey do? Like I said they hid their treasures and revered artifacts. I could tell you a story of the Black Abbey in Kilkenny regarding such hidden treasures which impacts what I think happened here only that was done when Cromwell ravaged Ireland during the English Civil War which he had just won by beheading King Charles I, but that would be over the top."

Susan was none too pleased with Ron's decision to cut off yet another tale which peaked her interest but she didn't want to admit that so she took another tactic. She got into his face. "Now you listen to me Ron De Cenza. You think that you have this whole scenario figured out what with all your history lessons and now with this Kilkenny story. But smart ass you do not. The Black Abbey is in southeast Ireland in the ancient medieval city where the Normans built a magnificent castle. Those were the same Normans which invaded Ireland because that original Lady Devorgilla ran off and married the MacMurrough guy and created a new alliance which strengthened Ireland. It has nothing to do with Mellifont, St. Malachy or St. Erc's Hermitage, so there."

Ron jumped off the rock on which he was perched and took Susan by the arms and held her close. "Did anyone ever tell you how cute you are when those emerald eyes sparkle with fury and the wind takes that flaming hair and wraps it about your shoulders like lace curtains?"

She shoved him away and looked at Jan, who shrugged her shoulders to indicate that she started it and now her brother wanted to finish it.

"Don't you get fresh with me honey child I know what I'm talking about."

"That's only partly true. The Normans in Kilkenny began building that castle two hundred years before St. Malachy built Mellifont Abbey with St. Bernard from France. Secondly, I only wanted to mention the Black Abbey because the treasure of which I speak was found hidden in its walls only four years ago in 1961. It was a sculpture of the Holy Trinity which was sealed up in one of its walls when Cromwell came and took over the church to make it a court house. None of that is important except for the part of the sculpture being sealed in a wall."

"Holy shit Ron, are you saying that the chalice is hidden in a wall somewhere in Mellifont?"

"Not quite Bob, but it is hidden and I think somewhere in the ruins of St. Erc's Hermitage. But I can't prove it right now and I looking at these ruins can see no walls from that period of history standing except for…" Ron pointed to the circular walls surrounding the well filled with rocks. "Right there."

"No shit, really…"

"Yes Bob, really but how can we prove it and if we can how do we get to it?"

Silence shrouded the group as they sat upon that hill overlooking the ruins.

As they pondered their next step, along a lonely road known as the LG327, the black Fiat made its way toward Beaulieu House. In that car sat Miss Tulley and behind the wheel was Fitz. As they drove up to the manor house, the Chief Inspector not more than six miles away entered the Drogheda Hospital and began to question Nancy Clancy about the woman who identified herself as the niece of the Lady Devorgilla and a certain rather large man who was with her.

"Now you've done it. I told you to stay on R166. Where the hell are we?" asked a flustered Bridget Tulley.

"Hold your tongue woman or one day it will be your end. I don't need to take your shit any more. If it wasn't for me we wouldn't even have that brief case and those notes."

"And what good are they written in Latin?"

"Fuck! That is a problem. Look there; it's Beaulieu House where I was head of security before I met you. That asshole Professor tore the crest off mi jacket, see here. She liked me she did, I bet she would let us use their phone and we can make a call to him. You know so that he can meet us and translate the papers."

"Christ Fitz, you in charge of security? My have I underestimated you. Pull over and we'll do just that."

Gabriel Konig better known under her race car driving name of Gabriel de Freitas answered the door. "Good heavens, is that you Mr. Fitzgerald? Come on in."

"Thank you madam, I do beg your pardon to come unannounced but we got turned around coming from Drogheda on our way to Slane."

"Is that so," she led them into a sumptuous reception hall with portraits of original nobility who built the house centuries ago. Over the doorway was the crest with highlights of blue coloring which matched that which was torn from Fitz's jacket. "Now I'll call for some tea and you must tell me all about your life since you left us." She pulled a cord next to the white marble fireplace and then sat herself on a baroque chair gilded in gold leaf across from the sofa on which they sat.

"There's not much to tell Madam. I have been working with…oh this is Miss Tulley the assistant curator of the Dublin Museum."

"How do you do Miss Tulley. My, you are so young to hold such a prestigious position. Why just the other day I was talking with a Mr. Hugh O'Neil who asked if he could visit my Library with a certain woman by the rather strange name of Devorgilla MacMurrough. I half expect a call from him today as I told him that I would be home. The recent wet weather has delayed the planned race. In any case, he hasn't called."

Bridget Tulley became quite uncomfortable as Gabriel went on to speak about her boss and the woman they just saw dead in the morgue. Should she share that story? If not, what would she talk about in regards to why they were out so far from Dublin? Fitz decided for her by chiming in.

"I am so sorry to tell you that the woman you call Devorgilla is dead. It was a God awful murder it was. They found her bloody on the rocks of Mellifont and took her to Drogheda Hospital but it was too late."

"Oh my Lord why would someone who was working with Mr. O'Neil and he studying the history of our land be killed?" asked a shocked Gabriel de Freitas. "He was to use the library here. She I'm told was most interested in some of our historical texts."

"Yes it's so sad indeed Madam. But now as to our unplanned visit, would you allow me to show Miss Tulley the Library. She being with the museum would certainly find it most interesting. Maybe she might be allowed to call Mr. O'Neil and alert him of her presence here and save him a trip."

"By all means, come young lady and let me show you our special volumes. How are you with the ancient Irish language and Latin? I'm afraid that I am quite poor with the ancient tongue but my Latin isn't too bad. Fitz, now that's what the young lady calls you. I didn't realize you had such a nick name but then who am I to speak of names as I use a stage name as it were. Anyway dear man, you would know that weakness in languages now wouldn't you?"

Eamon Fitzgerald suddenly became tongue tied. Bridget flipped some strands of the brown hair wig off her face. She did so with a flare to hide her shock and realization that of course original texts centuries old would not be translations into English. "Oh…look at me your man Fitz had the windows open in the car and I must look a fright." she then hesitated not knowing how to address the lady race car driver.

"Just call me Gabriel young lady; that will do. And you were saying?"

A knock on the door startled both of them as they crossed the entrance foyer on their way to the library. It also saved Bridget from having to answer the question. At the same time Bridget realized she had another problem. Fitz had introduced her as her real self and her real self was a raven black not chestnut brown haired woman. She jabbed him in the ribs and leaned into him.

"Now on all days when no one is about except the cook we have more visitors. Do go on Miss Tulley; it's right through those doors." She pointed towards double solid oak doors opposite them.

With a smile on her lips but boiling with her new dilemma she locked arms with Fitz and dragged him off. "Why the hell did you have to introduce me as my real self?"

Gabriel pulled on the heavy front door inward and held onto it as she saw three young people standing on the steps. "Well Good Morning to ye. I'm afraid if you're here for the garden tour that it doesn't operate today." The tenth generation descendant of Sir Henry Titchbourne who founded the manor house and protected it during the turbulent wars of the 1600's stood with a grace one might not have expected from an upcoming race car driver. But here she stood in gray slacks and a dark green blouse over which she wore a black wool vest as the morning chill hadn't quite dissipated. Her short sandy blond hair was cut short and contrasted with the long flaming hair of the young lady who stood at her doorway. The reason for the vest became apparent when a swirl of cool breeze entered and the young woman shivered a bit as it did.

"Oh excuse us but we are not here to view the gardens though Henry tells us that they are quite lovely and rival their own at Slane Castle."

"Henry you say, as in the son of Frederick the Earl of Mount Charles?"

"The very one madam…"

"Well do come in and forgive me keeping you at the door. You have come when I am quite alone save for my cook but we shall have some tea in any case. I am Gabriel de Freitas…"

"Oh yes we know," answered Ron. "Henry showed us photos of you next to that white racing car you used recently. He loves…I mean he's a great fan."

"Oh such a fine lad, I had no idea that he was just an avid fan given his father's position and all. Now then do sit and tell me all about how you came to be at Slane Castle as they too are on the garden tour and would be closed today as well."

"Actually, we aren't on a tour more like an exploration to solve a mystery as it were," began Susan. "But first let me introduce you to our leader Ron De Cenza and his Watson…I mean friend Bob Wentz. My name is Susan Liguri and we are all from America."

"Ah the states, how nice for you to visit Ireland, I am most pleased to meet you but do tell me why did you refer to this young man as Watson?"

Bob squirmed with embarrassment in the same chair where Fitz had parked himself, an ornate 18th Century antique. Susan found herself explaining that they were helping a Chief Inspector named Rory O'Connor with an unfortunate incident. Gabriel already having been told of the death of the Lady Devorgilla made the connection as she eyed the young people up and down wondering how so young a trio could help with a murder investigation. Nevertheless she encouraged Susan and heard the tale of how Ron and Bob were a team of sorts who helped with solving crimes and how she and a few others who were back at the Castle helped out. She marveled at their talents as the Italian adventure and the saving of Renaissance art work was told.

"Well you lads and lass must be rather disappointed with the quiet life here in County Louth after that frolic in the Italian Alps. But we shall do our best to welcome you. I shall go for some tea and introduce you to the others who also arrived this morning. I'll get them from the library on my way back with the tea."

"You are most gracious Miss de Freitas." Once the lady car racer was out of the room Susan ran to the doorway and pointed up. "Ron look at that, it's the crest on that cloth in your pocket."

"Holy crap," Ron pulled out the cloth torn from the jacket of the Professor's abductor. "It is but what's the connection? Maybe that thug was just wearing a souvenir jacket like I'm wearing this Slane Castle sweatshirt."

Bob walked to the opposite doorway and peeked out into the foyer from where they entered. "Bullshit, there's more to it I'm thinking." He looked about the lavishly furnished room and then back into the entrance hall. "This isn't a castle but it sure looks like a palace. And she races cars to keep up a place like this... some woman."

"You're right. From the Professor's description he didn't strike me as the type to go on a garden tour. I think I'll ask Miss de Freitas..."

"Ask me what young man," Gabriel placed the sterling silver tea tray onto a small oval table held up by three legs which were joined half way up as one pillar holding up the tabletop. The Irish lace runner hardly moved as she placed it down."

Susan and Ron walked over to the table. Susan offered to help pour.

Ron showed her the torn cloth. "Well Madam the Professor, the one whom we are all helping with research on the Mellifont Abbey's construction and gifts given to Saint Malachy by a noblewoman named Devorgilla

MacMurrough, found this." He held out the brightly embroidered crest emblem. "We think it's from one of your souvenir shirts or jackets perhaps."

Gabriel asked if she could hold it and examine it. She rubbed her fingers across it. "This is not a souvenir Master De Cenza. It's an actual embroidered piece which means it came from me or my staff when they wear official attire such as when the garden tour is conducted. For instance, my Chief of Security who is in the library would have had such emblems sewn onto his jackets and coat." She remembered her other guests. "Oh my I need to get two more cups for the tea and ask them to join us. Isn't it strange that he would come today and inform me that a woman with that same name was killed the other day and here you are talking about her namesake from our early history."

Sparks began to fire in the synapses of Ron's brain. He asked her to describe this security person. When she pointed out that he would be larger than the rather amply bodied Bob, he about jumped out of his skin. Controlling himself he asked for a name. When given the name of Eamon Fitzgerald there followed a slight hesitation. He had to make sure if the person she was talking about was the same one he was thinking of.

"And did you have a nick name for him Miss de Freitas?"

"Heavens no, but the young woman who came with him did. I found it amusing that she called him Fitz, you know short for Fitzgerald I would imagine."

"Oh my God, Mam you did say that you were alone, save for the cook is that correct?"

Gabriel answered that she was quite alone now that even the cook must have gone out since no one was in the kitchen and she had to make the tea herself.

"Bob, close that door and stand firm against it. Miss de Freitas, I think you have a criminal in your house. What did the woman look like? Susan close that other door, Mam can it be locked?"

"Yes by key which is in the desk under that portrait."

Susan ran to the small desk under the 18th Century portrait of a noble gentleman in flowing robes indicating membership in the House of Lords in the British Parliament.

"But young man, Master De Cenza this is all too much Mr. Fitzgerald worked for me and I don't know the woman but she's obviously well-educated and is in my library as we speak. She is dressed in a well-tailored suit with long nut brown hair and just enough make-up so as not to be considered…well you know one of those brazen hussies one hears about these days."

As this conversation about who Fitz might be took place inside the library he was paging through an ancient text. Bridget Tulley had located a phone on a small table with a marble top from the Victorian era. It would be of interest to Miss Tulley from a historic point of view; were it not for her becoming filled with anxiety. She picked up the phone and gazed out of the window overlooking the tranquil gardens with their perfectly trimmed hedges and flower beds one of which was filled with the pale yellow Aquilegia plant which drew her attention as it was one in her grandmother's garden. She called it the Granny Bonnet. She shook off the budding memory. The tranquility offered by the view would have no effect on her. She was now consumed with worry that the Lady of Beaulieu House was given her true identity but in the disguise of the murdered woman's niece. Her hand shook as the phone call ended. She had hardly offered a word. She slowly turned away from the view outside that window. Seeing Fitz frustrated in his efforts to figure out what the book he held had to offer, she ran to him and grabbed the frail book from his hands and shoved it, though gently, into her purse.

"He says to bring the book. He'll be able to translate."

"Right the old goat didn't happen to say where that would be which didn't have the Garda all about, did he?"

On the grounds of Slane Castle in the ruins of St. Erc's Hermitage the Professor had his assistants spread out from the Amphitheater slope to the slender tall stones marking the grave of the saint and his followers to the walls surrounding the ruins which were of interest. Forming a jagged peak were large white pointed stones which offset the dark limestone rocks forming the wall underneath. Looking out over the wall Andreas and Dominic took in the sight of the village below where they stood. Their hands rested on those white stones as they for a brief moment eased their hands over the rocks as if caressing them until one rested on top of the other. They said nothing until several cows left a small herd grazing on the hill leading down to the village. They lumbered their way up toward the wall as if they wanted to visit these two striking young men who were certainly no farmers.

"Would these cows only have a clue for us," mused Dominic not so much to Andreas as just speaking aloud.

Directly behind them were the stone markers of the saint toward which Andreas now turned ignoring the visiting cows who Dominic was now patting on their heads. The fleeing moment of reflection and affection was ended.

"They're cows bambino, now these stones have a tale to tell." Andreas walked to the tallest of those standing stones and stroked it as if it was a crystal ball ready to reveal some truth. "Just maybe we could dig up the grave. Maybe what we seek is buried with the saint."

Dominic saying farewell to the bovine visitors sprinted toward him. "Andreas, you are a soldier obviously and not a historian. This Saint Erc predates St. Malachy by around six centuries."

Andreas turned to take hold of the strong arms of one who was his hidden love. He pressed him against that tall standing stone releasing his arm which then came to squeeze him as he closed in on him their tall frames almost matching in height bringing a vivid contrast between the fair haired one with sparkling blue eyes and the dark haired research assistant with eyes like those cows; ones which rivaled those of Ron. Andreas teased about Ron's eyes often to make him jealous. Now he looked into those eyes and smiled.

"And so you think because I am a soldier of the Vatican's Swiss Guard, that I am ignorant of such things." His lips came quite close to those of Dominic who now became filled with the hope of what would follow and at the same time nervous about who might be about to witness this demonstration of soft strength between what Susan would call models for Michelangelo's statue of the David. Suddenly Andreas dropped his hold and fell to his knees. Instinctively Dominic waited, like a statue of marble, for what he thought would be an expression of Andreas' love for him.

Instead Andreas was not looking at him but at the flat stone covering the ground of the grave. He was rubbing it gently. "Gaudare... look at this stone. You think I didn't know the Saint lived long before the one whose chalice we seek. But who is to say that when the troops came to destroy this place that the monks did not invade the tomb to hide what was most precious to them." Turning his head ever so slightly and looking up those long legs fitted tightly in jeans and up toward a broad chest heaving with different thoughts and onto the stunned closely shaven smooth face, he added. "Com'e bello."

The spell was broken. Those strong arms developed while on archeological digs were brought across that chest. "So the rock is beautiful and as rocks go, perhaps it is."

Laughing aloud, Andreas grabbed hold of Dominic's belt and pulled him down with such force that he fell on top of the Swiss Guard and they tumbled along the grass until they crashed against that wall of stone beyond which those same cows stood waiting for their new friend to appear.

"You think that I call a stone such a name?" Andreas continued trying to use English as he spoke.

Owww! My head you're potso, crazy man…"

Andreas' composure changed like a chameleon which swiftly changes its coloring. "Dio mio, bambino, did I hurt you?" He threw himself off of Dominic, pushed up on the standing rock and slipped behind it not wanting to let his amico, his friend see the tears in his eyes. He was a soldier and not supposed to show emotion.

Dominic lay against the rock wall rubbing his head and regretting that their moment washed away like a wave upon the sand. He saw himself as that wave bathing the moment that could have been into nothing but a bump on the head. He curled himself up into a reflective posture and just sat there knowing full well what his soldier friend was doing behind the standing rock in front of him. He couldn't keep quiet any longer. He jumped to his feet and ran behind the rock.

Andreas was leaning against the limestone rock slightly slouched and gazing out over the ruins. In the distance he could just make out the Professor and the others through his blurry eyes filled with tear drops about ready to fall again.

"Caro amico…dear friend I didn't mean to hurt you."

Andreas remained with his back facing Dominic and looking out over the ruins. "It is I who hurt you not the other way around."

Dominic inched closer and placed his arm around the heaving chest breathing heavily trying to control emotion. "It's only a bump on the head…"

Andreas attempted to turn around in that embrace; his water filled eyes catching the sunlight and glistening like diamonds at the corners of those crystal blue pools. He broke the hold and gently placed his hand on Dominic's head. "So I did harm you in more ways than one. Let me take a look." On his fingers he noticed some drops of blood seeping out of the thickness of the black hair. "Madonna mia, Dominic you are hurt. We must get you to the Professor. He has a first-aid kit."

"Stop fussing, I am fine just a scratch."

"Look here, you are bleeding. It could get infected and then what?"

Dominic relented and let Andreas hold his arm and lead him to the professor who was standing around the large rock filled well of St. Erc's Hermitage. Along the way Dominic insisted on knowing what Andreas meant by saying he had hurt him in more ways than one. The Swiss Guard with all the courage he could muster began to talk about the beauty of rocks and the beauty of his friend and that the one is nothing but a lifeless thing while his friend, his *caro amico*, was full of life and joy. And to stifle that joy, to endanger that life force was unthinkable; that was the hurt to which he referred.

Standing on the edge of the circle of rocks the Professor was reflecting aloud as Alessandro and Jan listened while holding hands and wishing that they could have been off to enjoy the view beyond the walls of the ruins like Andreas and Dominic had done.

"Imagine what these rocks could tell us," the professor stooped down and picked up a fragment of stone. He held it up towards the young couple and looked at it as if waiting for it to share its story.

Alessandro smiled down at Jan and whispered. "I think this Professor is like Hamlet as he held the skull of his friend and wishing that it could speak to him." He pulled Jan closer to him.

"Alessandro, stop your nonsense; but you are right about one thing. It sure looks like a scene from a Shakespeare play."

"Centuries old stone, speak to us mere mortals. Tell us of the monks who lived and taught here, speak of the horror of Cromwell coming to destroy that which you were once a part, talk of the faithful coming to this well to draw water to be blessed so that the many could be baptized."

Jan broke the spell. "Professor Pettigrew, are you okay?"

"Oh my, of course dear girl I am fine just a bit lost in history. Now let's get back to our task…where are your brother, Susan and Bob? They've been gone for quite some time."

CHAPTER TWELVE

Escape from Beaulieu House

The Lady of Beaulieu house, Gabriel de Freitas, paused as she handed Susan the tea pot to finish the pouring. "Now I wonder what's taking Mr. Fitzgerald and that nice Miss Tulley so long. Do finish Miss Liguri, I'll go fetch them."

The three exchanged confused mixed with shock glances as she spoke Tulley's name.

Just as Gabriel opened the door of the sitting room and entered the entrance hall the front door squeaked open as a rather strong breeze came rushing against it. She went to the door to shut it. A loud roar of an engine met her ears as she did so. Swinging open the door she saw Miss Tulley entering the Fiat and off it went. She called out to them but to no avail but the call did attract her other guests in the sitting room. They ran into the hall just in time to look over the lady's shoulder and see the car kick up the gravel of the driveway as it pulled away.

"Now why do you suppose that they would go off like that without so much as saying a good-bye?"

"If you are missing one of your ancient texts then I could give you a guess," answered Ron. "But for now, we must go after them. Do forgive us, but if they have what I think they have, then the Professor who we work with will be in danger, at least that which he seeks will be."

Ron paused on the stairs looking at the Trinity College van. "Oh Jesus have mercy but we'll never catch up with them in this thing. Come on guys, we'll give it the old college try."

Gabriel de Freitas followed Susan and Bob down the stairs as they ran out the doorway. She stood next to Ron. "I think young man, I may have a solution to your dilemma. Follow me."

Ron sprinted up to her after calling out to Bob and Susan to follow them. The two caught up and they hurried along to a stone building with large wooden swinging doors which were painted red.

"What gives?" asked Bob.

"No clue but she has an idea that will help us catch up to those two she talked about. It's my guess that the man could be the one who assaulted the Professor. And right now I'm convinced that the woman is really ONeil's assistant or at least pretending to be her."

"Oh my God are you saying that we are going after murderers; no not again Ron, call the Chief Inspector."

"Bob's right. We need some muscle…"

Ron glanced her way with a look of disbelief or was it more like "I can't believe you just said such a thing to me who caught the murderer in Italy." He ran up to the red doors and turned to Gabriel de Freitas. "Mam, so why did you take us here to a barn?"

She stood there for a moment without a word absorbing what she had just heard. "Young man, if this is not just about a theft of a book perhaps your friend is correct. I shall call the police."

Ron ignored the part of the comment about theft and murder and focused on calling the police. He walked up to her after giving a burning look of how time was being wasted to his friends for their lack of support for him and totally rejecting that the comments were given out of love for him and keeping him safe. For they knew full well how he almost got killed in Arona Italy on more than one occasion when they once again had set out to save the professor and his discovery.

"Mam, we don't have any time to lose they are already minutes ahead of us and all we have is that old van. So again I ask; why did you bring us to a barn?"

Gabriel with a side glance toward Bob and Susan decided to answer his question and help him catch up with Tulley and Fitz. She pulled on one of the large red doors while directing that Ron do the same to the other door. As they doors swung open inside it was quite clear that this building was not a barn. "As you will see this is not a barn but my garage." She walked up to a vehicle of some kind which was covered with a large canvas cloth so that only the black tires were visible. In one sweeping motion she tugged on the piece of canvas and then pulled it off revealing a gleaming white sports car with red markings and also painted in red the number 43.

Ron's mind flashed back to the photo he had seen of her standing next to a sports car. It was however in black and white but there was no doubt in his mind that the number on the car in that photo was "43" so he spoke his mind. "Mam, is this the car you use in your races?"

She patted the hood. "That it is and she has given me a good run. But to the point, you may use it to catchup with that Fiat. Fiats look quite sleek but they are no match for this Austin Martin with a Ferrari engine that I can assure you." She leaned over and opened the glove box as the model had no roof but was a convertible style onto which a solid roof could be attached. Pulling out the keys she turned to Ron. "Can you drive a stick shift young man?"

He gulped hard as a flashback to his days of first learning how to drive. It was in a 1959 Chrysler sedan which drove like a tank, but his father was quite proud of it even though it wasn't new. The grinding of the clutch came to mind as he recalled those lessons which required him shifting from first gear to second and then to third. Looking into Gabriel's car he noticed that it was not a column shift but one on the floor board between the seats. He had no clue if it would shift in the same manner or not.

"Well I did learn on a stick shift," he began knowing full well that was only a brief period as his father then got a Ford LTD automatic because he felt it would be easier for him to drive. "And that Trinity College van is also stick."

Bob coughed and poked him. Leaning into him he spoke quietly. "Are you nuts Ron, you never drove the van only Andreas and Alessandro has and this thing is worth a fortune."

"Shush your face Bob. Do you want to catch those creeps or not?"

With a shrug Bob walked back to stand with Susan whose emerald eyes were about to pop out of her head as she watched a Ron she didn't recognize take on a flair of James Bond as he caressed the car and smiled at Gabriel its owner. She took hold of Bob's arm. "Can he drive it Bob?"

"I really couldn't say. We only drove his dad's Ford and he crashed that up good one night. Almost killed himself but thank God didn't." He squeezed her hand on his arm. "Don't worry; Sherlock will figure this out wait and see." He could only bring up a nervous half smile.

The lady race car driver placed the keys into Ron's hands. "If I am correct they would be taking the back roads and not go onto the N2 as that's where the police will first go after I call them."

"Right the police. Do get hold of Chief Inspector Rory O'Connor, he has gone to the Drogheda Hospital to identify the body of the Lady Devorgilla and then should you be so kind to call the Marquess at Slane Castle and inform Professor Pettigrew of what we think has taken place."

"Good lad, now just follow my drive out onto L6327 and follow it to R166. You should be able to see them around that time if you hit fourth gear."

"Fourth gear..." he gasped. "Sure." Of course he only knew about three gears

"Now you probably won't have to get into fifth gear as that would really get you flying but just in case, it's there and the power is available." She pointed to the number on the base of the shift stick. The round ball top of the shift also had the locations for each gear engraved onto it. "Now then hop in and I'll make the calls. What about your friends?"

Ron did as directed and jumped into the seat adjusting it and then grasping the wheel to get a feel for it. He called out to them. "Susan, you take the van back to Slane castle with Bob. Tell them what's happened and..."

"No way Ron, I'm coming with you." Bob jumped into the passenger seat. "Susan can handle the van."

"Well of course I can handle it but I will meet you at Trim Castle first."

The two guys and the Lady Race Car driver looked at her with inquisitiveness. "No not Trim Castle, I said Slane Castle," called out Ron.

"Yes, Ronnie I heard you but I think we should go to Trim Castle as that what it is written on this piece of paper I found on the driveway." She pulled out the slip of paper from the small brown leather purse hanging on a gold chain about her neck. "I said nothing because I thought that a tourist may have dropped it but then I remembered that the garden wasn't open today so unless this belongs to Miss de Freitas, I am thinking that those two who were in the library may have taken notes of some kind." She held up the slip of paper. Under the name of Trim Castle was written N51 and then Dublin Gate.

Ron instantly became sullen and disappointed. "Well then, if that really is a note of some kind, we know where they are headed and don't need this car to catch up to them."

"Nonsense young man, even if it is to Trim Castle they head you will need to get there first. You see Dublin Gate is the entrance near the Boyne River where there is what is called a water gate which leads to the ruins of the Great Hall. I have been at the castle many times but not on the River and through that gate."

A broad smile crossed Ron's face and the look of James Bond in control returned. "Then that's it then. I will follow them. You Bob will get out and drive the van directly to Trim Castle. I will not have Susan go there alone."

With a muffled "shit" expressed Bob got out of the car and took the keys from Susan. "I'll drive." He stomped off out of the garage and turned. "Well come on Susan, we need to get a move on and Ron needs to get his ass in gear."

Calling back to him, Susan told him to stop at Slane Castle and pick up the others and meet her and Ron at Trim Castle. "We may need the strength of that Swiss Guard and Alessandro."

Bob gave no direct answer but went off mumbling something about "so much for Sherlock needing his Watson. No one asked me if I could drive stick shift." He kicked the gravel like a young lad pouting over his woes.

Ron in the meantime was not thrilled that she singled out Andreas and Alessandro for their muscle. "Let him go Susan and get in."

A bit confused as to what had just taken place, Gabriel affirmed that she would call the Chief Inspector and clarified that she should send him to Slane Castle. That was where Ron was sure the Professor had determined was the location of the St. Malachy Chalice. "Now remember

Mr. De Cenza that you are looking for R161 and then follow the Boyne River roads to Trim."

"Right and thanks so much for the loan of this spectacular car." Ron turned the key and the engine roared. With just the slightest crunching of the gear shift he rode off in first gear shifting again as he reached the driveway and soon he was speeding down the gravel road to the black top one lane backroad all the while making an effort to stay on the left side of it which really wasn't crucial as it was only a one lane street.

Susan pulled up the silk like souvenir scarf depicting those very places which now had become a scene of murder, a possible location of a hidden heritage treasure and castles withstanding wars and centuries of neglect. As the rushing wind whipped through her long crimson hair she tried to keep it from becoming tangled knowing full well that the one sitting behind the wheel would not have noticed if she was disheveled or not. His focus was on the gear shift and the road ahead.

"Keep an eye out for that black Fiat."

She was right; it was all about the chase and capturing who he thought had attacked the Professor though he didn't know that to be a fact as yet. Nevertheless she continued the effort to tuck her hair in the scarf as Ron shifted from third into fourth gear and they just about flew across the pavement.

Bob pulled up in front of the entrance area of Slane Castle and jumped out of the van. Instead of going to the front doors he ran around the rather imposing building seeking the ruins where he knew the Professor and his friends would be. Out of breath and starving half to death as he would often say to Ron when they were on one of their journeys of discovery he stood on the crest of the natural amphitheater hilltop and looked down onto the ruins of St. Erc's Hermitage. Not a soul was in sight.

"Shit, now where are they?" he called out in frustration thinking that Ron and Susan could be in danger by now.

In the Library of Slane Castle he would have found the Professor and his friends. They had been called in for refreshments and tea but once inside were informed that the Chief Inspector had called from Drogheda Hospital ordering that everyone wait for him in the castle. No other explanation was offered to the Marquess as to why he needed to see everyone once again.

The Professor with Dominic at his side decided to make the best of what they knew and was examining the ancient maps in the new display case. Dominic with pen and pad in hand jotted down notes as the Professor translated the Latin words notating areas of the map. Andreas was left with Jan and Alessandro, the young Count of Pianore. The three of them were being helped by Hugh O'Neil as Andreas had opened on the table the book he took from Trinity Library.

The Lebor Gabala Erenn was written in the ancient Gaelic Irish language and O'Neil would serve as the translator. They were seeking if there was any mention of St. Erc's Hermitage or the Mellifont Abbey in its poetic rendition of the History of Ireland. And if so would it refer to the St. Malachy Chalice. With the Professor's brief case stolen and his notes and documents with it, they had only the Professor and Dominic's memory to rely on concerning what was found in the Vatican Archives.

"Mr. O'Neil thanks for your help with this," began Andreas. "Alessandro and I are okay with the Latin but not with this language of the Irish."

'You are too kind Sir but Dean Drumond would be the one who could get through this with ease for if I'm not mistaken this volume has the mark of Trinity College on the inside cover. Now where could he have gone off to?"

Their conversation was interrupted by the Marquess who told them that the Dean was driven to the Hill of Tara where he had a colleague working on a dig there. The butler was acting as his driver for the outing as he knew the area so well and what with the Curator having gotten lost in that area on the day the Lady Devorgilla was murdered.

"My son was to go with them however he decided to meet with some friends in town instead at the last moment. I will be off to fetch him shortly as I would think by his order that everyone was to be here in the castle the Chief Inspector meant me as well as my son."

As this explanation ended the library doors swung open and a panting Bob stood trying to catch his breath. He tried to speak but hadn't the breath to do so as yet.

"We need to save…" Bob took a deep breath. "It's Ron and Susan…"

Jan screamed as Alessandro ran to the near hysterical Watson to Ron's Sherlock, his Tonto to Ron's Lone Ranger. "Dio mio, Roberto what's wrong? Where are Ron and Susan?"

In two seconds flat Jan was tugging on Bob's arm. "What are you saying Bob? Where are my brother and Susan?" She began to shake him.

Alessandro pulled Bob away from Jan as Andreas and Dominic ran to her side to console her. He led the distraught lad to the tray with the pot of tea and a pitcher of water.

"Va bene cara mio, we will see what the problem is; it will be okay, I promise." Alessandro lifted Bob's head and looked into his aqua blue eyes filled with terror. "Amico, now breathe deeply and tell us again, where are Ron and Susan? Here take a sip of water; you look like hell; what's happened?"

Bob was beginning to breathe in regular patterns as he slowly sipped down the glass of water. He once again tried to not so much to explain but to call them to arms if they had any. And to that end Bob looked at each of his friends, the Professor, Curator and Marquess all of whom were standing like statues in the Vatican museum frozen in place.

"They're after him, the one who attacked the Professor in Dublin and the girl with him. We have no time to lose," he turned to run but Alessandro held him back.

"Hold on; the Chief Inspector is coming. He told us to stay in the castle until he arrived."

"Don't you get it? We don't have the time. If that guy is the one who tried to kidnap the Professor who knows what he'll do to Ron and Susan when they catch up with him at Trim Castle? And what about that woman who called herself Miss Tulley? Let go of me. I have to save my friends."

Bob was no match for Alessandro in ordinary circumstances but this was not one of those times. He broke away and ran to the door of the castle. Jan was on his heels and Alessandro with her. The young count placed himself between the door and Bob. Jan trying to push the young Count aside.

"Alessandro, Count of Pianore, you had best get out of my way or so help me I'll globber you where the sun doesn't shine."

"But then what would happen to our chances to have children," he broke a slight smile.

"I…well that's…what did you say?"

"I said that we should think calmly and then go after Ron and Susan and whoever these people are whom they are chasing to God knows where." He dropped all mention of his deepest hopes for him and Jan's future.

Everyone was now spilling into the Grand Entrance Hall with the Curator, Hugh O'Neil wondering if the woman was indeed his assistant curator and how they knew that it was she. Bob dropped his arms to his side telling Alessandro that he would explain first but then he had to let him go.

"Va bene, explain and then I shall open the door for all of us to go with you, Chief Inspector or not."

"Yes Bob, we are with you," called out the Professor."

"But he said Miss Tulley was with them," shouted O'Neil. "How can this be? She was attacked when the Professor was; it can't be her."

"Well that's what Miss de Freitas at Beaulieu House called her. Maybe His Lordship can call her, as all I saw was a young woman with brown hair and dressed in a gray tweed suit. She climbed into the car with this football player hulk of a guy and drive off like a bat out of hell, if you pardon my expression." Bob pushed through the now crowded hall and ran to the tea cart with Jan right behind him. He grabbed the pitcher and tried to pour another glass of water. "I'll probably have to pee in ten minutes but all that running has made me thirsty." He glanced at Jan who took the pitcher from his shaking hand to pour.

"It will be all right. We will get to Trim Castle and make sure they are safe."

Gulping down the water rather than sipping it made him choke a bit. "There's no time to lose Jan. Tell them that they can't stop me. Sherlock needs his Watson more than ever."

"I thought you were Tonto." She grinned. "I know my brother needs you and so does Susan who may love him but still doesn't know him with that brain of his always churning up ideas and plans, his blushing over the slightest off color remark, and his ability to see what others cannot like right into their very soul."

"Holy crap Jan, I had no idea that the little sister had that kind of insight. I thought all you two did was fight over the TV." He took another gulp of water and began to choke again as it went down the wrong pipe as Ron's Dad would say.

"I'm full of surprises so if you're done drowning yourself," she slapped him on the back and turned to the others now congregated at the library doors watching the scene unfold. "Now listen to me all of you. That Chief Inspector will be here God knows when but my brother needs help and doesn't even know it. He thinks he's being the hero again and therefore like up on that statue in Arano. So Alessandro and I are going with Bob. The rest of you can cover for us until we get back."

Alessandro stood quietly in the back of the gathering still contemplating what had not been addressed and that was Jan's ignoring what he said about having children. When he heard his name in conjunction with Jan going to save Ron and Susan, he brightened up. "Jan's right, we all shouldn't go, the Chief Inspector will be upset at best. Clear the way, we have to get going *veloce*…ah fast."

Trim castle was only seventeen miles from the town of Slane and a bit more from Beaulieu House outside of Drogheda in eastern Ireland. The white Austin Martin with the Ferrari engine made short work of the road and soon Ron could see the huge gray stone ruins of Trim Castle off in the distance on the other side of the river. The Keep stood tall above the broken walls and gutted great hall which actually was the newer part of the castle having been built in the 14th Century while the Keep dated back to the 12th Century. But he wasn't listening to Susan as she read those historical facts of the Norman built castle from her guide book.

"Susan can you see the black car? I thought it went down that gravel road but if we go that route they may see us coming. Where is the Dublin Gate located? This place is gigantic."

Ignoring his lack of enthusiasm for the history she found the gate in question next to the ruins of the Great Hall which was closest to the river bank. "See that stone bridge there to the right; I think if we follow that path it will lead us right to the Dublin Gate."

Ron thought it best to do just that; get to the bridge and get to the gate before Fitz and Tulley got to it. One thing was for certain and that was not to park the rather striking looking sports car in the parking lot on the other side of the castle. So he pulled over onto a dirt road near the river and parked behind some brush.

"Here goes nothing Susan. We'll hike down the river a bit to that pedestrian bridge and hopefully find those two." He held out his hand to help her out of the car not through the door but over it. She hesitated before taking it but when she did she thought it to feel quite warm and firm not a tremble at all. This obviously meant that he had no affection for her whatsoever or so she thought.

Now Ron had a history of sexual reactions whenever he touched Susan as it caused him to get an erection. As soon as she landed on the soft grassy embankment he turned and began the trek toward the bridge. This was accomplished without that embarrassing situation arising. His focus was on that ruin on those who were going there but as to why he hadn't a clue. He was mulling over the idea that perhaps everything they had suspected about the location of the Malachy Chalice was wrong. Perhaps the monks did manage to hide it in Trim Castle while leading others to think otherwise.

He turned to make sure Susan was right behind him as he broke into a run. "Luckily you wore those short pants today; a skirt would be a problem."

She didn't know what to think about the statement so stated the obvious. "These are Capri slacks and now I wish I was wearing jeans like you. This grass is still wet and is making my leg and socks all damp."

Wisely dropping the commentary on fashion, Ron returned his focus to the bridge and getting to the Dublin Gate. "So what does your guide book say about the Great Hall; maybe there's a way to get into it so that Fitz and that Tulley woman don't notice us."

Susan recalled that Dublin Gate was more than an entrance to the Great Hall area of the castle. It also had a water gate below it which blocked entrance from the river itself. While she was describing what a water gate was they had arrived at the foot of the bridge. On the other side was a dirt path which seemed to surround the castle thus if one went left they would go to the Castle Keep or living quarters for the soldiers and nobility and to the right to the ruins of the Great Hall.

"Look there Susan," Ron pointed to the path on which not a soul was seen. "Looks like we beat them here…"

"Or they went into it already from another side."

"Maybe," Ron leaned on the stone railings of the bridge on which flower pots were attached to dress up the site. Red Geraniums filled those pots but he wasn't interested in them at all for he had spotted a small skiff, a rowboat like craft peeking out from under the bridge. "Look down there, it's a boat." He climbed down the embankment and tried to reach for the bow of the craft. A rope was hanging in the river and was caught on some rocks along the shoreline. "This is our lucky day Susan. Come on down. We'll enter through that Water Gate you've been talking about."

She was quite pleased that he had actually been listening.

Helping her jump onto the boat without falling into the river having been achieved he had to make the short leap as well. She grabbed hold of him and they fell, he falling on top of her with a stifled shout as he placed his hand over her mouth. "I'm so sorry but they might be near here." He removed his hand.

"Well you can get your body off me Ron De Cenza. I feel…well I just feel uncomfortable."

"Oh shit, I mean oh my…well I don't know what I mean." He rolled off her as best he could in the cramped quarters of the skiff and onto one of the oars which struck him in the ass. "Shit, that hurt."

"Oh my God, Ronnie, are you hurt?" She used his family's familiar name as she usually did to show affection, concern or aggravation.

"Only my pride," he began to laugh but quietly. "Well I had best get rowing. I bet some guy is looking for his boat right now. From the looks of it just floating there under the bridge it must have gotten untied and the current took it here." The oars splashed in the water and a spray of it hit Susan.

"Good heavens," she pulled out a hanky from her purse and dabbed her face. "Should I row? I think I can do it with less of a flare."

"Don't be a smart ass. I can do it myself just fine."

"Whatever you say Ronnie," she dipped her hand into the river and cupped her hand. With a sudden smooth motion she swung up her arm and threw the water onto him. "So there, now we're even."

"What the hell, I didn't do that on purpose," he stood which was not a wise thing to do. The boat rocked and he fell over onto her once again. "You are something else Susan Liguri that's all I can say." Then without so much as a by your leave he planted a kiss right on her rosey pink lips. Jumped back onto the board seat and took up the oars. A smile crossed his face. He had done it and nothing happened. He was sure that it was more than lust but the thought was short lived. A tingling sensation could be felt in his lower abdomen area and into the groin. His thing began to waken and discomfort followed as it tried to find room to grow which was restricted by his tidy whitey briefs and equally tight fitting jeans. He squirmed and fidgeted and tried in vain to hide his issue.

During this sudden silent awakening of what had just taken place, Susan sat touching her lips. There was no quick remark, no slap in the face. In fact there was no response or reference to what had just happened at all. Just the touching of her lips and those emerald eyes sparkling in the sunlight burning into his cocoa brown orbs twinkling with delight that he had finally done it.

Distracted and feeling a mixture of "wow that was so cool and crap how will she react" he hadn't noticed the stone archway which once held the iron gate so that boats could not slip under the Great Hall's floor. The thud of the bow of the boat brought both of them out of their stupefied reaction.

"Holy shit, Susan, I think this is the gate; now what?"

"Huh? Oh, well first I'd say lower your head so that it doesn't hit those stones."

Ron ducked pushed the boat off the side of the archway and pulled on the upper stones to bring them into a small lagoon lighted only by sunlight coming from the archway gate area and a stream of sunshine above the stone stairs worn by the centuries of weather and people using them to secretly come and go out of the castle. Maneuvering the boat toward the rocky platform onto which the stairs met he then jumped out, erection or not, he was not to be distracted any longer. His lack of attention to his predicament soon had the issue subsiding. Holding onto the bow rope he tied it to a rock and held out his hand to help Susan out of the boat.

"I can do this myself," she didn't want it to sound the way it did but it did.

"I think that's how we got into the situation in the first place."

"And I think it happened not because of me but by you foolishly standing too far on one side of that thing called a boat."

"I found the result to be not too bad," he was trying to act cool as he stood there with outreached hand.

"Boys…that's all you think about," then she changed her tune. "Well it wasn't too bad at all." She smiled and took his hand, "So what now Sherlock?"

Ron became a bit tongue tied and had no retort or suggestion for that matter. He just stood there holding her hand. He had not even realized that despite her objections she had taken it into her own. Looking up into his eyes now glowing, she pulled away from him and with her went her hand. He felt the jolt as if a bolt of electricity had been introduced into his body and then suddenly vanished. He gazed down at his empty hand.

Susan watched as he slowly came back into the real world. The transition was too much like a turtle racing the proverbial rabbit and this time losing. "I said, what now Sherlock?"

This time the words sank into those temporarily frozen brain synapses. He shoved his hand into his jean's pocket like a cowboy might have done as the slit to the pocket was horizontal on top. The movement did not go unnoticed.

"I thought you were Sherlock and now you're trying to be that Lone Ranger guy."

"Huh, what are you talking about?" He lifted his hand and dropped both it and the other one to his side. "You don't know what you're talking about. Where the hell is Bob when I need him?" Bending over he secured the rope on the rock. "Now those two must be here by now. All we can do is to wait and listen."

"Well I'm for going up those worn old stairs behind you and searching the castle grounds. What if they don't come to this place?"

"But they will come here. We saw them walking towards this part of the castle ruins. Shush, I hear something." He pulled her to the stairs and both sat on the second to the last cold stone step. "Can you just keep your opinions to yourself for one minute and listen?" He held his finger up to his lips.

Softly she responded. "Really, listen to me smarty pants you're the one who has an opinion on everything at any given moment."

Footsteps clumping across the crushed gravel which covered the floor of the great hall above them ended their banter. Ron began to crawl up the stairs not knowing where it actually led and if he could be seen once at the top of them. Susan was right behind him.

Trim Castle

CHAPTER THIRTEEN

THE GREAT HALL REVELATION

The floor of the Great Hall of Trim Castle ran up to the open area of the stairwell. It was obviously designed so that a water escape or entrance could be made from or to it. Prancing back and forth and stopping every couple of steps was Fitz who was kicking the gravel when he paused.

"Where the hell is he?"

"Be a little patient; he said he'd be here and he will." Bridget Tulley tried to calm him but the event at Beaulieu House had made him unhinged.

The thick blackish hair was just coming up from the opening of the staircase; this was followed by those cow-like cocoa brown eyes. In an instant it was back down below the floor level. "It's them; but who is that woman? She doesn't look like Miss Tulley."

Susan didn't have time to answer. Another sound of footsteps could be heard and a voice followed them. "There you are. Where is the book? I don't have much time."

Bridget turned and held up the stolen book from Beaulieu House Library. Before she could answer Fitz exploded.

"What the hell are you talking about old man? We've been here waiting for you and almost got caught at the lady race car driver's house."

The hulk of a man pranced up to get into the older man's face and looked down at him. The trench coat he wore concealed his stature and the cap he wore covered almost all of his graying hair. But he didn't hesitate to shove Fitz aside. "Step aside if you want to see any of the money."

Tulley shot a look of disdain toward Fitz and handed the book to the man in the trench coat. "I hope it has what we need. That de Freitas woman knows who we are and if she gets hold of that chief inspector we're screwed."

His hands trembled as he opened the book to where a ribbon was placed. "Well there my dear woman you are safe. For only Fitz can be identified. She thinks you are the niece of that dead Devorgilla lady since you appeared as you are now." He turned and glanced at the still steaming muscle man. "And as for you, thank your lucky stars that you got this book to me. The Chief Inspector is probably at Beaulieu House at this minute and will be on his way to Slane Castle soon. He called the Marquess as I left to meet you." Running his finger across the ancient Latin text he muttered about twenty-five years of searching and the treasure of that lifetime search coming to an end. "Here it is," he pointed to the line. "It lies not in the Mellifont ruins but in the bowels of the St. Erc's Hermitage. Those maps in the Slane Castle Library will confirm the location as it's near the well and at the end of a tunnel structure of some kind." He closed the book and began to leave. "I will meet you in the ruins at Slane Castle. Have to get back before they miss me. You will excuse me Miss Tulley?"

"Miss Tulley," Susan squeaked out in shock.

Ron held his hand over her mouth.

"What was that?" the man in the cap and trench coat turned back. "Check it out. I need to leave, he's waiting for me." He glanced about the vast area of the Great Hall or what remained of it. He saw only crumbling stone walls and the fields beyond the ruins.

Fitz however was running about the area checking behind the half fallen walls and out the stone arched windows. Tulley ran to the man in the trench coat to calm him and suggested that they remain quiet and let Fitz do his thing. And that's exactly what he was doing when he noticed the depression at the end of the hall opposite of where they had entered from the castle keep area. He headed toward the opening at the edge of the dirt floor. Ron and Susan couldn't get down the stairs quickly enough. There was nowhere to hide save a narrow strip of rock at the side of the staircase. There they clung onto each other and the stones next to the water where their skiff lay. That tiny boat was in full view to anyone coming down those stairs. Both realized that but hadn't the time to jump into it and paddle back onto the stream which led from the river under the castle ruins.

"Oh my God Ron, what now; if that creep comes down here we're sunk," Susan paused and cracked a smile. "No pun intended," she pointed to the boat.

"Just hold onto me," he kicked a loose stone breaking away from the stairwell. "I think I can get hold of a rock next to my foot." Bending down he attempted to take hold of it. He began to lose his balance at the same time Fitz's voice sounded an alarm.

"Shit, will you look at this; it's some kind of stairway."

Tulley called back to him as she urged the scholar to leave. "Wait for me, just in case someone is actually down there wherever that leads."

Before Fitz could quip that she'd be of no help to him a bellowing voice drowned them both out.

"Ron, Susan are you in here?"

Tulley instinctively pushed their partner in crime through the stone archway. This led onto a grassy area which sloped down to the river. That river fed the lagoon which was partially under the castle's Great Hall.

"Thank God, that's Bob's voice, I'm sure of it." Ron still holding the rock turned ever so slightly to face Susan. "I think Watson has arrived to rescue us." He planted a kiss on Susan's cheek.

She did not say a word. Rather she placed her hand on his cheek and returned a kiss but to his lips.

Their brief encounter was interrupted with shouts. Bob was calling out to Fitz who was watching Tulley disappear.

"You, Sir, have you seen a young guy and girl around here?" Bob began to run toward Fitz. Appearing behind Ron's Watson was Ron's sister Jan and her Italian Count boyfriend, Alessandro.

There was nowhere for Fitz to go except down those stairs or face the now shouting Jan. "You there, say something. My brother was coming here with a girl, cute with red hair, the girl that is; my brother has black hair and big brown eyes and is rather lanky but strong never fear."

"Jan, I think the man doesn't understand you."

"Don't be ridiculous Alessandro; I am speaking the Queen's English and this is Ireland where English and Irish are both spoken." She stopped to look up into that well chiseled face like that of Michelangelo's David. Just for a moment she almost melted but took hold of her senses and broke into a sprint pushing Bob aside as well. "Listen here, you…answer us."

"Don't even try to stop her Alessandro; just try to keep up to her." Bob gave chase and the young Count did likewise.

Not liking the odds Fitz was already jumping from step to step down to the water level. Seeing the boat he jumped into it and began to untie it when he saw Ron and Susan clinging to the rocks making up the steps. "You, I saw you at Beaulieu House."

"Nonsense man, we've been here all day and you just wrecked our… shall I say intimate moment."

"Fuck you, you little twerp; you were at Beaulieu House not more than an hour ago." Fitz having unfastened the rope pushed away from the ledge with the oar. He was not more than two feet from Ron and Susan as he paddled like he was in a Condola in Venice.

"Little twerp… we'll see about that asshole." Ron pushed himself off the narrow ledge and leapt onto the skiff. Colliding with Fitz he bounced off the huge body of a Viking-like Warrior and found himself falling into the water with a crash and scream echoing up into the Great hall.

Fitz was out of the underground docking area and through the iron gates by the time Jan, followed by the guys, reached Susan. Together they pulled Ron out of the dark waters of the lagoon and laid him on the damp stones. "Ronnie, are you okay?" Jan was in panic mode.

The big cocoa brown eyes opened as a bit of water was spit out. "Calm down, I'm not drowning." Glancing up at the four looking down on him as if he were at death's door, he squeezed the water from his dripping wet sweatshirt. "Looks like we lost him," he grabbed hold of Bob's hand and was pulled up to his feet. "Come on we'll have to take the land route; he has to get to the parking lot where their car is and speaking of the plural did you see her?"

"Her, who's the her?" Jan replied for all as Bob shrugged with ignorance as his focus had been on the big guy at the stairwell.

"I'll explain on the way up and out of here."

Fitz was paddling on the river over which was the very bridge that Ron and Susan had crossed when they saw the duo from Beaulieu House enter the castle ruins. His focus was on the oars and crouching low so that he could easily push under the bridge. As the skiff emerged on the other side there hung Andreas, the Papal Guard being held in place by Dominic who let him go just in time for him to fall onto Fitz in the skiff.

One of them being built like a linebacker for American football and the other sleek but tall and well-formed as one would expect a soldier to be was just too much for the little craft to bear. The sheer force of the impact sent them both flying off the now capsizing craft and into the Boyne River. Nevertheless once emerging from the rather cool water the two of them began to throw punches. Andreas not really knowing if the culprit he fought was indeed the murderer they sought was being shouted at by Dominic hanging over the side of the bridge. The momentary distraction allowed Fitz to push away.

"Be careful Andreas…"

The words had hardly left his mouth when the thud of the oar paddle clunked the Papal Guard on the side of the head which was followed by the long pole end being twisted up between his legs and crashing into the family jewels. Andreas let out a howl followed by "Asshole…" as he grabbed the pride of the bedroom action in pain and then went limp in a daze.

At the parking lot, the Black Fiat stood out in stark contrast to the Trinity College white van, as the red racing car of Gabriel de Freitas was far behind in a clump of brush, which flanked it. Bob pulled on the door of the Fiat.

"Too bad, they had the sense to lock it." He peered into the windows on the driver side. "No book in here that I can see."

Susan grabbed hold of Ron's arm and looked up into a concerned face with water running down it from his saturated hair. He shivered a bit.

"Shit…" he replied to Bob as he patted Susan's hand which didn't go unnoticed by his sister who tugged on Alessandro and pointed to the gesture taking place.

The young Count just smiled back knowing that Jan had a wish to fix her brother up with Susan since day one of their meeting on that Alitalia flight from Chicago to Rome when they by chance met. That plan was placed on hold by Susan herself as she promised that she would not challenge God's calling Ron to be a priest.

"All right, so they got away but how did that huge guy get here before us?" Ron looked around to his friends waiting for a possible answer. When his gaze crossed over to his sister, he saw a slight smile. "What's so funny? So I'm all wet because some guy twice my size got the better of me and tossed me." He twisted his soaking sweatshirt from which quite the puddle formed from the water issuing forth.

"You're freezing in that thing. Let me take it off." Susan pulled up on the sweatshirt without Ron fighting her, after all he had his shirt on underneath.

The problem was that Ron was soaked all over not just his sweatshirt. This Alessandro observed and remarked to the fact. "Here you can have my sweater but as for the pants…"

"Thanks Alessandro I get it. I'm too skinny to wear your pants even if you had an extra pair lying around." He took off his polo shirt as Susan took a hanky from her purse and tried to dry off his chest and back. He let her do it. "The boys will just have to freeze for a bit more." He pulled on his belt and shook the top of his pants.

That was over the top for Susan and Jan realized it. Susan stopped wiping him down and stepped away. "Here put on the sweater," she grabbed the Aran Knit sweater from Alessandro and tossed it over to Ron.

Clueless as to what he did to upset her, Ron caught it and did as he was told. "So that's it. We had best get back to the castle and tell the Professor this whole thing was a bust."

"I'd say the Chief Inspector will be there as well. Maybe he can get some of the Garda to search for them." Bob said with the hope that Ron would finally let go of the quest and let the police handle it. In that he would be wrong and Jan would be the cause of that chance to abandon his detective work.

"Ronnie, if you're quite done with the nonsense about your precious "boys" you might like to know that all is not lost. We have an Ace in the hole as Dad would say."

The dawning of his locker room humor finally coming upon him, he gulped hard and glanced with downcast eyes toward Susan. He would have liked to tell her that he wasn't pulling his pants like that so that she could see his manly pride but just to loosen the jockeys a bit so that he didn't hurt with everything being squished down there. But that seemed inappropriate as well so he said nothing and let the look say it all. Jan's words also filtered into his contrite brain. "Huh, what Ace in the Hole?"

"Just this brother dear, wait, you tell him Alessandro as it was your idea."

"Will someone tell me what's going on here?"

Alessandro looking every bit like the nobleman he was puffed out his chest. "Your sister, she is too kind with the words." His reddening face turned and he smiled down to Jan holding his hand. "The term Ace in the Hole from your Papa that means to keep something hidden and unknown so to surprise someone; isn't that right?"

"Yes but what's my father got to do with this situation?"

"Just this Ron, we placed Andreas and Dominic on a bridge over the river you fell in as what that Cowboy favorite of yours, the one known as the Lone Ranger I think, called back-up."

"No kidding, then that big dude didn't get away." Ron ran to Alessandro and hugged him. "That was brilliant. So we still have a chance to get to the truth of what's going on with that book, the map we saw in the Castle and the murder of that poor Lady in Mellifont." He was about to kiss Alessandro in Italian style when he came to his senses and let him go and kissed his sister on the cheek, something which was also out of character for him. "Don't screw your relationship up with this guy Jan; he's quite the man."

Bob had moved next to Susan knowing that she felt uncomfortable over the "boys" reference despite the fact that her first meeting Ron in the Abbey School for Seminarians revolved around his privates and his lack of control over them. He placed his arm over her shoulder. "I guess we're back in the game thanks to Jan and Alessandro."

"Bob, I would have it no other way. He has to do this to prove whatever he's proving to the world and himself and us."

Ron interrupted their exchange by squeezing between them and placing an arm over each of their shoulders. "The game is afoot again Watson. All is not lost." He looked across at the two turtle doves of his sister and the young Count and smiled. "They make a cool couple don't you think? Anyway, we need to get to that bridge and see what Andreas and Dominic have come up with." Breaking away from them he began to run across the parking lot back toward the river. A steady dripping of water was left in his path as he ran. The sound of his squeaking gym shoes crunching across the gravel added a sense of immediacy to what was to take place. "Well come on, what are you all waiting for?"

Across the river peering over the ruins of the outer wall of the Trim Castle keep or central tower a pair of bloodshot eyes followed their departure.

Dominic was cradling Andreas in his arms as they sat on the bank of the river just below the bridge where it all happened a few minutes before. The overturned skiff still floated nearby and the oar used as a weapon was caught on some rocks near the water's edge. Lying across those rocks to catch the sun now coming out with brilliance, was the Papal Guard shirt and two sweatshirts. Dominic was himself shirtless as well given that he also had to plunge into the river to pull out the love of his life. His olive skin tan of an Italian was glistening and muscular for a research assistant and not very different from that of Andreas other than the Papal Guard was fair. He was so fair that the sun was already causing his smooth chest and arms to display a tinge of redness. Dominic was using his shirt as a compress on the wound just over the right temple area on Andreas. It was more of an abrasion as the skin was not broken but it was swollen. With his fingers, he brushed away the golden hair and patted it down keeping it away from the injured area.

Upon this scene of tranquility with the slight wind caressing the tall grass along the river bank and the stone walls of the ruins taking on a mystical glow of their own entered Ron. Falling to his knees at Dominic's side he lost all thought of the big guy lost to them. "Dominic is he okay? I mean…"

It was Andreas who answered. "I'm as you say OK, just a little dizzy."

"Save your strength." Ron patted the bare shoulder of the Papal Guard who had become his friend in the most perilous of times back in Italy when they fought against a radical group seeking to overthrow the Italian government. "So what's happened Dominic?"

As he asked the question the others arrived. Immediately Susan and Jan came to the aide of Dominic. "Oh my God, your shirt is filthy with river water. Here use my scarf." Jan took the silk-like scarf from around her neck. The depiction of scenes of famous ruins in Ireland was emblazoned on it. Blarney Castle and the very one they were looking at across the river were easily identified in its bright coloring.

As they hovered over Andreas, Bob asked the obvious. "So what happened here? Where's the guy from Beaulieu House?"

Ron shot him a glance and without words it said a lot. "Now is not the time."

The questions however were asked and Dominic answered. "We almost got a big man. He was on the boat that you see in the river dressed in black leather. I held onto Andreas just before he jumped off the bridge right on him; but they fell and fought in the water and this is the result. I am sorry to say that he got away when I dragged Andreas from the river."

The crystal blue eyes of Andreas opened. "Dominic you are not to blame for any of this." He grabbed hold of his lover's arm. "We came to help when Bob told us of what happened at Beaulieu House. He got the better of me that's all."

The brightness of the sun became more pronounced as something snapped in Ron's brain. "Maybe that's not all Andreas; just maybe it's not over." His eyes began to sparkle and Alessandro's sweater two sizes too big for him made him look even thinner than he was but it was the eyes which let Bob know something was up.

"Sherlock's onto something; everyone just quiet down."

"Thanks pal but I think this is just a long shot. The black car which Susan and I chased here is still in the parking lot. So whoever this Fitz character was with…"

"You mean the niece of the murdered lady?" asked Bob.

"No, I mean whoever she really is. Where is she now with whoever she was with when we heard them in those ruins?"

"That's easy; the guy in the trench coat must have had a car and they went off," observed Susan.

"Exactly, and they left the car we chased and somewhere that guy Andreas jumped on is out there. We need to get back to that car." Ron began to run off along the river's edge just in case another soaking wet guy might be lurking about along the way. Since they saw no one coming to the bridge from their side of the river bank Ron was sure when Fitz got out of the river it was on the side where the castle ruins were. "Dominic, Alessandro you guys help Andreas back to the van. Jan and Susan follow me."

"And what about Watson; just chopped liver again?"

"Come on pal, you know I can't do this without you. That's a given."

The large frame of Bob never moved that fast as he sprinted to catch up to Ron. Huffing a bit, he was what the Irish would call "that proud" of himself for being able to do so. "Now I'd like our gym teacher see me. I bet I could do that mile in eight minutes."

Smiling Ron agreed and kept the teacher's goal of six and a half minutes to himself. The girls were right on their heels as they reached the gravel path leading up to the parking area. The spirit of all four evaporated instantly as they saw the empty space next to the van.

"Shit, he got away too." Ron kicked the gravel with his still damp sneakers.

"Not quite Ronnie," quipped Susan as she pulled out a sheet of paper from her purse. "I took down the license plate number. I bet our friend the Chief Inspector Rory O'Connor will be able to check out who is the owner of said missing car." She waved the slip of paper in front of Ron's face.

Before anyone had a chance to take in what Susan just said, Ron took her in his arms and gave her a kiss full on the lips. Like butter on a griddle her resolve not to challenge God's call melted away. She kissed him back as Jan smiled ear to ear and poked Bob in the ribs.

"So my dear Watson, I think you have a challenger."

"Huh, oh yeah…well so it seems; but never fear your brother will not abandon his pal. We'll just have to add a third character to our bantering." Bob was pleased with his analysis of what stood before them.

Jan on the other hand just watched and counted. When she reached five she announced that time was wasting and they needed to get a move on. It was at that time when the guys arrived; carrying Andreas between them on their arms. Their jaws dropped as the clinching continued. They howled their approval and that stopped the kiss right as it was getting heated.

The voices calling out their approval split the two instantly. They stood as statues once did in the ruins of Mellifont Abbey with immovable posture, frozen emotion and a lifeless gaze from stone. But within their breasts beat two hearts pumping a life force which would light up their world and fill it with something they had yet to come to understand in their challenging relationship.

Using her brother's own words, Jan broke the spell and brought them back into the real world. "That's enough love birds, it's time to catch the thief and murderer."

Sweat poured off Ron's brow though the day was mild and most of him still damp from cold river water. "Right Jan," he glanced around into the faces of his friends and fell into making excuses. "We were excited about what Susan just presented. Show them show them the paper with the license plate number."

Disappointed in his cavalier excuse of what she felt was their moment of truth to each other she held up the paper.

"See, all we need is to have the Chief Inspector trace the number and we'll learn who owns the car and the Garda can find it."

His stunned friends nodded their understanding.

"Well then let's get a move on," Ron headed for the thicket behind which was the Number 43 Racing Car. He turned, "well come on the show is over."

Susan echoed him, "Ron's right. If we are to find these people we need to move now. The show is indeed over." She forced out a smile and walked to the van. "Bob, you go back with Ron. Alessandro, you can drive this thing so get in the driver's seat."

The black Fiat was already nearing the Slane Castle grounds when the van pulled out of the Trim Castle parking area. The sopping wet Fitz was steaming as his hands gripped the wheel so forcefully as to turn his knuckles white. He felt she had deserted him. She had left him to be sacrificed as a casualty of their enterprise but he resolved that by the end of the following day he would have his revenge on all of them and take the prize as well.

Slane Tower

CHAPTER FOURTEEN

SLAIN AT SLANE CASTLE

Chief Inspector Rory O'Connor was none too happy as he paced the Slane Castle Library. After speaking with Gabriel de Freitas at Beaulieu House he along with Sargent Carrick stopped at her home to inspect the theft area. He by phone had directed that everyone stay at Slane Castle.

"Sir, you mean to tell me that all those young people have left the castle after I explicitly called for everyone to stay here until I arrived?"

The Marquess was none too pleased to be chided in his own home but at the same time given all that had happened with the apparent murder of his guest and now the robbery in his friend's home he held his tongue for the most part. "To be quite clear Chief Inspector, the young people were already about the grounds and left before the message to remain here could be delivered."

"There's just too many of them to keep track of, that's quite understandable. You all understand that one of them or one of you in this room…"

The Professor jumped to his feet and protested what he thought was about to be said. "Chief Inspector you cannot even consider that one of those young people could be the murderer after all they've been through in trying to save that poor woman?"

"You misunderstand me sir. What I was about to say is that each of you and each of them might very well be the next victim."

"Dear God," exclaimed Hugh O'Neil.

"Not in my house sir, impossible," added the Marquess.

The clock was chiming the four o'clock hour as the Chief inspector tried to calm them and Shamus appeared at the doors. Before he could speak O'Neil was in his face.

"Good God man, where have you been? Where's Drumond?"

"I'm right here Hugh not to worry about me. I overheard what the Chief Inspector just said and as you can see I am just fine, though disappointed in that the find at the Hill of Tara came to nothing." He took O'Neil's arm and walked into the library nodding a greeting to the Marquess. "Hugh all they found was a bit of pottery and not that ancient at all. So tell me what did I miss?"

"I'm afraid that the Professor's assistants have all disappeared from the castle and no one seems to know where they went or why."

"Is that so," he patted O'Neil's shoulder and gently guided them to the Professor standing at the new display case with the original maps depicting the layout of Slane Castle and St. Erc's Hermitage before it was destroyed. "My dear Professor, I am so sorry to hear that your helpers might be in danger."

The Professor looked up from the glass protecting the maps. Before he did so, he noticed dirt on the cuffs of Dean Drumond's pants. He studied its appearance in that it had a reddish tinge to it. Drumond Shannon caught the downward glance.

"You will forgive my appearance Professor. It seems that I have brought back some of that red clay of Tara."

"Not at all, it just reminded me of the digging we were supposed to be doing with those missing assistants; that's all."

Shamus in the meantime had wheeled in a cart with tea and biscuits. "Your Lordship, given the hour, I thought some tea might be in order."

The Marquess excused himself from Gabriel de Freitas. "Good man, now let's just take tea and hear what the Chief Inspector has come to tell us."

Rory O'Connor stood next to the display case deliberately while the others took their cups to the reading table in the center of the library. He soon had begun to explain that the woman in the Drogheda Hospital was indeed the Lady Devorgilla MacMurrough and that the book stolen from the Beaulieu House Library was related to what was displayed on the maps. As he continued to make the connection the Marquess saw his teenage son Henry running into the garden as seen from the window behind the Chief Inspector. He was not alone in that observation.

"We know this," the Chief Inspector continued. "One of those two people who visited Madam de Freitas was known to her…"

"That's true as I said; Mr. Fitzgerald was in my employ as security manager. But that woman who called herself the niece of that poor murdered woman but who my former employee called Miss Tulley was unknown to me."

"And as I said, Miss Tulley does not have that chestnut brown color hair as the woman you described apparently had."

"Thank you madam, Professor I was getting to those points…"

His words had hardly left his lips than the young Henry came bursting into the library. "Father…oh hi everyone; oh there you are Chief Inspector. Well I have something to tell you." He ran up to the Chief Inspector. "There's a naked man in the ruins."

"Henry, please, there's a woman present."

"But it's true father, honestly quite true I even saw his you know what. He's a big man in all respects and quite hairy and…"

"That will do Henry. Chief Inspector perhaps you should speak with my son and me in a more private setting."

"I don't think that will be necessary. Sargent Carrick, get down to those ruins and check out this lad's story."

"Yes sir."

"Now then everyone remain calm. I suggest that you all stay here except for Henry who I will need to identify the person if he is indeed found in such a natural state. Perhaps, Marquess you should come along as well given the lad's age and all."

Amongst the ruins stood a tall tower of what was part of the Friary and walls of the college founded there which operated for centuries. Inside that tower stood a naked man and it was indeed Fitz. His leathers had been tossed aside as they were still sopping wet from the fight in the River. The black Fiat was a distance away but in it were two suitcases one of which was his. Thinking it best to change his clothes in a more concealed area and trying to get near the spot where the prize of the St. Malachy Chalice was thought to be concealed he had made his way to the tower and began to change never noticing that Henry was returning home from the village taking the route through the ruins as he usually did walking his bike once on that rocky ground.

It was that bike which Sargent Carrick found abandoned just a short distance inside the crumbling walls of the ruins. As he inspected it the footsteps of a crowd crunched on the stones of the ruins about him. "Sir, I found this bicycle." He looked up to see the young Henry, the Marquess, his boss and behind them Professor Pettigrew of Oxford Univeristy, Drumond Shannon Dean of Trinity College Department of Antiquities, Curator of the Dublin Hugh O'Neil and the lady race car driver Gabriel de Freitas.

"That's mine sir," offered Henry.

"Indeed, well then as for this man in his all-together any sign of him?"

"Not as yet sir."

The Chief Inspector asked Henry to show them the route he took coming through the ruins. To do that they would have to backtrack as it was near the Tower on the other side of the ruins where he saw the man. Before they began that trek the Chief Inspector asked a few questions more to make sure that none of those following him were in danger. He was pleased to hear that no weapons were viewed though the lad admitted his surprise at seeing a full grown man in such a state took such a thought far from his mind.

Ron and Bob arrived at the parking area and spotted the Fiat first. They were examining the area of the open trunk in which contained only some tools to change a flat tire. Watching them from behind the very wall where Andreas and Dominic had their brief frolic watching the cows was a pair of eyes. The Trinity van pulled in and soon they were surrounded by their friends.

"Nothing here," we had better get back to the castle and report the car being here to the Chief Inspector." Ron was disappointed but Bob had spotted a puddle of water inside the car and then a trail of wet rocks as if water had dripped on them recently. "Watson, you're a genius," he glanced at Susan and then got back on track. "Come on, let's follow the wet stones.

Bob, you lead us as I am all wet and may confuse that which is the trail from what is being left by the water dribbling off my clothes.

Susan ran up to Bob and walked next to him. Ron watched as his friends all followed them save Jan and Alessandro who now flanked him. "So Ronnie what happened between you and Susan?"

"Nothing, why?"

"Don't be cute with me Ron de Cenza, I know you hurt her and she you that's quite evident, right Alessandro?"

"Don't get me into this Jan. I just figured Ron had to tell her that his vocation came first and she's miffed about it."

The young Count of Pianore had saved Ron from a long explanation which would only serve to relive what happened. "Alessandro is right; it's all about my vocation. Let's get going they're getting too far ahead of us."

Ron began to run which forced them to run after him but not before Jan had words with Alessandro. "And don't you think I don't know what you just did for my brother. You gave him an excuse and I know it."

It was impossible for him to protest too much as Shakespeare would say. Thus he left it for a later time. He pointed out that the issue was where those two, in the Fiat had gone off to?

The two groups converged on the Friary Tower almost at the same time. Chief Inspector O'Connor seeing the Professor's assistants coming toward the tower yelled for them to stop where they stood. And where they stood was just to the side of the arched stone doorway leading inside the tower. Ron however pushed through them and yelled back.

"Chief Inspector, we found the car which we saw at Beaulieu House in the parking lot back there. If you come a little closer you will see water spots on the rocks around this tower, and it's not been raining all day." He pointed to the rocks in front of the doorway.

O'Connor approached the doorway and picked up one of the wet stones. "Well you're right about it being wet," he turned to Carrick and ordered him to have all the men form a circle around the tower, "that goes for all of you so called assistant researchers of the Professor too."

The son of the Marquess, Gabriel, Jan and Susan were not to be left out and filled in the circle as well. That placed Henry facing the doorway.

"Sir," he called out to O'Connor. "That door was not closed when I came by. A ray of sunshine was like a spotlight on that naked man; that's how I came to notice him from just about where I am standing now."

"Good lad, all of you be prepared in case he runs out. We just need him to be delayed so that I or Carrick may get to him. Though it's unlikely what with all this noise and shouting that's been going on he's probably long gone."

"Not really sir," observed Ron, "his car is still here and he couldn't be far on foot I'd say."

"Quite right lad; now you just push on the door and I'll rush in."

Ron did as he was told and the Chief Inspector rushed in and tripped over something moveable and soft. He found himself lying over a naked man. Quickly rolling off the man he pushed himself up to his knees and looked about the corpse and the small area in which they were. Looking about he had realized that he tripped over a pile of wet clothing just inside the doorway. Ron standing in the open doorway behind which the sunlight once again poured into the darkened space first held out his hand to pull up the Chief Inspector.

"Sir, there's a suitcase on the other side of him. He must have been trying to change his clothes as he was all wet."

"And how would you surmise that young man?"

"Simple this is the man I fought with at Trim Castle not more than an hour ago. It's also the man who I saw at Beaulieu House with that woman who by the way is still on the loose and where is her suitcase. There was none in that car they drove and yet he has one. Why would he have one and not her if she is indeed the same person who went to the morgue in Drogheda?"

"Saints preserve us but don't you have a lot to say on this matter young man. Are you sure this is the man? I think we need it to be verified. Call for the lad and your friend not Susan given the condition of this man but your sidekick as you Americans would call him."

"Sir, we Americans would just call him a partner like Carrick is to you I'd say."

"Indeed, just go do it if you'd be so kind. I'll check out the body."

Ron turned to go when out of the corner of his he spotted a bright colored something amongst the pile of wet leather pants, jacket and shirt. He stooped and picked up what was a silk scarf while O'Connor examined the body. Just as he was about to tuck it into his pants pocket he realized that there was blood on it which meant that he interfered with forensic evidence. There was no time for guilt or contrition so he decided to play the ignorance card.

Outside the circle began to fall apart as it became apparent that something had happened though what was uncertain. Everyone was now congregating in front of the tower opposite the doorway in which Ron now turned after handing over the scarf to the Chief Detective.

"The Chief Inspector has asked that Bob and Henry please come into the Tower. Your Lordship may accompany your son if you so choose given his age and the fact that there is indeed a man in this tower but he is dead."

The Marquess took hold of his son as if to protect him from what he was uncertain, Susan and Jan took hold of each other as the clamor of shocked reaction took place. Bob standing next to the girls motioned to Alessandro to come by them. He then walked toward Ron reading his pal's face as to what was found. He took hold of Ron's shoulders, "Is it the guy you fought in the river?"

Ron looked into those blue eyes which had a calming effect on people. "The very one; now what do we do?"

"First let's get everyone together and plan how we will find that woman who was with him and secondly we need to find that Chalice first."

"Watson, you are my pillar," Ron glanced up the mound toward his sister and Susan but his focus was on the latter.

"Thanks but this time you need more than one. At least they can't accuse you of killing this guy."

"Small consolation in that I fought him and if he died from what happened in that river, I'm screwed once again. But let's get on with this.

Upon entering Ron and Bob found O'Connor on his knees with the blood stained scarf in his hand and exploring a gash on the dead man's right side of the rib cage. "Ron, would you call my Sargent as well? This is definitely a murder scene." He rose as the Marquess entered with his son.

One look at the naked body and he turned his son away from the sight. "Chief Inspector, is this really necessary? My son is only fourteen."

"I am so sorry Your Lordship but he may have been the last person to see this man alive. I need to know if this is indeed the man he saw and one more thing; young man, please come around toward me."

Henry turned and made his way toward O'Connor being quite brave and without glancing at the obvious gruesome scene next to him. Ron entered with Sargent Carrick as this took place.

"Good lad," began O'Connor, "now look at his man's face and tell me if he is the person you saw in the doorway."

Henry looked into Fitz's face and then down to the wound. "I can't say that I saw his face very well sir, but his size and all would mean that it was the man I saw but he was standing of course and holding his side when I passed and turned to face me which is why I saw everything."

O'Connor placed his arm around the lad and guided him back to his father. "Sir, you may take him back to the castle for now. Sargent Carrick we'll need some uniforms here and the Medical Examiner. In the meantime," he walked up to Bob, "and you young man, are you able to identify this man as the one who Ron fought at Trim Castle today?"

"Yes sir, it is the same guy and also he was at Beaulieu House."

O'Connor laid the scarf over Fitz's private parts rather too late to offer some sense of decorum but he tried. "Thank you, you and your friends will have to stay on the grounds. I will need to speak with all of you shortly. And as for you Ron, in that fight at Trim Castle did he and you have a knife?"

Bob swung around with the ghastly vision of Ron being embroiled in another murder. "No way, Ron just jumped onto the little boat he was in and they fought but he was too much for him and ended up in the river."

"I see; is that about how it happened, Ron?"

"Yes sir, that's about it. We then gave chase and Dominic and Andreas well really Andreas, he's a Papal Swiss Guard you know, jumped on him and they fought but this guy clobbered him with the oar and got away. That's why he and I and this guy are all wet. We all fell into the Boyne River at some point."

"So that is why you are also dripping water from your clothes. Well after I speak with this Papal Guard you and he may go to the castle and change into something dry. Carrick before you leave, send in this Andreas person."

Sargent Carrick left only to find the entire group racing up to the car park on the other side of the ruins except for Hugh O'Neil and Drumond Shannon. "Gentlemen, where are those people going in such a hurry?"

"Damned fools kids thought they heard a car's engine. I told them the Castle was closed today but they wouldn't hear otherwise and the blond young man who says he's a member of the Papal Swiss Guard gave chase with the Professor and that strange one who is always giving that fair young man something of a look of admiration or whatever was right behind and the others followed as well." Drumond responded.

Without hesitation off ran Carrick toward the car park.

"Well Hugh, this is all just obscene, imagine we of all people involved in such goings on."

"Drumond, the Lady Devorgilla was of an ancient family and sought to bring a piece of our heritage to light after centuries of concealment. It is our duty to find it and to bring justice to her and her legacy."

Carrick found Andreas sitting on the ground with Dominic fanning him with his shirt when he arrived at the car park. "What's happened here?"

Professor Pettigrew spoke. "Andreas here tried to pursue the car as it drove off toward the town."

"I am so sorry Sargent, just a bit dizzy still from that fight at Trim Castle."

"Andreas is right, he should never have tried to outrun a car after being hit in the head with that oar not to mention…"

"That's enough information for the Sargent don't you think Dominic?" Andreas smiled with close lips and a wink.

"Oh my…of course; well Sargent shouldn't you call the Polizia, the Garda or whoever?"

"Yes of course but first, Andreas if you are able the Chief Inspector needs to speak with you. But first please give me your knife."

"Knife, he doesn't have a knife Sargent. We're on a research expedition."

"Thank you Dominic, but let the Papal Guard speak for himself."

A hush surrounded Andreas as he checked his pockets. "Oh Jesu, I must have lost it."

"Then you did have a knife I take it."

"Just a Swiss pocket knife; we all carry one in the Guard. We are all Swiss after all."

"I see. And when was the last time you had the knife in your possession? You needn't answer that until we are with the Chief Inspector, please come along with me." Sargent Carrick took his hand and brought him to his feet.

As he did so a glimmering object could be seen squashed in the gravel of the parking lot. Andreas had foolishly tried to conceal it.

"I found it by the car and thought…"

"Hold that thought sir, and just move on." Carrick cut him off before he got himself in anymore trouble.

The others followed behind with Susan consoling Dominic who was trying in vain to control his emotions. "It will be all right; Ron will set everything straight, by now he has already solved the murder. The Chief Inspector probably wants to see Andreas as a formality to identify if the dead man is also the one we saw at Beaulieu House though why he didn't ask for me I'm not quite sure as I was there with Ron and Bob when all of this happened."

Inside the tower, the Chief Inspector was grilling Ron about how such an injury might have been inflicted. "As you can see, this wound is fresh and placed in such a way as to require time for life to leave the body."

"So are you saying that I could have inflicted it at Trim Castle after which he drove all the way here, came to this tower and was changing his clothes while dying and leaving no blood anywhere but on this silk scarf which surely does not belong to him?" Ron asked sarcastically.

O'Connor smiled. "Bright lad, no I am not saying that. What I am saying is that when the lad Henry came by and saw him holding his side, he may have actually been seeing him dying from this wound as death was not instantaneous."

"Exactly my thought Chief Inspector, and look here in the dirt. These footsteps are not just his or ours not there off to the side of the tower opposite the door. There was a scuffle of some kind here, he got stabbed and the killer got away before Henry saw the man in the raw or before the murder actually took place. I doubt that latter part though as we would have found him still alive given your theory of a slow death."

"Have you ever thought about entering police investigative work, lad?"

"Not really as I am going to become a priest."

O'Connor crossed himself. "Is that so, I would never have guessed that path for you given how a certain party looks at you and I don't mean how Dominic looked at Andreas back in the Trinity Library or even how your friend Bob here seems to be your right hand in these escapades of yours."

"We're just Sherlock and Watson, sir, don't read anything else into it," Bob quickly added.

"I wasn't suggesting anything …ah there you are Sargent. And this must be Andreas the Papal Guard I'm told." O'Connor saw the bruising on the side of his head. "And how did you get that bruise young man?"

Before Andreas could answer, Carrick handed O'Connor the Swiss Pocket knife. "We found this where he was on the ground by the car. It belongs to him."

O'Connor took the knife wrapped in a handkerchief belonging to Andreas as well. "And who touched this besides the Papal Guard or you?" He began to examine it and then opened it.

"No one touched the actual knife except Andreas Berne who this gentleman is. It's even wrapped in his linen."

"Actually you will find my linen as you call it to belong to my friend Dominic Fontana of the Vatican Archives and assistant to Professor Pettigrew. He used it along with his shirt as a compress for my wound."

"Then that would account for the blood on it, I presume. The forensic people will let me know if it's your blood or of another, let us say such as the person whose blood is on that scarf lying on the victim. And Sargent, get me that shirt off Dominic's back if necessary."

Everyone was gathered outside and sitting about the fallen walls of the old Friary and ancient stones of St. Erc's Hermitage. The Professor was telling them about the little known saint who was made a Bishop by St. Patrick and admired by the Apostle of Ireland as a man full of wisdom and sound judgement. He pointed to the standing stones as being the grave marker of Saint Erc, to the surrounding stone walls mostly destroyed by

Cromwell's Troops centuries later and to the Tower of the Friary itself which was the center of a college admired by many in Europe.

"Ladies and Gentlemen," began Carrick as he tried to get their attention away from the story and focused on him, "the Chief Inspector would like everyone to return to the Castle where he will interview each of you later."

Inside the tower remained Ron, Bob, Andreas, Chief Inspector O'Connor and of course the dead Fitz. "And now lads, the time for truth has arrived. I need to know what your involvement was with the Lady Devorgilla, this man on the ground brutally killed and a certain woman who identified herself as the niece of the murdered woman. And one more thing, what is the actual reason for your coming to Ireland?"

After exchanging glances indicating agreement to tell their story, Ron and Bob shared how they came from Italy in search of an Irish Heritage Treasure dating back to the time of St. Malachy and the original Lady Devorgilla MacMurrough buried at Mellifont Abbey in its hay day. He learned of the Malachy chalice created for Mellifont by the original Lady Devorgilla and how it had been saved from the soldiers of Henry VIII when he dissolved the Abbeys centuries later and the troops destroying all things Catholic by the troops of Oliver Cromwell decades after the dissolution of the monasteries. Once again he heard of the events at Mellifont when they witnessed the murder of the modern day Lady Devorgilla as she prayed on the stone over the grave of her ancestor. He heard of how they met Hugh O'Neil's assistant curator, Bridget Tulley but did not hear of Ron's opinion that she was part and parcel of the attack on the Professor and what happened at Trim Castle and Beaulieu House. That Ron felt needed to be proven and that couldn't happen unless she was given enough rope by which to hang herself. He also didn't hear about the documents and books which placed the location of the hidden chalice; that the lads felt also needed to be verified and that verification would come from them. They would not deprive the Professor or their friends from completing the quest to find the Malachy Chalice.

In Bob's rendition the Chief Inspector did hear about Ron and Andreas' bravery in Arona Italy the previous year. He did so to prove how back then they too were accused of murder and proved who the real killer was as well as uncovering a Socialist plot fueled by the Communists of Russia and Italy. But all that did was raise a connection to Professor Pettigrew who seems to have been at the center of the Irish murders and whatever happened back in Italy.

"This has been quite illuminating lads, but now as soon as my team has arrived, we must return to the castle."

St. Erc's Well

CHAPTER FIFTEEN

TRAPPED

Once again the Professor and his team of research assistants along with Dean Drumond, Curator O'Neil, had been gathered in the library to await the Chief Inspector's interview. Sargent Carrick had just left the Marquess in charge of their remaining in place while he took the M.E. and forensic team down to the Friary Tower. The lad Henry had been sent to his room in an effort to keep him away from further exposure to the sordid events unfolding on the castle grounds. The grandfather clock was announcing the seven p.m. hour when Shamus asked the Marquess what to do about dinner as the cook was not on duty.

The question was placed on hold when O'Connor entered with Andreas, Bob and Ron. He announced that since the hour was late that the interviews would be held in the morning when some of the forensic findings might also be available such as the blood work on the mystery scarf, Dominic's shirt and handkerchief. Dominic he noticed was not shirtless as he sat at the reading table. He had been allowed to retrieve one from his room. Pettigrew and his team, the Dean and Curator were to be guests at the castle while the police continued their search for the now stolen Fiat, the mystery woman and the ruins for clues most especially a knife which was not Andreas' Swiss pocket type.

As O'Connor was finishing up his explanation for the interview schedule the next morning, Shamus entered quite beside himself. "Your

Lordship, there is a woman out in the hall who says she's a Miss Tulley of the Dublin Museum."

A stampede followed led by O'Neil as all ran into the hall to find the very woman who the police had found tied up in a closet in Dublin when Professor Pettigrew's brief case was stolen while he was virtually kidnapped and placed in a compromising situation in that very woman's bedroom.

"Bridget, what on earth; where have you been? The entire police force is out looking for you and someone claiming to be you," exclaimed the Curator as he inadvertently gave her information. Something both Ron and the Chief Inspector noted as being too conveniently given.

She gently lowered her suitcase to the oak floor with hardly a noticeable sound. Then she removed her coat and handed it to Shamus, who upon getting the signal from the Marquess received it courteously along with a green silk scarf fastened about her raven colored hair. This revealed that she was wearing a gray tweed suit consisting of a jacket matching the skirt with a white cotton blouse fastened up to her neck. Her black rimmed eyeglasses gave her the look of the stereotypical secretary or perhaps a female Clark Kent.

"May I sit? I have been walking from Slane town with that bag for miles it seems."

Shamus showed her to the very chair which had been used by Drumond Shannon when he first arrived at the castle. The ancient chair of the High Kings of Ireland didn't mind her presence at all. O"Connor approached her but not in a threatening manner.

"So 'tis it really you Miss Tulley or do my eyes deceive me?"

"Truly, it's me sir. You certainly remember me when I was found in my closet bound and gagged."

"Aye, that I do but that seems to have been an age ago. Tonight we have yet another issue to resolve. Where have you been between the hours of 3 p.m. and this time being 7 p.m.?"

Bridget Tulley began her tale of being concerned about Hugh O'Neil the curator of the Dublin Museum of Irish Heritage. Since she was found as she was abused and bound she had been recuperating and worrying about her boss. "Not having heard a word since he left with all of you I decided to come to Slane Castle and offer what help I can to find the person, especially that big beast who tried to abuse me and bound me in my own closet."

All eyes turned toward the Professor and she beamed in on their gaze. "I mean that big burly man of course who tried to kidnap Professor Pettigrew," Tulley clarified. "I took the train to Slane town and arrived around late afternoon around five, I think. In any case after arriving there I sought out transportation to the castle and none was to be had. So I walked from the town to here after having a bite to eat as I've had nothing to eat since the previous day due to my nerves and such. I must look quite the mess and do apologize for it Your Lordship."

Ron listened but managed at the same time to get close to Shamus and thus Tulley's coat which he held. Like the red clay on the cuffs of Drumond Shannon, he noticed dirt on her coat which in his memory was almost exactly the same coloring as that of the woman he saw in Trim Castle. It was however dark and moist not unlike that which was spread on his still damp clothes as opposed to the dry reddish clay on the Dean's pants. He felt his theory of their working together was just shot down.

"Nonsense, Shamus we must feed these people. Young Lady, you may stay here at the castle with the others. My son tells me that in town there is what the Americans call a Pizza joint. I'm afraid that to feed so many on short notice; this may be our only option."

"You are most kind sir," responded O'Neil on behalf of all present. "Shall we all take an evening walk into town?"

"That I'm afraid wouldn't be possible given the circumstances of this evening's event," replied the Chief Inspector. "Perhaps Shamus might be sent to pick up pizza for everyone."

And so it was decided that pick up by the butler would have to do. It would be an evening out on the veranda overlooking the gardens and then an early night as the Chief Inspector made it clear that two uniform policemen would be on patrol outside of the castle through the night. He would be returning for the interviews around eight in the morning.

The Marquess turned on the garden lights and then retired for the evening wishing everyone a pleasant meal and rest. He walked upstairs with Andreas and Ron who were rather anxious to change into dry clothes.

"Gentlemen, I hope that the rest of this night will offer some rest for you. I bid you God's blessing for such a sleep."

"You are most kind Sir," they replied and went into their respective rooms.

Bob was sitting on the bed waiting for Ron. "I put out some jeans and a tee shirt and your underwear."

"Christ pal, you're not my servant; you're my Watson." Ron tore off his clothes and tossed them about. "But I appreciate it anyway. Turn around while I put on my underwear. Okay all done. So why are you really up here by yourself?" Ron slipped on his jeans and zipped up, grabbed the tee shirt which was a souvenir from Trinity College and pulled it over his head. All the while Bob sat there and didn't say a word even when he was told to turn around he gave back no quip about modesty to the extreme or Ron's lack of size in his manhood which would bring back a retort about being endowed well enough for a would-be priest who would not be using it in that way anyhow.

"I can't stand it. Tell me what's wrong. Why are you sulking?" He sat right next to his best pal and folded his hands in his lap in silence.

"You don't need me anymore; not even to get your clothes ready let alone to fight with you against that dead guy in the tower."

"So that's it; you're jealous of Andreas. I didn't even know he was on that bridge. You were the one with me…" Ron paused and realized that it wasn't the gay Papal Guard who was the problem. "Holy shit, you're right, it was Susan with me under the great room staircase. You can't seriously be jealous of her; my God Bob she's a pain in my ass most of the time."

"And the rest of the time she gets you all hot and bothered and can't take her eyes off of you and you on her."

Ron jumped away from the bed on which they sat. "Oh no, shit no, you can't be going all Dominic and Andreas on me; not now not when I need you to help find the murderer; not when we're sharing the same bedroom."

"Don't be an asshole; if I wanted to be with someone like that it certainly wouldn't be with you."

"Fuck you Bob and I mean it. What's wrong with me? Or are you only into Papal Guards?"

"There you go again; when you don't want to talk about something bugging me you go off on a sex tangent about something stupid like sex between us. I could throw up before that would happen."

Silence followed as Ron paced and Bob watched him with sadness in those sulking eyes. Finally, Ron plopped himself on the bed again. "Okay you can have me; go for it," and then burst out laughing and soon they were punching each other's arms and laughing their asses off. "I do love you pal and you know it just not in that way."

"Asshole, I know that but what about Susan? It's just not fair to lead her on the way you do."

"Lead her on; are you nuts or what? She practically follows me around like a puppy dog until today that is. Now even if there was a bit of truth in what you say it would be over. I'm poison to her after Trim Castle."

"So that's why she held my arm and wouldn't go near you. What happened? You didn't…I mean you didn't try something with her did you?"

"Just the opposite, I told her I had chosen the priesthood or rather she did that for me."

"Well which was it? Did you dump her and did she dump you?"

"No one dumped anyone asshole; I just chose to follow the call."

"Or she sacrificed and gave you up so that you could do that." Bob joined Ron who was now pacing back and forth in front of the four poster bed which dated back centuries to another time when things were so black and white, so clear or were they? Neither of the lads would have been able to answer that question so they just paced together until Ron broke the silence.

"So are we done here with the touchy feely stuff or what?" he stopped at the foot of the bed and watched for a response.

Bob twisted with a jolt and rushed Ron tossing him on the bed before he knew what happened. "You're such an ass; you do realize that don't you?" He looked down at his brother from another mother as the saying goes and grinned. "Yes, we're done; so what's really on your mind when you're not thinking about her."

Ron sprung up and poked his pal in the belly, not too hard just enough to make him feel a bit of discomfort and returned the grin. "Oh my pal, those who are about to become a priest aren't supposed to get boners so maybe you should stop that kind of thinking."

"Huh, no way; it's you who gets the hard on not me." Bob pulled down on his pants so as to give a little room to the problem. "Damn it; I'm not hard; it's you who get in such a state whenever Susan glances at you."

Rolling off the bed, Rom walked to the window overlooking the veranda where they were supposed to be at that moment. In the fading daylight he could see the Curator O'Neil having words with his assistant Bridget Tulley. She then walked off leaving him alone save for his sister, Jan and her Italian Count, Alessandro who were seated on a bench at the other end of the stone terrace. "Cool it pal. It's not that way. Come over here and take a look at this."

Bob dutifully did so and saw the couple holding hands on the wrought iron bench flanked by large pots overflowing with red geraniums. "See that, I bet Alessandro doesn't get all hot and bothered because my sister in holding his hand; but I do when Susan does. So am I a sex maniac or what?" Ron folded his arms across his chest and tried to return a stern look at his puzzled friend who couldn't find the words to answer the question without telling him that Alessandro probably did get an erection or lie and say he didn't which would affirm Ron's feeling that he was full of lust for Susan. So he avoided the issue altogether.

"Here's what I think. Sherlock and Watson should stop this sex talk and focus on what our next move will be." Bob shook Ron by the shoulders. "You do have a plan, right?"

"Not exactly; but I do have a theory; and that's a start."

Bob pulled Ron away from the window as it was too distracting and suggestive of other things. "So spill it before that Chief Inspector returns and grills us under hot lights like some kind of "B" murder movie.

Breaking away from Bob's hold, he looked into those eyes of his Watson, thought for a moment. "You're such a drama prima donna. No one is going to put us on the hot seat; this is real life pal. I would have thought you'd get it by now after all we've been through."

"Well for shits sake if this is real life then it sucks all around."

"Now you're just being cynical which by the way isn't a very good trait for a future priest; even worse than getting a boner. So do you want to hear me out or not?"

Returning to the edge of the bed Bob wrapped his arms around one of the pillars holding up the canopy as if to give him purpose or steadiness. "Okay, I'm holding on just in case the earth begins to shake with your brilliance."

"Oh my God, you are such an ass but here goes nothing. What do we know so far? And don't answer that was a rhetorical question; you do remember what that means. Well first we know that the Malachy Chalice is real and worth a fortune on the Black Market. Second, the Lady Devorgilla killed at Mellifont thought she had found a way to find the chalice. Third, there are people who want that chalice so badly that they are willing to kill for it."

Bob couldn't help himself, "the earth isn't trembling yet."

Ignoring the comment, Ron went on with his laundry list. "You may have noted that I said 'people' which is plural. I used that plural form because I think we are dealing with more than one person."

"No shit Sherlock and one of them is dead in that tower," Bob pointed to the window where the silhouette of the tower in the approaching evening hours could be seen at the far end of the castle grounds.

This time Ron couldn't ignore the comment. "Very true Watson but that second murder is not related to the first and yet at the same time it is."

"Lordy, Lordy, I do believe I can feel a trembling in the universe as if God's hand is about to strike."

Ron lunged for Bob. "I could just clobber you right now and get it over with but instead…" Ron hugged his pal. "Watson that's it; there's going to be another murder if we don't stop whatever I just saw out on that terrace or veranda or whatever it's called."

"What are you saying? And you can let go now before I get stiff."

Ron jumped away as Bob laughed. "Works every time; are you that smug as to think you can give even a guy the hots for you? Don't answer it's a rhetorical question. So we saw Jan and Alessandro holding hands; oh my God Ron your sister is in danger."

"I don't think so but just in case let's get them up here with us." Ron ran to the door and turned elaborating on his thought. "No it's Miss Tulley or Mr. O'Neil who I also saw and they were having words before she went off toward the ruins and he into the castle."

Ron pulled open the door and there stood a shirtless Dominic with fist made ready to knock on the door. "What the hell?"

"Sorry Ron but Andreas and I were lying down and you know having a quickie just to make sure everything was in good working order after the fight with that dead guy when he was alive of course back at the river by Trim Castle..."

"Cool it Dominic, I get the picture after all we were there as well and in that river."

Bob was now peeking over Ron's shoulder. "So are you saying that you have to go to confession?"

Dominic smiled and Ron scowled.

"Does everything have to be about sex?" Ron shouted and then clasped his hands over his mouth. "The answer would be yes in this case guys. I think I get how the first and second murder may be related."

"No kidding, that's why I came to get you. Come to our room." Dominic tugged on Ron's arm and Bob followed.

Upon entering Andreas was just pulling his gold color Papal Guard shirt over his head. "Good, he told you then."

"Told us what?" asked Bob.

While Dominic put on a Vatican City sweatshirt, Andreas brought Ron and Bob to the fire place situated on the interior wall but not the one which was shared with Ron and Bob's room. He asked them to kneel in front of the hearth and look into it. At first all they saw was some burned logs and the fire screen but Andreas told them to really focus as he removed the screen. There was no brick wall inside; rather they could see another fire screen to keep the sparks inside the fireplace which was shared by two rooms. Blushing so badly as to even make his ears turn red, Andreas went on to explain that as they were making sure everything was in working order some voices could be heard coming from the room which shared the fireplace.

"Of course by then we were in shall I say a compromising state given that we were naked and all but that didn't stop us," continued Andreas. "We silently crept off the bed and knelt at the hearth..."

"Luckily there was no fire burning at the time or..."

"They get the picture Dom, no need to be graphic. So how do you Americans say it? There was anger in the voices… no worry… no fear… no not even that; it was a mix of all those things. The man was upset with the woman."

"But Andreas there are no couples in our group or as guests of the Marquess. Who is assigned to that room anyway?"

"Didn't I say? Why it's Miss Tulley the Curator's assistant."

"But I just saw her on the veranda with Mr. O'Neil; she went off into the gardens toward the ruins."

The Papal Guard and Pettigrew's right hand research assistant gulped with embarrassment. It became clear that it took them a little time to get dressed and make sure no one was around before Dominic slipped out of their room and showed up at Ron and Bob's door.

"Time enough to allow her to get downstairs and outside," Andreas noted.

"But who was the man with her?" asked Ron knowing that it couldn't have been O'Neil. He knew the answer had to be the Dean at Trinity College or the Butler of the Castle as everyone else was accounted for unless it was a totally different person unknown to anyone. The later he dismissed as a stranger could never get past the officers at the front entrance to the castle. "So guys, which one was with Miss Tulley? Was it Drumond Shannon or Shamus the butler?"

"How does he do that Bob?"

"Please Dominic, don't give him an even bigger head than he already has. Okay Ron, stop the nonsense and tell us which one was in the room with her."

"It had to be the butler as we haven't seen the Dean since just after the Chief Inspector told us not to leave the grounds and order pizza. It can't be the Marquess or his son and it isn't Mr. O'Neil as we saw him out by the garden with Miss Tulley and their words obviously were upsetting to him; thus he hadn't heard from her earlier."

"Dio mio Ron, you are like a Sherlock Holmes from the stories," a dazzled Andreas exclaimed. "It was the Butler, Shamus, and he told Miss Tulley that he was being sent out to get pizza on the Chief Inspector's orders so she had to go tell him what happened in the tower."

"Him, who's the 'him'?" a puzzled Bob asked.

Ron answered. "Drumond Shannon of course as he's the only one unaccounted for except for the Professor but he's one of us and is in the clear that's for certain."

The four of them peering into the next room through the hearth became silent. Andreas then asked what their next move should be. Ron thought it best that everyone, including the professor should come together and move as a unit back to the ruins. But first they needed to get into Miss Tulley's room. First they removed the partially burned logs and then climbed through knocking over the fire screen on the other side. It didn't take long to search the room as Miss Tulley had just arrived and hadn't even time to unpack. Her suitcase was still lying open on the bed but unpacked. Out from under the bed a strap stuck out and Bob tripped on it.

As he tumbled over onto the carpet depicting the battle of the Boyne his foot remained tangled in the strap pulling out what was attached to it.

"What the hell was that," cried out Bob as Ron tried in vain to catch him before he hit the floor.

"You found the Professor's brief case Bob, that's what it is." Ron pulled him to his feet as Dominic took hold of the brief case. "And that confirms it."

"Confirms what?" asked Andreas and Dominic in unison.

Ron explained that as he and Susan hid in the stairwell peeking into the ruins of the Great Hall at Trim Castle they easily identified Fitz who was with a woman, the same one they saw at Beaulieu House. She disappeared with a man in a trench coat as Fitz confronted them and the fight ensued which left Ron in the water and Fitz later getting away from Andreas in the black Fiat they found in the car park later right at Slane Castle.

"Then not more than an hour ago this Miss Tulley shows up somewhat disheveled and with a story about her worrying about Mr. O'Neil and yet just now I saw them having heated words on the veranda. Now we have the Professor's brief case, which by the way is empty. It obviously was in the possession of the one who stole it from the Trinity College security room. I propose that our Miss Tulley is really ONeil's assistant but she is also the one who seduced the Professor, posed as a niece of the murdered Lady

Devorgilla and again as herself but looking like the niece which was not her mistake but Fitz's for it was he who called her Miss Tulley at Beaulieu House. And now he's dead."

The proposal was plausible but had a flaw which Dominic pointed out. He presented the fact that Miss Tulley and the seducer even if they were one and the same person could not have been in the ruins of Mellifont and seducing the Professor at the same time. Ron agreed but also proposed that was the very reason why someone besides the dead Fitz was part of the picture.

"So maybe the butler did," laughed Bob.

"And just maybe you are right pal; after all he was in this room with Tulley on the pretext of announcing the orders for him to fetch some pizzas for the guests of the Marquess. Or and that's a big OR, he really did go and look for O'Neil on the night of the Lady Devorgilla's murder and murdered this Fitz guy over the contents of the Professor's brief case which would help them find the chalice before we do. And that brings us back to one person in this who done it puzzle."

"Si, amico," began Andreas, "the Signore O'Neil says he got lost on the night of the Lady's murder which we came upon. Maybe he was the one we saw run from the ruins in Mellifont."

"Very possible but I just now saw him with Tulley; and it wasn't a friendly situation."

"My God, you're not suggesting the Marquess or his son who was gone from the castle supposedly with friends in town." Dominic felt like biting his own tongue for even suggesting it.

"Of course not; remember what I said earlier and this time focus on his pants; he had mud on his pants cuffs when we returned to the castle this evening."

"Mud! Come on Ron, we all have mud somewhere on us just by standing around that tower in the wet grass."

"True quite true Watson but still has anyone seen our esteemed Dean of Antiquities, Drumond Shannon, recently?"

"The Dean, are you out of your mind? He's like what sixty years old? And besides, he's an accomplished professor in his own right. It would be like our own Professor Pettigrew being accused."

"In any case," interrupted Dominic, "didn't we see him at the tower when the body was found? I thought he was talking with Susan at one point."

Ron in panic mode bolted for the door yelling that he had forgotten all about her and being told that she took a walk into the ruins. The three ran after him as he flew down the oak staircase on the wings of Mercury it would seem. Jumping off the last step with lightning speed he pulled open the heavy entrance door only to find two uniform policemen preventing his exit.

"You don't understand; I need to get to Susan…"

"Sir," we have orders. "No leaves the castle grounds. You may enjoy the evening in the garden area."

"Aye, perhaps your girlfriend is waiting for you there under this bright moonlight," added the second officer. And with that he stepped in forcing Ron backwards and closed the door.

Bumping into the three who had caught up, he turned and ran for the Library through which one could get to the garden. "He called Susan my girlfriend. Am I the only one who doesn't see that?" Pushing through the glass door off the library he ran into the garden where Jan and Alessandro were enjoying that moonlight just holding hands while seated on that same stone bench.

Bob yelled back trying to keep up as he did so, "Ron when it comes to matters of the heart you ain't no Sherlock Holmes that's for sure."

Andreas and Dominic paused and pulled the young Count to his feet as Jan shouted to her brother. "Ronnie, what's happening?" She broke into a sprint toward him.

Ron paused at the crumbling border wall surrounding the St. Erc's Hermitage ruins and scanned the grounds for signs of life, for this girl who got him all excited, who frustrated him, who teased him, whose emerald eyes seared into his very soul and who until she became missing, didn't even realize that all those reactions meant something more than friendship.

Jan grabbed his arm. "Ronnie, what's happened?" She pulled him around as the guys lined up behind her.

In the moonlight the glistening of crystal-like droplets streaked down his smooth cheeks from those huge cocoa brown eyes. He pulled away not wanting her and the guys seeing his state. She wouldn't have it. "Ronnie de Cenza, you tell me what's going on here or I'll call Mom."

The word 'Mom' stopped him in his tracks. With disbelief and a slight grin much needed comedic relief entered his spirit. "Mom, she's in Chicago…"

"That would be Oak Park Illinois as you so often point out young man." Bob smirked. "You know the village across the street from the city boundary line." It was what Ron needed to get back into focus.

"All right, all right, you've got me cornered as they would say in a Cagney movie. You don't have to call Mom and get her all upset that I'm about to die or something and then Dad would get out the shotgun and come over here with his brothers to really set things straight."

Jan smiled and nodded in agreement that what he just said would probably really take place. She looked back to the guys. "He's back to being Sherlock. You can find out what the plan is now."

They formed a circle around Ron as he explained the urgency of what he thought happened to Susan. "Did anyone think of bringing a flashlight?" Ron looked up at the moon now being veiled by floating clouds. Alessandro of all people had one as he and Jan were exploring the gardens and using it to shine on the path as they strolled through the garden. "Great, you lead us to the tower where that Fitz guy was killed. From there we'll spread out across the ruins. If they haven't taken Susan off the grounds there're not too many places to hide.

As they approached the murder scene, Ron called for them to stop. "Did you hear that?"

In the stillness of the growing darkness, a muffled cry could be heard. It was coming from the scene of the murder of Fitz, the Friary Tower. His mind was running wild with thoughts of finding yet another murder victim and that being Susan, as Ron broke into a run. "Surround the tower guys. Jan, you stay back just in case."

"In case of what, that some guy is out there and panics and shoots me or something. No thanks, I'm right with you." She squeezed her petite body between her brother and Alessandro who took her hand.

"Don't you let go; no matter what." Alessandro brushed back her bangs; no amount of hair spray would hold anything in place in the dampness of the Irish evening.

"You're like a Knight of the Round Table or better but I think I can handle this." She continued to hold his hand nonetheless and sealed her comment with a kiss on his cheek just above the hair line of his beard now starting to appear since their departure from Rome.

Slowly they crept across the rocky ground filled with centuries of stories from the days when St. Patrick invested St. Erc with the Order of Bishop, to the establishment of a thriving college to its destruction not once but twice thanks to Henry VIII and Oliver Cromwell and now as a tourist attraction of Slane Castle. As they neared the tower, the sound became clearer and it was more of a moaning than a cry for help.

"Listen, someone is in there," Ron motioned for them to spread out around the tall structure which perhaps survived almost a millennium of history. The door of the tower was closed. He placed his ear to it and heard the moaning again. It was definitely a woman. At first he gently pushed on it and it didn't budge; something was obviously holding it in place on the other side. Bob came to help as he saw the effort to open failed. They both used their shoulders to crash into the door. It budged a bit but didn't open. The moans were changing to a hoarse voice making an effort to speak, "help." They slammed against it again and budged it a bit more and again it moved slightly. They could peer through the crack along the framework.

"There's someone on the ground for sure Bob. Guys, come and help us."

The others lined up and were about to become a human battering ram when Ron noticed the reason for the door not moving. "There are rocks holding it in place," he smashed his face against the frame and looked inside again. "There's a small window on the other side. Come on, I think we can do this."

Ron ran around the tower as the others followed. He had seen correctly. There was what was a window at one time but elevated so as not to be able to reach it from the ground unless of course you had help. A flashback to a memory of what he and Bob did back in the Abbey when they first entered the seminary erupted in his thoughts. "Okay Bob I'll climb on your shoulders and squeeze through the window. Andreas, you're a soldier find something like maybe all the belts of the guys and link them. I may need a rope to climb back out if I'm right." Bob stooped and Ron placed his foot on his bended knee and then wrapped his legs around his neck. Bob stood as Ron used the wall of the tower to steady himself as he reached for the window ledge. He easily pulled himself into the opening and looked down into almost total darkness. And yet he could see that crimson hair and those green Capri pants she was so found of. "It's her guys; it's Susan."

They cheered in silence as he backed out and then entered again backwards as he pulled himself through; his thin frame was now a blessing rather than a curse. In this manner he could hold onto the bottom of the window stones and drop to the dirt floor hopefully missing Susan as he fell.

Susan rolled over and looked up; her hands and feet were tied. Blood streaked her face coming from the left side of her head where he could see a gash. "It's you; I can't believe it." The words were hardly audible.

Ron let go of the ledge and dropped to the ground tumbling over and rolling right into her. They were face to face. "We've come to save you."

She managed a smile. "And me looking like something the cat dragged in."

"No time for nonsense; don't talk unless you can tell me who did this; save your strength until we get you out of here." He was untying her feet and then her hands and then his intent was to connect the two pieces of rope together. When he was holding her hands he leaned over and kissed them. "Did they hurt you? I mean are you badly hurt; I can see the blood and everything like that of course; I mean thank God you're alive. I was so worried and…"

"And what, Ronnie?" she grimaced but put her hands on his shoulders.

"Oh Christ help me but I don't think I'll ever be a priest Susan."

"You won't. Those words are like a choir of angels singing to me; glad it's down on earth and not in heaven just yet though."

"You drive me crazy but boy am I glad that you do. I think I love you. Is that what this feeling is?"

She leaned against him. And they held onto each other, Ron now having the sense to take his handkerchief and pressing it against the wound on her head as they did so.

Outside Jan called to her brother. "Ronnie, is everything all right in there?"

Their two heads perked up from resting on each other's shoulders. "Oh my God I have everyone here looking for you. I knew right away…I mean I am so sorry we fought and that's what caused you to be well be tied up and everything." He called up at the window. "Susan is fine; I will lift her up on my shoulders and you guys get ready to help her."

Dominic immediately jumped onto Andreas and stood up on his shoulders easily peering into the window opening. "Amici, my friends, it's good that you found each other."

The two still holding onto each other smiled up at his beaming face. "Cut the mush and get her out of here." Ron helped Susan to her feet. "Can you climb up on my shoulders and reach that ledge?"

"I think so Ronnie, I'm still a bit dizzy from that tramp hitting me in the head with a rock but I think so." She stepped on his knee and like he did to Bob wrapped her legs around his shoulders. "It feels different than when I did this same thing with Bob to get in here."

"Well I hope so Ronnie," she decided not to elaborate and save her strength.

"Now just give Andreas the rope and he'll send it back down here to me so that I can climb out." Ron shouted to the guys. "Be careful she's wounded on the head and is dizzy."

Bob took hold of Alessandro and dragged him to Andreas holding up Dominic. "Now we'll wait here and Dominic will lower Susan to us; so we'll keep her from falling and gently bring her down to the ground, got it?"

"I'm a Count not an idiot," replied Alessandro with a grin.

"Well I'm sorry but this is precious cargo more so than even what we seek as far as Ron is probably concerned anyway."

"Si, I got it Bob; we'll link our arms and Dominic will lower her into them. Jan mi amore, you stay close to me, won't you?"

"Si, my love, I'll be right here to help Susan."

"Oh my God not you too; I'll have no one to talk sense with me." Bob grinned ear to ear.

The rescue went off like clockwork as Ron's Dad would say when a plan actually worked out. Jan was kneeling next to Susan who was resting against the tower wall as Ron hovered over them and the guys were asking him what next. Susan began to explain that when she ran into the garden she had parked herself on the wall overlooking the pasture and just watched the sheep who had taken it over. She was steaming mad at the time and didn't notice a thing until some voices interrupted her thoughts. She recognized the voice; it was that of the butler, Shamus. She jumped down from the wall just a couple of feet and looked for a place to hide and ran into Miss Tulley. They tussled for a bit but Tulley knocked her on the head and she dropped in a daze. With clouded vision the owner of the voice she recognized came into sight and he was with the Professor and another person she couldn't identity as he was in a trench coat and broad rim hat in the increasingly dark evening. She laid motionless less they think she could recognize them and it worked.

Shamus ordered Miss Tulley to hold onto the Professor who it turned out was bound by ropes, his arms behind his back. The two men then dragged her into the tower. Careful not to damage the police crime scene tape crossing the doorway, one by one they brought in rocks to hold the door closed. Shamus remained inside until the end and rope was sent through the window to pull him out just like Andreas did for Ron with the rope and belts.

"And that was it; I was left alone and have no idea where they brought the professor." Susan concluded her story.

"But I think that I do."

All eyes turned toward Ron. The game as Sir Arthur Conan Doyle said through Sherlock was indeed afoot again.

CHAPTER SIXTEEN

RESCUE AND DISCOVERY

The moonlight became brighter as they spread out across the ruins, Dominic reciting out loud all that he could remember from the translations of the documents found in the Vatican archives. The clouds were sent on their way but the flashlight was still a fortunate item to have as Ron shined it into the nook and crannies of every corner of the ruins. Suddenly, Dominic came to a part which resonated with Ron. It was how the 12th Century Lady Devorgilla donated the chalice in the first place to St. Malachy as part of donations to help build the Mellifont Abbey with the help of St. Bernard who came from France to help him. She would die and be buried in the chancel of the chapel under that stone on which the 21st century Lady Devorgilla was killed. When Ron photographed that blood soaked grave marker her name was clearly evident. It proved the writing of the found documents to be true. The problem was why the lady in black of today was killed in the first place.

Ron understood that the murder victim was a descendant of the original Lady Devorgilla but why would she be killed for that, he wondered aloud. All she seemed to be doing on that fatal night was praying some ancient Irish poem. Then in the midst of this thought it dawned on him, "so here's a connection; the poem she recited was taken from the Irish book we borrowed from the Trinity College Library. It talked about the ancients who came to settle Ireland and the symbols they used to settle the land. The chalice over time began the Holy Grail symbol of Ireland to many.

There has to be a connection between the Malachy Chalice and one of those sacred symbols. Who remembers what those were?"

Dominic of course being the right hand man of Professor Pettigrew understood the connection and also recalled what those symbols of the ancient Nuatha settlers were. "Ron, remember when we found the book and began to translate it? We made a list of those very items thinking they were a key of some sort to find the chalice." He called out to Bob, "don't you have that list on the notepad in your satchel?"

Bob ran over, the always present leather satchel hanging over his back and quickly opened it. "Here it is; wait a second this is the part about the potential location of the chalice." He flipped a few more pages. "Oh my God Ron here it is, the list of the Nuatha gifts. There is the Dagda's Cauldron, the Spear of Lugh, the Stone of Fal called Lia Fail and finally the Claioth Solais or Sword of Light but really more like a glowing bright torch of sorts or so you put here in the notes."

"And that guy is why he's my Watson." Ron ran to Bob and gave him a hug.

"Stop the nonsense, you'll get Susan jealous." He pushed Ron away dramatically.

"Not any more Bobby, not anymore; he's all mine," she sashayed up to him and planted a kiss on his now blushing cheeks but no one could see their brightness really given that the bells of the Town of Slane's churches were ringing out the eleven o'clock evening hour.

"Well if this is becoming a love fest, I don't want to be left out," with that Jan kissed Alessandro right on the lips.

"Hey, that's not fair; we can't do that in public," called out Andreas.

"Who says so," replied Ron. "Go for it."

With that the Papal guard in full view of everyone planted one right on Dominic's quivering lips. "And to hell with everyone who has a problem with us; I love this guy and I don't care who knows it."

Shaking from head to toe, Dominic brought everyone back to focus on what was just read off by Bob. "That was quite nice and also quite the announcement to the world but I think we just hit on a clue as to why the Lady in Black might have been killed and why the book was stolen from Beaulieu House just to name a couple of things."

"But why kill Fitz? He was one of them," observed Alessandro.

Susan was able to enlighten them on that point for as she was dumped in the tower and locked up Shamus was chiding Miss Tulley she told them. Apparently he was quite upset as was the other man that Fitz had been killed. But Bridget Tulley was not; she told them that the big oaf confronted her about leaving him behind at Trim Castle. He wanted to teach her a lesson and pinned her down in the tower where she just happened to see him as he was naked and changing into dry clothes. He confronted her with fury. So furious was he that he actually told her that he would show her what a real man felt like not like that British professor she lured into her bedroom. To ward him off she offered an apology and lifted her skirt to invite him to enter. She flirted with him and soon he forgot about vengeance and sought pleasure. He never noticed her slipping something out of her purse as she dropped it to embrace him. As he pulled at her panties, she jammed a knife into his side. He lurched backwards and probably the last thing he saw was Miss Tulley smiling as he fell to the ground, his manhood deflating rapidly.

"Her description was all too lurid and disgusting but it put the two men in their place and they said no more about the death of Fitz. I just feigned total unconsciousness so that she wouldn't do the same thing to me."

Ron wrapped his arms around her. "Come on let's find them. Fitz's murder is not connected with the Chalice or one of the items on our list. The Lady Devorgilla was killed it appears because she knew that there was a connection between where the Malachy Chalice was hidden and with it one of these famed sacred items. And I think I know where they may be if the map in that display case is accurate."

The seven of them no longer spread out but gathered in close proximity as Ron guided them across the ruins of St. Erc's Hermitage to the multi-story stone walls of the ruins of the original Slane Castle. As they approached the end of the Hermitage ruins and could see the walls of the castle ruin, Ron remembered that the map showed that part of the hermitage consisted of a cave like connection, a tunnel really in which crops could be stored to keep them cool, and priests could hide during the persecution under Oliver Cromwell. He flashed the light looking for such a structure and its beam shone through a small window-like opening.

"Follow me." Ron ran to the opening and stuck the flashlight into it. A long tunnel was illuminated. "Guys, look at this," he stepped back and each of the six took turns looking into the tunnel-like structure. "What if this window wasn't visible when the Hermitage was destroyed? What if this just seemed like another mound of rocks to the marauding soldiers?"

"But there is absolutely nothing in there except a small wall dividing it. Someone was in there and took out whatever was in it," noted Jan after peering into it once more. "There's nothing but rocky walls curved in an arch over the flat floor with that little wall separation."

"Very true but in the time of Catholic persecution many castles, Manor Houses and I suppose, even schools like this was had what are called priest holes. The Catholic clergy were hidden from Cromwell and his troops in them. We need to get in there and check it out."

"But what about Tulley and company; they are out there somewhere. Shouldn't we handle them first?" asked Bob.

"You're right of course Bob, first we catch the murderer and then we prove the Lady Devorgilla correct."

"Correct in what Ron?"

"Correct in her theory that the Malachy Chalice rests with one if not all of the gifts of the Nuatha of ancient times, Dominic. Maybe we should split up. You and Andreas go to the old castle ruins with Bob and using our notes try to locate anything which might be a priest hole and hiding place in its day. We'll stay here and I'll crawl inside this tunnel and check it out."

"I don't think splitting up is a good idea."

Ron paused for a moment soaking in her concern. "Okay Susan, we'll all go to the old castle first."

It was done. The search for the hiding place of the Malachy Chalice would have to wait so that the murderer of the Lady Devorgilla could be captured. The seven were in agreement and they set off for the old castle. They hadn't gotten very far when their flashlight beam met the beams of several others. The opposite beams seemed to stop their progression. Soon Ron's flashlight beam was quickly raised and shone in the faces of those behind the sources of the other beams.

"It's you," Susan shouted and made for Bridget Tulley. Jan held her back as in Tulley's hand was not a knife but a revolver.

"Very smart young lady; just keep her calm. I thought you were dead as Fitz. You seem to have a cat's life."

"Forget all of that," a low and familiar voice cautioned. One of the beams of light now skipped across the faces of the other six with Ron. "These young people may be of use to us."

All of them knew that voice. Ron flicked his flashlight to the source of the voice in shadow beyond Tulley. There stood the butler, Shamus. Their lack of surprise upset the butler. He rather fancied himself as being successful in presenting himself as a servant. He too was holding a small hand gun. He waved it at the seven and ordered them backwards.

"Take us to wherever you just came from." Shamus turned to the man in the trench coat who was holding papers which Dominic immediately recognized as those from the Professor's brief case.

"Where is Professor Pettigrew…you didn't, no you wouldn't do such a thing," he pleaded.

The man in the trench coat moved his light so that its beam shone upon the entrance area to the original Slane Castle. There on the ground propped up against one of those border walls was the Professor bound and gagged. "As you can see, no real harm has come to him; save that which occurred in a certain bedroom back in Dublin, if I am to believe what the Chief Inspector shared with me."

"That voice, we know it guys." Ron flicked his beam and there stood Dean Drumond Shannon of Trinity College. "You, I just knew it was you all along. You were faking your helping the Professor with the translations and locations for the chalice. You're a fraud, a liar and a thief…"

"Say it young man, say it all…and a murderer; isn't that what you were going to add?"

"Asshole, don't put words in my mouth."

"Watch your tongue or none of you will leave these ruins breathing the fresh air of Ireland or anywhere else. Now then, let's get down to why the Professor is our guest and why you are going to help us."

Shamus ordered the seven to sit on the rocks about them as Drumond laid out his plan for them.

Up in the castle Hugh O'Neil who many thought was the brains behind the murders and theft of the brief case had gone to his room furious that his assistant was so rude to him on the veranda. Her sudden appearance and what happened in her apartment to the Professor bothered him. He decided to call the Chief Inspector and share with him his concern. He had picked up the phone and once again there was no dial tone. This time he pulled up on the connection line and soon saw that is was severed from its source. Running out into the hall on the upper level of the castle he came upon the Marquess who having seen lights flickering about the ruins was about to check them out.

The concerns of both having been shared, they went to the entrance door of the castle and summoned the officers on guard there. One radioed O'Connor while the other went to check on Henry the teen son of Lord Conyngham who everyone just called the Marquess. It was soon discovered that the main phone line to the castle had been cut. It was fortunate that a squad car was left for the officers. Officer Shields was assigned to guard the boy, the Marquess and Curator. When Chief Inspector O'Connor arrived with Sargent Carrick and two more officers some fifteen minutes later he led the others onto the veranda. Through the garden they descended into the St. Erc's ruins through the old castle ruins.

Totally opposite of where the police entered was Drumond with a gun pointed in Ron's back and lamenting what had brought him to this unfortunate situation for Ron and his friends.

"For thirty years I have searched for the Holy Grail of Ireland, the Malachy Chalice and then as it was soon to be in my grasp when along came this woman who called herself the Lady Deverogilla Macmurrough. She had presented herself to Hugh and he called me all excited that the treasure of the century was soon to be found. Would I be interested in helping with the discovery? What was I to do but feign a similar excitement and join forces with them. Hugh was to go to Slane Castle and speak with the Marquess and I was to search out the ancient texts for clues to the location of the chalice in order to validate that woman's information. Me a research assistant, me the Dean of Antiquities serving as her lackey; it was all too much for any person of my stature to take."

Ron remained unsympathetic much to Susan and the others' concern. "Yes, I suppose it's hard to realize that you're an asshole and once you realize that to become an even bigger one."

The resulting blow to the side of his head with the barrel of the gun gave Ron pause but did not bring on a more respectful tone let alone silence. "So what now, are you going to kill us all for a trinket of the 12th Century?"

Drumond shook with a building rage as he grabbed hold of the neckline of Ron's sweatshirt and shouted in his face. "How dare you speak to me in such a manner. I'll kill you right now as I did that creature calling herself the Lady Devorgilla."

"So then, you did kill that poor woman," Ron looked down at the aging hands holding him. "What a shame that such a record of service must end with you dying in prison."

"Ronnie, stop it; you're provoking him," Jan shouted.

"Please Ron, don't say anything more," added Susan.

Shamus and Tulley told them to quiet down and worry about the Professor. Andreas removed the gag so that he could breathe better despite a warning from the butler. "You can't kill all of us; one of us will get to you," Andreas replied.

They had arrived at the opening of the tunnel just discovered. Drumond still holding onto Ron shone his light into the cavernous space. It was easily determined that Ron could climb through the opening and another would have to help him find anything which might appear to be a false wall of some kind. To the naked eye those walls appeared to be carved limestone creating the tunnel which given its close proximity to the location of the Well of St. Erc may have also been a source of water for the Hermitage and College until the well was filled in with rocks by the local farmers during the desecration and destruction of the chapel and Friary save for the tower.

"You smart ass will climb in there and look for a false wall." Drumond shoved the barrel of the gun into Ron's ribs. He looked at Bob, "and you bend down and give him a boost to get in."

Ron tossed in his flashlight before Drumond could stop him. "I'll need the light to look for human tampering with the walls." He then stepped into Bob's clasped hands and was hoisted up so that he could pull himself through the opening.

"Miss Tulley send me one of the girls; he'll need some assistance to hold the light while he picks at the rock."

She pointed her pistol at Susan, "you the girlfriend; how about a romantic final night with your lover?" She waited for no response. "Get a move on."

Lifted up by Bob, Susan shimmied through the window and was caught by Ron as she came over the ledge. The two of them looking up at the opening now saw the face of the butler. He threw down a pick-axe which was to be used to chip at cracks which might present a false wall creation. "Watch out below."

The tool came down with a heavy thud as they jumped back. This was followed by Drumond's face appearing. "Now then, I would begin at the far end of the cavern. It's nearest to the Well and seepage may have weakened any newer addition to the surface."

"Drumond are you sure this is where the map indicated the chalice being hidden?" asked the butler as everyone now sat on the ground waiting to hear anything and others planning to escape when Ron and Susan found a way to distract their captors.

The only light was the faint moonlight at the opening of the window and Ron's flashlight which was needed as they approached the far wall. Susan shivered a bit and Ron noticed. "It's kind of chilly in here." He began to take off his sweatshirt.

"Yes, but you'll be cold without a shirt."

"Well you're not exactly dressed to be caving in the middle of the night. Here take it, see I have a tee shirt on underneath. I'll be fine."

"Always the knight in shining armor, aren't you?"

"Really now, when I'm half frozen and we're about to die?"

"But I'm not trying to be funny. You are my Sherlock turned Lancelot; wait maybe it should be Arthur himself because you know the other guy went for the king's wife as the legend goes and well you know what happened then."

"Whoa, that's a lot of you knows being said. But I get it," Ron chopped at a crack on the ceiling a few feet from the far wall of the structure. "I saw water dripping and thought this might be soft and therefore conceal something. But no such luck."

Several pieces of rock showered them as he loosened the plaster-like sealant covering parts of the ceiling and walls.

"Go further back," yelled Drumond who was standing on Bob's back, wobbling back and forth. He could only see shadows in the darkness and the beam of light pointing at a particular part of the wall.

Again Ron noticed water seeping in but this time along the wall. He rubbed his hand across it and tasted it. "It tastes like crap but it's better than nothing. Here, take a lick off my hand."

"A lick, okay," Susan tasted the water cool but not refreshing. "Well not too bad. I'll get some in my hand while you chip away."

Ron had an idea as he swung the pick into a wide crack along the wall where the water was seeping through. "Hey asshole, I think we found something. Want to come and take a look? I see something through the crack something shiny."

Drumond became ecstatic. He insisted that he be lifted up so that he could squeeze through the opening. It was the perfect time. Tulley and Shamus went to the portal opening and watched each taking a turn to keep a gun on the captives on the ground. The Dean landed with a groan but managed to right himself up and began to walk toward Ron and Susan. Using his flashlight he now could see them clearly.

"Show me, show me the spot," he commanded.

"You'll have to look into that crack to see it," Ron stepped aside as Drumond placed his eye on the crack.

"I don't see a thing…"

Ron jumped on him the flashlight went flying a shot rang through the tunnel. Outside Bob jumped up crashing into Shamus who dropped his gun while Andreas tackled him to the ground while Jan took hold of Bridget Tulley and soon had her on the ground. Dominic untied the Professor as the others used the rope to tie up the butler and museum assistant curator.

A roar of more gun fire came from the tunnel. This was followed by crashing sounds as rocks splintered and loosened and fell from the ceiling. Drumond was thrown by Ron as the rocks came crashing down and then pulled Susan to the far wall. In seconds they were separated from the Dean of Antiquities by fallen rock. Only a small opening more like a slit of light could be seen over the top of the pile. But there was no way for Drumond to get to them. He had been hit by a falling rock and lay on the ground in rubble. He tried to call out but his voice could not be heard as others voices outside drowned his out.

The Chief Inspector and his Sargent, along with Hugh O'Neil, the Marquess and three other officers had arrived and soon had Tulley and Shamus in handcuffs. As they were escorted past the Curator O'Neil and the Marquess both expressed their regret that such a fine future for Miss Tulley was destroyed by fury and greed. And as for the butler, his days of hosting would soon be the cleaning of prison tables.

Sargent Carrick was lifted to the portal window and squeezed through. He found the injured Dean lying with a bleeding head. It not appearing serious, he cuffed him just in case as the gun was not to be found. It wasn't found because it had bounced off the stone wall and ended up with Ron and Susan on the other side of the pile of rocks.

Outside Bob and Jan were being held up by Dominic, Alessandro and Andreas so that they could call out to Ron and Susan through the portal. The Sargent called out as well.

"We're behind the pile of rocks Sargent; tell everyone that we are not hurt, just cold." Ron turned to Susan. "Shall we let Drumond know what's with us besides his gun?"

"By all means," she snuggled into him as he patted what fell from the wall.

"Oh, and tell the Professor that there's a small chest here with us but we haven't opened it but it looks mighty old and is made of bronze."

Drumond groaned as Bob and Jan relayed the message and cheering could be heard.

The Chief Inspector began shouting a series of orders on how to get everyone out of the ancient structure while not destroying it more than the pick-axe had already done. The squad cars came as close as they could to shine their headlights into the area. Andreas and the Professor fit through the portal and helped Carrick remove the fallen rocks. Hours would pass. On the other side of the pile Ron worked to take down what he could without the loosened rocks tumbling into their small space with limited air coming in. As dawn drew near enough of the rocks were removed so as to allow Ron to boost Susan up and over the pile and into the waiting arms of Andreas. Next over the pile came the chest, which the Professor carefully received as Ron popped his head over the rocks and slid down into the Sargent.

"Sorry about that Sargent; lost my footing." Without a further word he embraced Susan. "I can't promise such an adventure every time we go out on a date, but then just maybe we would enjoy a movie with popcorn and a Coke."

"Why Ron de Cenza, are you asking me out on an official date?"

"Huh, I guess I am," and with that he planted one right on her lips in front of the groaning Dean, elated friends and Sargent Carrick. The usual reaction not withstanding he enjoyed the moment rather well given everything which had transpired.

It was decided as the last of the tunnel rescuers were pulled from the tunnel, that being Sargent Carrick that the chest would be opened but not at the site of such violence and fear. They would walk to the ruins of where the chapel once stood by the old castle ruins and open it on sacred ground. It was the crack of dawn as they formed a circle around the chest with the Professor kneeling next to it. There was no clergy to lead a prayer; the closest one to ordination would be Ron and BoB and the former had pretty much given up his vocation that night with Susan behind a pile of fallen rocks. So Bob was asked to lead them.

He chose the words of St. Patrick about St. Erc in whose Hermitage they knelt. The faint sound of bells from the town filtered into the ruins announcing the dawn. Those he had written on the notepad in his satchel.

"O God who granted the blessed Saint Erc a deep understanding of justice and wise counsel, grant us who benefit from his faithfulness a sound judgement in all things, a stillness of body, mind and soul and a faithfulness of heart that in all things we may honor your name and proclaim your glory; through Jesus Christ our Lord who lives and reigns with you and the Holy Spirit, now and forever."

All responded, "Amen."

"And now let's open the chest," Bob ended with glee.

The Professor once again thanked all for saving his life once again and for the privilege of the moment to present to the world the hidden treasure of Ireland, The Chalice of St. Malachy. The chest creaked open with a little prying from the blade of the Swiss Army knife. He lifted from the decayed linen fabric a gold chalice emblazoned with gems and trimmed in silver in the fashion of the Medieval period with a long stem holding the cup and a broad base supporting it. The first light of the day streamed into the site and bounced off the chalice giving it a mystical appearance so as to take away the breath of those who marveled at the treasure and the joy of it surviving to once again become a symbol of faith and endurance.

Evening arrived before sunset for the Professor and his team of research assistants. Their host the Marquess had wined and dined them along with the Chief Inspector and his officers. Hugh O'Neil would take the chest with its treasure back to Dublin under the protection of the Chief Inspector and his team. It was decided by the Professor and O'Neil that the discovery would not be placed in a museum but rather in a place of worship where it was meant to be. The Cathedral of Dublin would be that location.

As for Drumond Shannon, he was already being taken back to Dublin on the charge of murdering the Lady Devorgilla in the Mellifont ruins. Bridget Tulley in a separate squad car was on her way to Dublin as well under the charge of murdering her accomplice called Fitz. And as for Shamus, the butler, he too was on his way as well charged with attempted theft, murder and removal of a national treasure.

It was over, their adventure in Ireland wasn't quite what anyone expected but that thought was for another day for as the adrenaline subsided and fatigue returned all that came to mind was sleep.

Ron and Bob shared a room as usual and as usual placed a line of pillows between them. It had become a standing joke but just between them. Ron lay in his gray sleep shorts and white tee shirt and Bob in his blue pj's with jumping sheep over clouds bought for him by his mother much to his chagrin.

"So it's over; we're alive. What shall we do now? I mean now that you aren't going to become a priest," asked a slightly saddened Bob.

"I don't know; probably finish out the semester and then transfer to Loyola University's Rome Campus after all that's where my sister and Susan will be." Ron attempted to turn serious just for a moment. "You know this is probably the last time we'll bunk together if you get my meaning."

"I know," Bob's eyes moistened but also contained a bit of mischief. "At least, I won't need pillows at my back anymore just in case your pecker would poke me in the back."

They both began to laugh.

Bob turned on his side to catch a glimpse of his pal. "One more thing; I think the Professor was a little disappointed that all we found was the St. Malachy Chalice. He really thought you had been able to locate one of the Nuatha symbols."

"Just the chalice; it's like the Holy Grail of Ireland."

"I know that but still…imagine if your theory was true."

"Hmmm, well then perhaps on the morrow the gang and we should take a stroll back to that tunnel thing. Just maybe it wasn't just my imagination; I mean the glimmer of something gold in the hole left after the rocks almost fell on us."

"Holy shit, no kidding! You mean the ancient book and the map were on target?"

"Well pal, let's just sleep on it." Ron quickly changed the subject. "So what do you think about asking everyone to come together on the Isle of Capri for a vacation adventure before the next term begins?"

"Please Ron anything but an adventure. How about just eating, drinking and perhaps a dip in the Mediterranean?"

There was no reply; just the sound of restful breathing which could now be heard throughout Slane Castle. And in that hole in the wall of St. Erc's Hermitage a bright object reflected a beam of sunlight announcing its presence but no one was there to take note of it. At least until the morrow would arrive.